THE BIRD SAVIORS

ALSO BY WILLIAM J. COBB

The Fire Eaters

The White Tattoo

Goodnight, Texas

THE BIRD SAVIORS

William J. Cobb

UNBRIDLED BOOKS

Unbridled Books

Library of Congress Cataloging-in-Publication Data

Cobb, William J. (William James), 1957–
The bird saviors / William J. Cobb.
pages   cm
ISBN 978-1-60953-070-9
1. Parent and child—Fiction.   2. Environmental degradation—
Fiction.   3. Southwestern States—Fiction.   I. Title.
PS3553.O199B57 2012
813'.54—dc23
2011045575

1   3   5   7   9   10   8   6   4   2

BOOK DESIGN BY SH · CV

First Printing

For Elizabeth & Lili

PART ONE

The government killed more than 2.7 million "nuisance" animals last year, including starlings, troublemaking birds that destroy crops and contaminate livestock feed. Also killed were wild turkeys and chickens, black bears, coyotes and wolves. The animals were mainly killed because they threatened livestock, crops or people in airplanes. . . . The largest number of animals killed—2.3 million—were starlings. . . . Critics say the poison used also kills owls, hawks, magpies, raccoons and cats.

—"'Nuisance' Animals Killed in U.S. Program,"
New York Times, *11 September 2005, 17*

Horses in Red Snow

LORD GOD IS TALKING AGAIN. HE DOES
love to hear himself speak. A graybeard loon, he sits hunched
over the kitchen table, his arms sunburned, nose hooked, hair
thin and wiry, ranting hoarse-voiced about sinners and socialists.
Outside the foggy window Smoke Larks flutter liquid as living
shadows to perch atop the woodshed. When they settle the morning sun backlights their black silhouettes like burnt figures on a
woodcut.

Ruby shifts the baby girl in her lap and thinks of the birds,
how they must be cold of a morning like this. She's seen twelve
this week whole. She counts the birds and invents her own names.
She knows people call them by another name, but she calls
them Smoke Larks. Swirling in vast flocks in late winter, they
look like smoke from a great fire, burnt souls twisting in the
wind. Purple-black, dusky, and speckled, the short-tailed birds
scatter among the twisted junipers in the backyard, pecking in
the dry hay grass.

Ruby began counting all the birds two years before, when she noticed how quickly they seemed to be dwindling. They are disappearing and someone has to note this, to keep it in her mind if nowhere else. The going away of things has to be noted. Especially a thing as perfect as a bird, even the squawky Blackjacks, or an old Grief Bird with claws like voodoo earrings.

Only a handful of Smoke Larks came this winter, rare as snow. She remembers home-school years not so long ago when both snow and larks were common still and taken for granted. She remembers being trapped in the house and staring out the windows, watching the birds, wondering when she would go to school like normal children. And when she did, at age thirteen, she wasn't prepared for it. The smiles and touches. The looking at you and teasing, the telling you how funny you talk, how pretty you are. After years of harsh soap and chores and the warnings against vanity and foolishness. The wanting something from you, something unspeakable but familiar.

She remembers the Smoke Larks in her home-school years, outside her window, her untouchable friends. The cottonwoods in the gulch used to wear them like black leaves every February. Now more often than not the skies are clear and hateful, not a bird shadow or silhouette to be seen. Taken for granted are fires in the foothills and dust storms off the plains.

The world has gone wrong. They pay men to hunt and shoot birds. The fever has the city people spooked. They blame it on the birds, stupid stupid. It's a shame is what it is. Nothing to do but count to the last one. Ruby hasn't seen a Moon Bird in over a year, and Squeakies are just a flicker of what they used to be.

Baby girl Lila tugs at Ruby's nipple and puts her hand on her breast. Lord God says the world is Lila's to inherit and see through to the end. Ruby wants her to grow up in a world of birds and the beauty of spotted feathers. She worries that the last of the birds will be gone before Lila has a chance to recognize their leaving.

Things don't stay around forever.

People don't either. Like her mother. She's been gone for two weeks and Ruby can't take life without her. Life in this house. With its mouse scratchings and bacon grease and Book of Mormon on the table. The sense of Lord God breathing down your neck. Ruby's eyes well with tears as Lila's hand rests against the pale skin of her breast. The baby girl's eyelids blink as if in slow motion, her arms creased with fat wrinkles at the wrist, fingers splayed like the rays of a starfish.

Across the kitchen table Lord God is going on about how he needs to trim the toenails of his one good foot. And the danger of the bears. How in droughts like this they come down from the mountains. How you have to be careful. They could be out there, lurking behind the woodshed. They can smell bacon five miles away, he says, his voice raspy as that of a biblical prophet.

Ruby turns her face to her pancakes. She doesn't want to hear such nonsense. She doesn't feel right herself this morning. Her nose has been running and her cheeks feel hot and flushed. She fears the fever but doesn't dare say a word. She will pretend Lord God doesn't exist if for one second he will just shut up. He holds out a plate of bacon and eggs, urges her to eat. He has cooked their breakfast and the least she can do is enjoy it. She

5

needs to put some meat on her bones, she does, and he has blessed the food especially for her.

She lifts her face and tells him Lila is almost finished feeding, she'll eat in a minute. She speaks in barely a whisper, stares out the window at the parched fields of prairie and high desert, the Sierra Mojada in the west turning pink with the sunrise, above it a wall of dark curdled clouds. Opposite the mountains comes the day's light casting its long morning shadows onto rabbit bush, sage, and bunchgrass.

Behind the shed the crooked wooden fence posts lean this way and that like tombstones on a wind-bitten hillside. Lord God's land is miles outside Pueblo, off Red Creek Road West. The edge of nowhere, its face to the hills and back to the town, true to his isolation-scenario mind-set. The fence is a last stand before the coyote howls of emptiness beyond.

Wind gusts make the power lines hiss and whistle. In the west the sky above the mountains looms russet and solid, an ash cloud of trouble coming. Like wet walls of the Red Sea parted and waiting for that moment to swallow up the world once again. The weather people don't know what to make of it. Snow and dust storms at once, a thing both strange and ordinary now as a sky without birds.

Lila falls asleep with the nipple in her mouth. Ruby does her best to tune out Lord God. She strokes her baby's cheek for a moment, heartbroken at what's in her own mind, the anguish she faces. She eases Lila into the wicker bassinet between the kitchen table and the woodstove. Before the stove she squats to open its black cast-iron door, adds a couple split pieces of aspen from the cardboard kindling box. A wisp of smoke belches out, the gusty wind backing it down the stovepipe chimney. The heat makes her face flush, a smoky tang sharp in her nose.

That's enough, says Lord God. Until this wind dies down it's a bother. Another gust and this house will be smoky as hell.

Ruby stands and refuses to look in Lord God's direction. She rinses plates and cups at the kitchen sink. Outside the window a pair of Grief Birds perch on the fence rail. These are bigger than crows, lonely, speaking in tongues of portent. The closest Grief to the house croaks and shakes its ruffled neck feathers like an African lion its mane. Lord God is asking her something, again, but she doesn't catch what he says. She has to concentrate to decipher the sounds that issue from his perpetually hoarse voice.

You aren't ready for the world, he says. Do you know what it's like to live in a Muslim house? I've seen it. I've fought in their streets. You leave the house without your face covered? They scar you with whips. You fall for a man not your husband? They stone you to death. It's a circle of shame there and they want to make us their slaves. I've seen it. I know. And now I'm returned to set right the scales of justice in this fallen, sinful world of Mammon.

He cuts a bite of pancake and waits for Ruby to lift her voice. She dries a plate and stacks it in the cupboard.

I've shouldered weapons among the heathens, he says. I've struggled with them close enough to smell the spices on their breath. I have tasted the ash of anger and have seen my leg lying in the street, blown clean from my body. And in this greatness I have been given the grace of a new leg and now I walk to preach the tongue of a righteous Lord.

7

Ruby squints at the portrait of Jesus on the wall opposite the kitchen table—his expression merciful and angelic, a tenderness in his eyes she has never seen in a living man. Beside him hangs a portrait of Joseph Smith, high cheekbones and narrow chin, eyes burning like a madman, full of fire and conviction. Lord God insists the two martyrs stand side by side, both sacrificed to teach the sinful and the righteous a lesson.

Ruby asks if he has heard anything from her mother.

Lord God chews, his face turned to the window, a slat of morning sun reflecting within his artificial eye. The glass orb glows golden, opaque. He closes his eyelids as if to savor the food. His face wrinkles with maniacal certainty and anguish, crease lines on his chin visible through the gray tangle of his beard. His lips are lost in the coarse hair, even his cheeks and neck covered, as if he is becoming a half-man, half-bear creature of legend.

Your mother is gone, he says. But she'll be back. She will see the error of her ways. It may take time is all.

Ruby finishes drying the dishes. She turns to find her baby girl awake now and watching, a slight smile on her lips. Lila has a perfectly round head. Her grandmother calls her Baby Lollipop with such affection that it melts Ruby's heart. And now she's gone and not here to help with Lila.

I miss her, says Ruby.

Lord God is quiet for a moment. He chews his toast. Finally he whispers, I do too.

You should beg her back, says Ruby.

Lord God rocks back in his chair, stares up at the ceiling.

8

Girl? Haven't I taught you right? Never beg. Never rely on anybody else.

This is different, she says. It's Mom we're talking about.

We get by just fine, don't we?

Ruby makes a funny face for Lila, crossing her eyes and opening her mouth wide. The baby girl waves her hands in the air and makes a sputtering sound. Say what you want but it's not the same, living here without Mom, answers Ruby. The house is cold.

It's what I've been telling you, says Lord God. The house is cold because you don't have a husband. And with a child of your own too.

I'm doing okay, she says.

What? With me taking care of her, you mean? When you're off studying uselessness?

Ruby dries the dishes, counting the Smoke Larks. Maybe I should quit school? she asks. Besides, we won't be here long anyways.

You're just stubborn. You know how to solve this problem, says Lord God. Marry that man. They say he's a good egg. And he's got more money than he knows what to do with.

Why? she asks. Why would I do such a thing?

We could drop by his pawnshop and have a nice chat. He's a good egg.

You're not listening to me.

It's not you who takes care of Ruby when you're in school, is it? You need to be cared for. And kept from the wickedness of the world.

Daddy, don't.

A wickedness you have already tasted. And have been stained by.

My baby is not a stain.

I know. I also know there is more to the story. I have seen the wickedness, he says. It is amongst us.

Ruby sighs. Half the time I don't know what you're talking about.

We must keep you from harm, for your own good, he says. For Lila's sake. You haven't seen the evilness, says Lord God. And I hope you never will.

I've seen a little. I've also met some good people out in the world. They're not as bad as you say they are.

Lord God frowns and rises from the table with a faint pneumatic hiss.

That's a fine kettle of fish, he croaks. Man comes home from war, from getting his body blown to hell and back for your sake, so all the fat can sit around and complain about everything. His wife leaves him. His child mocks him.

I'm not mocking, says Ruby. I don't want to marry a stranger. Is that so crazy?

Lila grabs a skein of Ruby's red hair in her fist and cries. Ruby puts a pacifier in her mouth and rocks her, one hand on her belly. The pacifier muffles the sound until she spits it out and cries harder, her face turning purple.

She shouldn't get gas after feeding, not on breast milk, says Lord God. It might be something you're eating. You're not eating too much red chili, are you? She'll get those spices through your blood.

Ruby carries Lila to the wooden rocking chair in the living room. The crying subsides as she rocks, until Lila only whimpers. From the kitchen comes the sound of the clink of silverware and china, Lord God putting away the dishes.

Ruby rocks and waits. She needs to get ready for school. That is what she should be doing. But she watches the kitchen door and waits. Aloud she says, Because you have spoken nonsense and envisioned lies, therefore I am indeed against you.

Lord God finishes clearing the table and stands in thought. He is out of work and has given up looking for more. He lives off disability but it's hardly a living. He preaches now at the Lamb of the Forsaken Fundamentalist Church of Latter-Day Saints. His congregation is mostly lost souls and the lonely, living hand to mouth. He drinks his coffee and surveys the empty expanse of his day before him.

He walks with a thump and hiss to the doorway of the living room, where he stands and watches Ruby coddle Lila. A child of mixed blood, misbegotten in the hardest of times. The Lord gives us choices and we don't always make the right one.

Your baby girl needs a father, he says. Any fool can see that. You're going to marry Page.

Not a man with two wives already.

I had a vision, says Lord God. The Lord spoke to me. He told me Page is a good man. Better than you know or have known.

Says you.

Says the Lord God Jesus Christ. I'm right. And you know it.

Ruby takes Lila to her bedroom, kissing her forehead as she carries her propped against her hip. She changes Lila's diaper and finishes getting ready for school. She listens to Lord God talking to himself in the kitchen down the hall. It has become a habit with him, a kind of running commentary of his thoughts, spoken aloud in a whispery, intense tone. Sometimes he seems to be talking to her mother now that she's gone, arguing with her, firing back at her female sass. She hears him say, Is that what you'd have me do, Juliet? Is that what you want? Just tell me and I'll make it so.

Ruby slips a gauze face mask around her neck and arranges it at her throat like a white choker necklace. She can't stand the thing but school regulations require it, everyone insane about germs. With the fever that has swept the country, wearing face masks is now mandatory in public places.

Two years ago it was the fever snuck up like an ugly rumor and nobody believed it at first. Soon you saw people fainting at the supermarket. Later a shopping mall closed after a rent-a-cop discovered a Pakistani woman two days dead in the parking lot. They had to close down the unemployment offices to prevent the contagion in line. People out of work and sick too made it insult to injury.

In school that term Ruby studied Native American customs and learned that they had called it the Fever Moon. Somehow it made more sense than anything you heard from the talking heads on the screen. Doctors saying they have no cure but what can you do anyway? They don't know. They're making it all up. They like to hear themselves talk, to look important. They don't know when it will end. When the next thing will begin. They blame the birds.

Lord God calls out, You miss the bus, don't plan on getting a ride from me.

Ruby stands at the window, watching a lone Grief Bird on the railing. It stares back, like a shape-shifter waiting for her next move.

Lord God stomps his peg leg on the front porch. Ruby grabs her book bag and marches past him. She keeps moving down the front walk. Red Creek Road is a two-mile stretch of potholed dirt from their front yard to Highway 96. When she passes the junipers near the mailbox, she catches sight of the yellow school bus pulling away. She has to turn and head back.

It came early, she mumbles as she passes him.

You're late again, says Lord God. You'll be late for your own funeral.

Ruby stops and stares at the sky. Snow clouds bulge over the mountains. The wind whips dust into her eyes, makes her squint. She does not want to give Lord God the satisfaction of acknowledging his words and warnings.

I'll take you to meet Mr. Page on the way to school. He is just the thing you need.

She goes through the front door, back inside the house. Lila sits in her plastic play swing and smiles like a cartoon baby when she approaches. Ruby leans in to kiss her cheeks and forehead, trembling. Lila grabs a curling lock of Ruby's hair and holds on tight, as if she's holding the reins of a roan pony. A clear dribble of drool shines her lips.

Ruby disentangles her hair from Lila's fist, whispering, Mommy has to go now. I'm going to miss you and think of you every minute I'm away until I can come back and take you away too. Mommy loves you so much and she won't do anything to hurt you. For now Grandpa will take care of you.

Ruby's eyes well with tears as she kisses her baby's lips, soft and wet with drool. She tells her she's sorry. She swears she'll be back to get her as soon as she can. A day or two at the most. She covers her face with her hands and tries to stop her sobbing. She hears Lord God on the porch, opening the door, telling her to hurry.

He tells her he doesn't have all day. We have to get Lila dressed and in the car seat too, he shouts.

Lila puts her hands over her eyes and then pulls them away dramatically. She wants to play. Ruby's voice breaks when she says, Peekaboo! Lila covers her eyes again and Ruby starts to cry as she leaves the room. When Lila takes her hands away, the room is empty. Mama, she calls. Mama!

Ruby rushes through the smoky kitchen and out the back door. Lord God follows her but is several steps behind, his prosthesis slowing him. Did you hear me? he calls. You need to dress your girl. I'm not a taxi. You want a taxi you get a job and pay for one.

She runs past the woodshed, Grief Birds rising and cawing, her backpack slapping her shoulders. At the fence she tosses her backpack over, grabs a crooked post, clambers over the sun-bleached rails. She turns her body sideways to straddle the rough-hewn cross-ties. A rusty nail catches her jeans until she wriggles free.

For a moment she takes one last glance at the house—a faded

white box set against the redness of the sky beyond, a smoky plume rising from the stovepipe. Lord God on the back steps, bearded and angry as a statue of Brigham Young, perplexed and one heartbeat from judging her to have lost her ever-loving foolish female mind.

The high desert beyond the woodshed is brown grass sloping upward, toward the mountains. To the east dry gulches big as small canyons cut the bleached landscape.

Lord God shouts again. Ruby hurries on, the wind ripping her father's voice into the past. The field of rabbit bush and sage jiggles before her eyes. She cuts a zigzag path through cactus, cold air stinging her face.

The wind fills her ears with a loud buffeting roar. She stops to catch her breath. Behind her Lord God still follows, struggling against the gusts, losing her. She takes off again, her legs feeling thick and clumsy. To the west roils a dust cloud like a billow of sandblast. The early-morning sun reflects against it, against the clouds of prairie dust boiled loose by downdraft in the foothills of the mountains. The clouds churn, swirling tongues of dust spreading across the plains and heading toward Ruby alone in the murk.

SOUTH OF PUEBLO a red-tailed hawk perches on a telephone pole. It has not eaten in two days. Below it a prairie dog scuttles into its burrow. Trucks thunder by on Interstate 25, drafting gusty diesel wind, ruffling the parched brown grass. Another prairie dog strays from its burrow until the hawk swoops low with talons outstretched. The prairie dog darts below. The hawk banks, curls toward the highway, and is flapping its wings to regain height when a passing truck clips it with a shiny side mirror. Caught by the wind, the hawk's body tumbles into the right lane of traffic.

Passing vehicles run over it twice before a Subaru slows and pulls onto the shoulder. The driver sets his emergency brake and turns on his flashers, watching the stream of traffic. He pulls on leather gloves as he rummages on his floorboard for a paper sack. He unfolds it, watching a tractor-trailer rig in the distance.

Ward Costello gets out of the car and stands in the shudder of tailwind gusts off the diesel rigs, hurries across the right lane. A truck blasts its horn. He eases the hawk's broken body into the paper sack, taking care not to crush the cinnamon-colored tail feathers. The truck honks again. At the last minute Ward trots to the shoulder and gives the trucker a wave, cradling the paper sack like a swaddled baby.

He opens the bag wide enough to give the hawk a preliminary inspection. The tips of its primaries are ragged, indicating stress from pollution or inadequate diet. One of its talons is broken off to a stump. He smooths the mottled feathers, waits for a break in the traffic, and stares at the dead hawk's red tail feathers sticking out of the paper bag. It looks like something being smuggled.

A northwest wind blasts a thin scrim of dust over his windshield. Ward turns on the wipers and merges into traffic. On either side of the freeway, tall white wind turbines straddle the interstate like an invasion of alien propeller giants. Their enormous blades rotate slowly. A herd of antelope grazes in the stretched-out morning shadows of the turbine towers.

He heads into the outskirts of Pueblo, a no-man's-land of abandoned strip malls with jagged-teeth windows, ratty vacant lots, and dusty Mexican restaurants. The blackened husk of a burned XXX adult bookstore. A dark brown sky spreads in the west.

His cell phone rings and rings. He fishes it out of the console, sees the caller ID display, and cringes: his sister-in-law. After the rings stop the beeps begin, telling him he has voice mail, telling him to be connected, demanding that he pay attention, for God's sake. Telling him no matter how much he wants to be alone he can't be. He listens to the message, the only way to stop the idiotic beeping.

Nisha's voice is all about broken promises, suicide-hotline desperation. The electric bill is over four hundred dollars, she says. If he doesn't pay, they're going to turn off the power. It's his house, so he has to pay it, doesn't he? Legally? Isn't he financially liable? This is a country of laws, isn't it? True, she happens to be living there now but she has no job and no money. What does he expect? It's his house she's sitting, right?

Please help me please. Why did you leave me? You touched me and that's okay. I wanted you to. But you left and you don't talk to me now? Are you ashamed of me? Of us?

Ward listens as her voice fades in and out on the spotty connection. Nisha's voice resembles her sister's. Like voice mail from the dead. This isn't her only similarity: The last night Ward stayed in his home he slept with Nisha. Even her body, her spicy smell, was like Sita's, like sleeping with a twin. Only needier. She wanted to marry him. She wanted him to bless her with child. She said her time was running out.

The next morning he walked out of the house, leaving her naked in his bed, her sleeping body sprawled atop the white sheets, her mocha skin and darkly painted eyes, arms wrapped around a pillow and black hair tumbled and thick. He will pay the power bill. If it comes to it, and it will, he will deed the house to her and assume both the financial and moral debt.

On voice mail she begs him to come back. Come home soon, she pleads. Don't forget me now. You can't forget me, can you? I know you can't.

ON THE OTHER SIDE of town George Armstrong Crowfoot tries to avoid the severed head. He has bad dreams and a thing like that, once seen, skyjacks your nightmares like a special guest star. Like a relative with a shot liver who won't go home and won't quit asking where you hid the whiskey. George has never seen a severed head except in movies, and he figures special effects are good enough.

Mosca won't shut up about it. The infamous head. Said to be that of outlaw Black Jack Ketchum, hanged in Clayton, New Mexico, in 1901. When the trapdoor opened and Ketchum's body dropped twelve feet to the noose bite, his head popped clean off, shocking the crowd of morbid onlookers. Now Jimmy Rodriguez, aka Mosca (the Fly), says he won it in a poker game.

Right, says George. I believe that.

What? You think I'm lying? You calling me a liar?

What I find hard to believe is you winning a poker game.

You never seen me play, says Mosca. I got a poker face. I got luck.

George Armstrong Crowfoot does not believe that either. Mosca works with him on patrol for the Department of Nuisance Animal Control, and George knows anyone who stoops that low likely isn't a lucky bastard. Not to mention that Mosca is skinny and tattooed, like an overgrown Chihuahua. Crowfoot frowns and sniffs. Oh, Jesus. What's that smell?

Mosca sniffs the bowling-ball case. Oh, Black Jack's got an aroma, yes, he does. Mosca worries open the zipper. Behold the mighty, he says.

The skin is leathery, shrunken. Stiff as dried masking tape. A rictus pulled back to evince a death-scream grimace, reveal a set of long yellowed teeth. A black mustache all wiry and tangled above the grimacing maw.

George frowns at the head and says, Black Jack Ketchum was hanged in 1901. This individual looks to be only a few years departed, you ask me. Wouldn't Ketchum be not much more than a skull by now?

It's Black Jack's head, says Mosca. I shit you not.

Whatever you say, *hombre*. But before you get your panties in a wad, maybe you ought to take this to the Antiques Roadshow people. One of those queens will set you straight.

I don't need any queen to tell me what's what.

Antiques Roadshow, repeats Crowfoot. They talk about provenance and whatnot.

What's provenance?

Proof of where it came from.

I don't need proof. I got a head.

Right.

He's well preserved is what he is. Like my grandmother. We had to dig her up for an inquest thing. To prove if my grandpa poisoned her or not. For the insurance, you know.

And did he?

Probably, but they couldn't prove it. Grandma looked pretty good, considering. Like she'd been dead only a month or two.

I don't know about your dear departed. But I tell you it doesn't take a genius to figure that ain't Ketchum.

Is too.

You been had.

Mosca considers the withered human head in his lap. The wispy black hair, ears like dried apple slices. A flake of yellow epidermis peels away from the edge of a sunken, gaping eye socket. Mosca picks at it, trying to neaten the skull. It's like trying to scrape the label off a mayonnaise jar. All he manages to do is to loosen a bigger hunk. He licks his finger and dabs at it.

Damn, he says. I didn't mean to do that.

George shakes his head and backs out of the driveway. You can probably hock it.

You think?

George shrugs. Hock shops value the odd. It might fit right in. I mean, it's a head all right. Even if I doubt it's Black Jack's.

Mosca stares at the grimacing, leathery mug. People will pay good money for the head of Black Jack Ketchum. Man I won it from said it was worth a grand at least.

Crowfoot shrugs. You might get something for it. I don't know about a grand. Maybe a hundred bucks.

Shit. I get more than that. He's a famous outlaw.

Ketchum was. This dude, he probably robbed a liquor store and forgot to grab a top-shelf bottle of tequila, the dumbshit. Crowfoot grins. That's if you ask me.

Mosca says, Fuck it. He stuffs the head back into the bowling-ball bag, crams it between his feet on the floorboard. I'm going to make some money off this head if it's the last thing I do.

That's just peachy, says Crowfoot. They drive taciturn and moody through the streets of Pueblo to the Department of Nuisance Animal Control office, where they check in and get their assignment for the day. Crows and cowbirds near a feedlot. Exterminate with all due diligence. The boss man Silas tells them to get started pronto.

Halfway across town Mosca says, You hear about the fatso kidnappings?

Crowfoot holds the steering wheel with one finger, his hand in his lap, staring at the landscape of pawnshops, strip clubs, and palm readers that clatters by the pickup's window like lemons and cherries on a slot machine. After a moment of silence he says, You want the truth? I bet Black Jack Ketchum's head is buried along with his name.

They're kidnapping fat people and liposuctioning them skinny to sell the oil on the black market. That's what I heard.

The sky looks darker the farther west they travel.

What do you mean, "they"? asks Crowfoot.

You know, says Mosca. The lipo gangs. The ones who sell it

on the black market to the illegals and migrants living in the box-cars down at the freight yards.

Crowfoot squints at the storm clouds massed before them. Looks like we're about to be in the shit, Señor Fly.

Jesus Christ. I don't need another day off, says Mosca. I need some work is what I need. By hook or crook.

George is thinking he needs a better pair of boots. And a better job. He used to think this grunt work was a step up from hauling trash since part of the job was shooting things. Years ago maybe George would have enjoyed the pure sport of it—the aiming, the hitting of the target—but now when he's called out to exterminate another murder of crows sighted near town, he feels the spider-on-your-neck creep of guilt. And today's detail is just pathetic, sent to the west side of town to track and kill a flock of cowbirds massing on feedlot scraps. A job like this would make Crazy Horse turn over in his grave.

Interested in a little extra cash? asks Mosca. I got something going on the side. Bet I could get you on, easy.

You're full of bets today, aren't you?

Mosca grins. I'm a betting fool, that's for sure. I tell you about this, you promise not to breathe a word? It's somewhat wide of the law, if you catch my drift.

Do I look like a snitch?

Mosca explains that he's part of a crew of cattle providers. With the price of beef higher than ever, a man can make good money liberating a few head of cattle at night, taking them to a slaughterhouse out of state. Black-market beef.

You have to know your way around a steer, says Mosca. I'm

guessing you probably do. Plus it helps to have some muscle. It's all quick and fast and these dudes I work with, they don't fuck around.

You're cattle rustling?

You could call it that. I like to think of it as a Robin Hood kind of deal. Taking from the rich and selling to the poor.

That's supposed to be giving to the poor.

We can't be that old-fashioned, can we?

I don't like the sound of it.

I didn't either at first. But once you get used to money, it makes you feel like the king of Denver.

They near the western edge of town. The wind picks up and grit blasts the windshield. Crowfoot flips on the wipers. The rubber blades squeak and shudder on the cold glass, clearing two arches. Mosca says they're screwed. No way in hell they're going to do any bird killing in this duster. They watch as the dust storm rears up in front of them. It comes on like a cloud of bricks.

Crowfoot and Mosca sit in the cab and wait it out. The sand sifts across the windshield in a hypnotizing swift drizzle. It's as if time is moving faster than it should. Mosca says sometimes it seems that the end is near and this is nothing but hourglass sand running out.

They watch as the dust storm swallows a billboard advertising topless dancers in the Wiggle Room.

After a half hour the storm slackens. The wind dies and the dust sifts down on the back side of the wind gusts. Traffic begins to crawl. Mosca and Crowfoot drive on, straining to see the taillights of the vehicles ahead.

Crowfoot asks for more dope about this cattle-rustling gig.

.   .   .

RUBY HURRIES ACROSS the prairie, the roiling bulge of the dust storm looming like the debris cloud of a demolished building. She coughs and squints, the grit in her eyes and mouth. A gulch opens before her. She stumbles at the edge and into the shadows she falls.

She trips and slides down the steep ravine walls. Cactus rakes her face, neck, and arms. She hits the bottom of the gulch hard, landing in a jumble of stones and grass. When she comes to a stop, she winces and rocks in pain. Her left arm burns and aches. She clutches it to her side. She feels for wounds, finds a swelling on her head. Her hand is wet. She holds it before her eyes. She can see nothing but a finger and palm shadow in the brick-red haze.

The dust storm swirls above the gulch like a bloody tornado. She huddles in the hollow of a boulder, finds a windbreak behind it. She curls on the grassy floor of the dry-wash streambed, feeling the stab of cactus spines embedded in her cheeks and arm. She can feel the sand trickling into the gap of her collar and down her back. After a time she rubs crusty tears from her eyes and can see again. She pulls off the gauze mask and sits up, coughing and wheezing. All about her dust covers the grass and stones. She struggles to her feet, cradling her arm close to her side. Her elbow is swollen and shot with hot pain.

Not far away a coyote stands motionless. She stares numb and confused in its direction for several moments before she notices it, still as the landscape, the gray of its fur contrasting with the dust-covered boulders and stones.

She stares at it and takes a step forward. The coyote drops its head and backs away, keeping its eyes on her, until after a few feet it turns away and trots down the middle of the gulch floor.

She follows the coyote's prints in the dust. The gulch is a dozen feet deep, with sides of steep, corrugated dirt. At its lip are hard-packed overhangs, pocked with the mud cones of Cliff Swallow nests.

She comes upon two illegals in white cowboy hats, carrying *bolsas*, their faces covered by bandannas. Only their eyes and black hair are visible in the wedge of skin above their noses and below their foreheads.

Ruby pulls her gauze mask over her nose to hide her face. She stands coughing as they near. Her heart beats so hard she feels faint.

The illegals look like sand people. One of them has a bandage on his hand, brown blotches on the gauze, the stain of blood seep. They nod at her and pause.

She nods back and takes to coughing again.

One of the illegals removes his hat and holds it in both hands. *Está enferma?* he asks.

Sí. Mi boca está lleno de arena.

Lo siento. Puedo ayudar?

No, gracias. Estoy bien.

The man nods. *Bueno.* He looks behind him, in the direction she's headed. The one who has not spoken, who has the bandage soaked with blood and coated with dust on his hand, removes his hat and slaps it against his leg, brushing free a plume. A rifle hangs from his shoulder.

Ruby moves away. *Vaya con dios*, she says.

Dondé está su casa? asks the one with the rifle.

She keeps walking. She listens for their movements. She tenses to run even as she yet steps carefully through the sand and cactus. Her heart in her throat, she struggles to suppress her cough and to breathe, to be able to hear any sound of movement behind her.

Ruby moves toward town slowly. She feels snowflakes in her eyelashes like the smallest of blessings. A glorious hush falls upon the world. With the dust storm behind her and the snow squall upon her, she has no sense of east or west, past or present.

She thinks of the warmth and comfort she could find if she reaches the vet's office where her mother works, if she reaches someone to take her fever, to hold her up. To keep her from falling. To keep her safe. To return her to her baby girl, to squire them both away from Lord God and all his righteous rants and ravings.

She's faint and weak and begins to doubt her eyes. The falling snow looks red, soft crystals floating down like bloodstained feathers. She knows she's close to town but suddenly a quartet of horses appears galloping, snorting and shaking their heads.

One is a palomino, a pale golden blur in the blizzard of red snowflakes. The others are chestnut and roan, shaggy manes and arched tails. Their eyes are bright and wild as they gallop past. One of the roans, a stallion, slows and whinnies, tossing his head up and down.

Ruby remains still, frightened by the power and excitement of the horses. They canter around her for a moment, this quiet girl eerily motionless in the middle of a desert field, a girl out of place. It's like something out of *Lives of the Saints*, a miraculous girl there to tame the wild heart of the horses, only it is the animals who seem puzzled by her presence, who gallop over the hill to flee from this curious pilgrim of the cactus and prairie grass.

At Pueblo Boulevard, the hiss of tires on snow-wet asphalt. A siren Dopplers in the distance. It sounds like Lila crying, trapped in a wooden box with Lord God, watching out the windows as the world becomes swallowed by dust. A car's deep bass speakers throb. Ruby limps through the weedy parking lot of an abandoned Circuit City next to a defunct Blockbuster Video. The haggard facade of a beauty shop tagged with gang graffiti. Smashed windows of a camera shop next door. Shattered glass and fast-food paper bags litter the asphalt.

Ruby crosses the wide boulevard, forced to hurry on her sprained and swollen ankle through the honking traffic. The vet's office is a few miles farther. She reaches the median and waits for the walk signal. Cold spray from the passing cars' tires wets her cheeks. She slips her gauze mask over her mouth once again and stares stoically at the signal of an amber hand. Cars honk.

Mosca and George Armstrong Crowfoot sit in a line of cars at the red light and see Ruby trying to cross, standing in the median, covered with red dust. It's freezing cold and the jacket she wears is thin. Mosca rolls down his window and tells her, Get inside, honey pie. Get warmed up. No sense being out in the cold like that.

She shakes her head and won't look at them directly.

Come on, sweetheart! Where you headed? We take you wherever you want to go. You're going to catch your death out there.

Ruby hunches her shoulders and stares at the traffic signal.

Come on, *chica!* Get in here and we warm you up! We won't bite. Promise. 'Less you want us to.

Crowfoot feels sorry for her and watches as she hurries through the traffic, darting behind their pickup, to the other side of the intersection, caught by a green light halfway through, running with a hitch in her step in the pink snow.

Cars honk behind the pickup until it roars away. Finally the light changes and Ruby crosses the second lane of traffic. She limps down the sidewalk beside a snow-covered golf course. A Christmas stillness envelops it, the rolling greens coated a pure pinkish white, strips of red storm dust visible in the hollows of the sand traps. She passes a cemetery beside a seedy business district. Colored Christmas lights festoon the eaves of Vietnamese massage parlors and shabby strip clubs/casinos promising all-nude dancers and half-price drinks. She walks beneath a sign proclaiming, ALL NUDES, ALL THE TIME! The snow settles upon cinder-block liquor stores and palm-reader shops advertising *visiones del porvenir, amuletos para buen suerte, y pocíones contra mal ojo.* She walks on, feverish and dizzy.

On Polk Street Ruby comes upon La Iglesia de los Niños de Jesus Cristo. Her skin burns. A heavy weakness fills her bones. She can no longer see clearly. She rubs her eyes and holds out her good hand, watches the snow settle upon it like pink icing.

The sky above ripples. Ruby limps through the churchyard, tears the gauze mask from her face, and gasps, spots in her eyes. When she reaches the steps of the brick church, her vision clouds purple. She sits on the cold steps.

The snow grows heavier, falling in great fluffy flakes. Her hair is soaked and limp. Near her stands the church's nativity scene, a small hut of recycled lumber, a roof of juniper bows and straw, papier-mâché wise men, Joseph and Mary, a wheelbarrow in which lies a plastic doll, the baby Jesus. A square of straw-strewn earth surrounds it.

She rises and limps to the shelter of the hut, bone-weary and feverish. Into the wheelbarrow she curls her body around the doll, its blue plastic eyes open wide with artificial lashes fat and spiky.

She lies there, shivering, delirious. A flock of seagulls hovers over the crèche, their black eyes like polka dots upon the swirling red snow. After a time a nun appears. You cannot sleep here, she says. Please. It is a sacrilege.

Ruby only blinks at her, blood and scratches on her face. The nun makes the sign of the cross and hurries back inside the church, leaving Ruby there, holding the plastic baby Jesus in her arms.

IT HAS BEEN TWO YEARS and thirteen days since ward Costello's wife and baby girl passed away. On the outskirts of Pueblo he passes a billboard that reads, WHEN AMERICANS BELIEVE IN GOD, GOD WILL BLESS AMERICA. A dark blue deportation bus roars by, filled with illegals, mainly women and children, their sorrowful faces near the windows. They watch him through the smeared glass of his windshield.

He feels swollen. As if it is all too much for him. He's had this odd itching for a while now, since his wife had and daughter have been gone: a feeling that all his past, all his memories, is just a blink away, the width of an eyelash, the click of a tongue, everything, right there. The slightest movement or hiss of wind can bring it all rushing back. A trapped sensation that there's nowhere to go, nowhere to hide, from this tsunami of the past. The more he focuses on the present the more he can't wish or will it away.

This he remembers: her long, dusky eyelashes, her incredible warmth, the smell of her and her alone on the cotton pillowcases, the feel of spooning next to her, the curve of her smoothness against his lap. The bliss remembered. Waking up to call her by name, a single word, baby.

He exits I-25 in downtown Pueblo. He drives west, the sky ahead like a hammered sheet of copper, traffic moving in fits and starts. He passes a truck hauling cattle, the whites of their bovine eyes rolling at him through the slats in the cattle trailer. He heads down 4th Street, through a moribund district of brick shops long closed. His eyes burn like they've been soaked in Tabasco. His heart beats too hard and fast and the dividing stripes in the road seem to rise in the air above his car like flying white snakes.

He rolls down his window to let in the cold. When his scalp begins to tingle and goose bumps cover his arms, he rolls it back up. The heater blasts hot air, so he feels cold and feverish at once. He worries it could be a touch of the sickness, even though he's supposed to be immune now.

He heads toward an odd darkness in the sky, toward the prairie that divides Pueblo from the Sierra Mojada, foothills to the Rockies, where he plans to do his bird-population study. After sleeping in the car and no shower, he smells sour and homeless. He keeps expecting a motel to pop up on the western edge of town, where it would be convenient. None do. Hispanic teenagers in muscle cars rumble in the other lanes, blasting Tejano hip-hop.

Sitting at an intersection he closes his eyes and the next thing he knows a pickup behind him is honking and he's faint and frantic, pressing down on the accelerator and giving the driver behind a guilty wave. He passes pawnshops and massage parlors and Mexican restaurants. He squints at the street signs and sees he's crossing Pueblo Boulevard, on the edge of town, a sign indicating to turn right for the city zoo. All the billboards are in Spanish. He keeps driving until he realizes he is beyond everything. The landscape here is tan and rust-colored rock on cliffs above the road, and below it cottonwoods and Russian olives, pale green and dusted with road drift, along the banks of the Arkansas River.

Here what little is left of town looks like Mars conquered by Cortés. In a sudden moment of panic he loses his way. A cloud wall of dark red dust swallows the road and he slows to a crawl before pulling onto the shoulder. The car shakes in the wind. Sand and dust pummel the windshield.

Ward closes his eyes and leans against the steering wheel. His thoughts bob and float. A memory lurches up like a zombie: how as a boy he would mow the grass of an aunt and uncle's house. His mother would drive him there on weekend mornings and drop him off, return to pick him up hours later. The mowing didn't take long and he'd have hours to kill in the musty-but-clean house of the old couple. He must have been eight, nine years old. His cousin was much older and was already grown, but in his old room there was a large box of vintage comic books. Richie Rich, Caspar the Friendly Ghost, Archie, Spiderman, the Flash. He remembers how happy he was just to sit in the room and read the comic books. How peaceful it was. How long ago it seems.

Later he wakes in a daze, a spot of drool on his crossed arms. He rubs his eyes and sees that the storm has passed. Weak and brain-befogged, he does a U-turn in the empty road and heads back toward town, crosses the Arkansas River and the railroad depots. A neon sign the shape of a buffalo, upon which rides a cowgirl holding the loop of a lariat. The Buffalo Head.

He pulls into the parking lot and kills the engine. The car ticks like the sound of his brain defusing. He stares at a horse tied to a stanchion near the office. A faint snow begins to fall. Ward rubs his eyes and blinks. A horse? He wonders if the fever is affecting his vision. The snow looks pink.

In the motel office Ward stands at the check-in counter, blowing his nose. His head is clogged, each beat of his pulse causing a throb of ache in his temples. To his left is a platter of glazed doughnuts, a coffee machine with an urn full of black liquid. He takes a seat on the ugly brown sofa near a wall-mounted, taxidermied buffalo head. The lobby paintings are all cowboys herding steers across a river or coyotes against a full moon. The lamp-shade stand is made of deer antlers. Ward sits and stares at the painting of cowboys and steers as if stunned by a slaughterhouse air gun. His face is pale and he can smell himself, feel the waxy sweat upon his fevered forehead.

After some time he awakens in the chair, his bladder full and hot with pain.

Are you okay?

It's the clerk. She's behind the check-in counter now, leaning forward to see him. A bleached blond chewing gum. Hey, mister. You okay? she asks again.

He finds himself staring at the garish electric sign of the motel. A cowgirl with loopy neon lariat, riding a stylized buffalo. The yellow-and-blue light streaks like glowing tattoos upon the deep blue skin of dusk. No, he says. Not really.

H I R A M   P A G E   opens his pawnshop with a premonition of something wonderful about to drop into his lap. Not one month ago he saw a red-haired preacher's daughter sitting in a pew of the Lamb of the Forsaken temple and knew she would become his third wife. He has a way with these things and it isn't to be argued with.

Hiram is forty-eight but looks older, discount-store distinguished. He's a tall, broad-shouldered man with a wide, shrewd face, a high forehead and white hair. Handsome enough to use his looks for his own gain. Although raised in a Mormon family, he enjoys a drink now and then, but who doesn't? The chastised pride themselves on overcoming vices, but it takes a man to manage them for his own enjoyment.

The secret to success is constancy of purpose, he often says, a quote from no less than Benjamin Disraeli, a British prime minister from the nineteenth century. The man was an accomplished as a British statesman despite being a Jew. Hiram attends an FLDS church every Sunday and professes to believe in the mirage of the one true prophet. A foolish idea if there ever was one.

His pawnshop lurks on Northern Avenue, at the edge of Mexican town, a good place for poor folk desperate to sell something for much less than it's worth. The shop itself is an ex–convenience store, its wide glass windows girded by burglar bars. In place of the Slushy machine stands a firearms display.

This morning the sunlight slants through the steel bars covering the windows as into a prison cell. In the distance a train howls. Hiram starts the day with a nip of bourbon and its mist still warms his throat when a man-child in plaid western shirt and faded jeans stumbles in, struggling against the wind, face masked by a bandanna. Standing just inside the shop like a shy bank robber, he pulls down the bandanna and puts an asthma inhaler to his mouth. After a moment of wheezing he removes his cap and shakes it clean.

Hiram watches the dust settle onto his recently swept tile floor. I appreciate that, friend, he says. I was just telling myself how my clean floor needed some dirt.

Hiram has a Gregory Peck voice, rich and deep. A voice you hear on wildlife documentaries.

You the owner?

Hiram raises his chin. I might be. Long as you're not about to point a six-shooter at me and proclaim this a stickup.

I'm not sticking up anyone.

The newcomer puts his Colorado Rockies baseball cap back in place and tries to stand up straight, but it's as if his body is slightly crooked. He opens his mouth to speak and pauses. The fluorescent lights fill the white cap with a glow, giving him the aura of a farm-team Jesus, eyelashes long and girlish.

Hiram pushes a bottle of hand sanitizer toward the rockabilly. Do the honors, would you?

The man takes the sanitizer in a submissive way, rubbing his hands and then reaching out for a Kleenex to dry them.

What I hear is that you and me are family.

Hiram purses his lips. How so?

My name's Jack Brown and I'm your wife's second cousin. Honey Davis. Davis is her stepfather's name. Her real father was a Hostetter, and my mother is Dorothy Hostetter, his cousin. So Honey's my second cousin. Or third, I don't know. You just ask her. She'll tell you.

I'm sure she'd sing like a bird, says Hiram. But for the moment, let's say you're telling the Lord's truth. What can I do you for?

You've got a reputation, you know that? People always talking about what a shrewd customer that Mr. Hiram Page is. I even hear you got two wives.

Hiram blinks and again purses his lips almost imperceptibly. Both are sweet and pretty. And they smile when I walk up.

Jack Brown grins. You got me there.

Did you come in just to get acquainted? asks Page.

Brown steps forward, speaks in a hush. Thing is, he says, I need to borrow some money. I got to buy a pickup.

You do.

I know what you're thinking. Just 'cause he's my wife's second cousin he thinks he can saunter in here like the king of England and get some money for nothing. But that's not it at all.

It's not the half of it, I'd wager.

How much you give me to borrow off a carat-and-a-half diamond wedding ring? You know, as collateral.

Carat plus? That's a big diamond.

You're telling me. I'd say it's worth twenty grand.

Hiram raises his eyebrows. These days you can buy a house in Little Pueblo for less.

I got no use for a house.

Hiram sighs. A pock-faced teenager scuffles in the door. He smells like weed and looks like trouble. His oil-black hair hangs in his eyes and between the bangs his gaze slides by Hiram and Brown like they're museum pieces and he's on a high school field trip.

Hiram paces down the counter, away from Jack Brown and toward the kid. What can I do you for? Let me guess. You're looking for something? A birth certificate?

The kid is chewing gum and pauses in midchew. He shakes his head. He wears sneakers with the laces untied and spiderweb tattoo sleeves decorate his arms.

Is the drum set in the window for sale?

You bet it is, says Hiram. And if you can play a drum solo, I'll drop the price 40 percent. Hiram looks at Jack Brown and winks.

The teenager smiles. I'll try.

You interested in that diamond ring or not? asks Brown.

Let me see what you have.

I don't have it here with me.

And you want to know what it's worth?

Ballpark figure, yeah. I mean, what I could borrow for it.

I can't estimate a value on a mythical ring, says Page. King Solomon had three hundred wives, but he still knew you have to bite gold.

I can get that ring. This afternoon, most likely.

The teenager gives the drums a steady roll and drowns out Jack Brown's voice.

Pardon? asks Hiram.

I can get it, shouts Jack Brown. It! he shouts. The ring! Later today.

So where is this Star of India?

It was my grandmother's! He shouts again to be heard above the drum noise. Two teenaged girls who have just wandered in cringe and go wide-eyed.

Hiram nods. Let me guess. She's no longer among the living?

Died two years ago.

The kid kicks into a drum solo. Jack Brown shakes his head. After a moment the kid stops and calls out, I get that 40 percent off?

You got it, Ringo, says Hiram.

The whole set?

The whole set. I'll even throw in an extra pair of sticks.

The kid smiles and extricates himself from the drum stool. I'll be back later with the money.

You do that.

Hiram calls out to the teenaged girls in the electronics aisle and tells them to give him a holler if they have any questions.

Now, where were we? he asks Brown. Oh, yes. We were taking a diamond ring off your deceased grandmother. Right. Have to dig her up and soap her finger, do we?

I gave it to a woman is what I did. Now I'm having second thoughts.

Hiram smiles. Clear as mud.

I asked for it back. I'm going to pick it up later. It's early yet.

And this Ophelia? She's happy to return said expensive romantic keepsake you gave her free and easy? She hasn't sold it already?

Not if she knows what's good for her.

Hiram steps away, wiping his hands, mock Pontius Pilate. You bring the ring and I'll take a look.

I'll be back before you can get bored watching the two fillies there on aisle two.

Hiram stares back into his eyes. Okay, Cousin Jack. I'll be waiting. But remember what Margaret Thatcher said about patience.

Margaret who?

Thatcher. Former prime minister of England. I assume you've heard of the nation of England? Beef eaters and blood pudding? Soccer hooligans? Ring a bell?

Don't be talking down to me, okay? I know you got me over a barrel, but there's other pawnshops in the world.

Yes, there are.

So tell me already. What did this Margaret lady say that I should remember?

She said, I'm extraordinarily patient, provided I get my own way in the end.

LIKE SOMETHING out of legend, an equestrian patrol officer appears before La Iglesia de los Niños de Jesus Cristo on a chestnut horse. He dismounts and ties his mare to the crèche, squatting down to get a good look at the girl in the hay. The nun meets him and they speak for a moment. Both wear gauze face masks, struggle to hear each other over the shovel scrape and high-pitched beeping of a passing snowplow. The nun mentions the word *fever*.

Officer Israel James comes to stand above Ruby curled in the wheelbarrow. He shakes her shoulder. She does not respond. He calls in a report to the dispatcher. She tells him that all the ambulances are busy, that he should transport the girl to the hospital himself. He explains that he's on horseback. The dispatcher tells him to wait while she directs a patrol car his way. He listens and nods, replaces the wireless unit in his shoulder harness.

The girl has the fever no doubt and to touch her is forbidden if you are anyone but family or a doctor. He guesses a lawman fits somewhere between the two categories. A risk of his life it is and he will do it without thinking, looking at this pale face. How can you turn away? You can't. If it's your time to punch the big clock, so be it.

The chestnut mare shakes her head and mane, whinnying high-pitched and petulant.

The policeman takes a handful of sugar cubes from his pocket and holds them out, the horse's tongue warm against his cold fingers. Now, calm down, Apache, he says. This girl's hurt and I think you can wait a few minutes till the wheels arrive.

Before long he sees a patrol car turn at the intersection and head his way. He stands over Ruby for a moment, plants his feet wide, hefts her into his arms. He carries her to the patrol car, her body limp and lifeless. He waits as the patrolman opens the door and, grunting and breathing hard, he maneuvers her into position on the rear seat. She parts her lips and moans, her eyes half open and dreamy.

Later Officer James is called to defuse a domestic disturbance. At a motel no less. The dispatcher says some couple is shouting and threatening mayhem. Sober guests have complained.

Israel James does not like motels. They bring out the worst in people. The good take home a bar of soap or vial of shampoo, the polishing cloth for a shoeshine they will never use, maybe the Gideon Bible in times of spiritual doubt. The bad rip the blow dryer out of the wall, burn a hole in the carpet, then strangle a hooker to death after failing to perform, leaving her body beneath the bed or stuffed in the closet, covered with a blanket, behind an ironing board. And the people who are torn between good and bad? They hear the devil whispering, and they listen.

The Buffalo Head Inn has seen better days, perhaps during the Dust Bowl of the 1930s, when the Joads offered to sweep and mop to pay for the room. It's two stories of bleached and weather-beaten wood done imitation-ski-lodge style, with pine railings adorned with bucking-bronco woodcuts, plank walkways outside the rooms, and room numbers wood-burned on aspen cuts.

Israel James rides his horse to the office breezeway and dismounts, the leather of his gunbelt creaking. Apache snorts, her shoes popping the pavement. The carport roof above the breezeway catches the sound. He ties her to a wrought-iron bench.

You behave now, girl, he says. Don't bite the paying customers.

The parking lot is spotty with old pickups and new Minis, cars so small you expect a troupe of clowns to emerge at every stoplight. Cigarette butts dot the asphalt amid the deadbeat jewelry of broken glass.

Inside the lobby, a bleached blond sniffs a magazine perfume insert and watches Israel approach. Country music sad-sacks out from a radio. Behind her sits a bassinet with a sleeping child in it. A handwritten sign above the sign-in counter advertises HAPPY HOUR 5–7 IN THE WAGON WHEEL LOUNGE, FREE BEER & WINE.

Her ID tag reads, Fufu. You must be here for the honeymooners, she says. They're in 117.

You know anything about them?

Fufu shrugs. The gal's been staying in the room alone mostly. I think lover boy just showed up and if I'm guessing right, she's pissed he found her. Maybe she's just not that into him. Or he wants into her, and she wants out.

The female must be an Amish schoolteacher, right? A looker?

Fufu pulls a face. Nothing special. My guess is she's the kind of woman men like. You know. For their earthly pleasures.

James is thinking of Fufu along similar lines. It's the devil on your shoulder in the motel zone. She wears a tangerine western shirt with pearl-snap buttons and saddle stitching, a gap between the snaps revealing a peek of lily-white bra cup. He guesses she's sometime past high school and somewhere before second divorce.

Well, it's my job to keep the peace. Should I be worried about these two?

Fufu shrugs. He smells like lowlife, you ask me. Like he'd beat a dog if it took to barking.

You're saying maybe I should use some caution.

Fufu smiles. A horse cop trying to break up a domestic? Maybe you should call in the Mounties.

You watch my back, would you?

She grins. I could do that. But I got to watch him first, she adds, indicating the sleeping baby.

Officer James takes it slowly, counting his paces down the warped wood planks to the stairway. He passes a room illuminated by the glow of a TV flickering against the drawn curtains, laughter and loud voices. At another room a woman holds a door open for a man carrying a baby in a car seat. An alarm honks from the used-car parking lot, no one nearby.

Although Israel Franklin James is a man of the law, supposedly he's a descendant of Jesse James, hothead outlaw and one-time Missouri boy. He suspects it's just a family myth. Kin always get a little vague when asked for proof, citing some long-lost letter from Independence, Missouri, with Jesse's name on it. Israel figures Jesse wasn't much of a letter writer, what with the bank robbing and all. His hands must have been full, holding six-shooters and bags of cash.

And he doesn't particularly like the name Israel. He's uncomfortable with the biblical, Red Sea tone of it. He isn't a Bible thumper and doesn't want to be confused with one. But a name is a gift one doesn't give back. Friends call him Elray. His sister named him that. She gave it a hillbilly twang, just to yank his chain.

Elray hears bedlam before he reaches the top of the stairs. A man and woman both talking at once is what he'd say with his eyes closed, which they are in effect, just a pair of voices somewhere above and down the breezeway to the right. The woman raises hers loud and clear, calling for the comfort of the public sphere.

You touch me I'll scream, she says.

Nobody's touching nobody, the man says. Touching time is over and out.

Possession is nine-tenths of the law, says the woman.

Yeah, well, the other tenth is what matters, and it's my grandmother's ring. So turn it over already.

You don't scare me.

Give it back and let's just close this door and move on. That's what we're going to do here, less you got twenty grand cash to buy it straight out.

You're crazy.

Right. You don't have it, do you?

I have a ring is what I have. A diamond ring you gave me. Fair and square.

You got a broken heart and a rock that don't belong to you, is what you got.

Jack Brown is breathing hard and pulls his asthma inhaler out and takes a breath as he watches the law approach.

Come on, now, Brown says to the woman. You're making a spectacle of yourself.

She sees Elray and her eyes stay on him as she speaks. Don't tell me to clean it up. You're the dirty one, not me.

Brown holds her elbow. Great, he says. Now you're going to end up in court. Everybody's going to get a good laugh.

See here, says Elray. Let's you two just calm down and be nice.

Brown shakes his head. We got no use for you here, Officer. Just a civilized disagreement is all.

That's a lie, says the woman, trying to twist away from his grip on her arm. He's trying to take my engagement ring is what he's doing.

That's between us, Becca.

I'll be the judge of that, says Elray. Let her arm go why don't you?

Brown doesn't budge. This is my grandmother's ring.

I don't give a shit whose it is. I said let the woman go.

I'm not letting her take my—

In two steps Elray has Brown's ear in his right hand, twisting.

Pardon? says Elray. I don't think I heard you right.

He gave this ring to me, says the woman. He gave it to me, she repeats. He called it off but once you give an engagement ring you don't take it back.

Jack Brown grimaces from his ear being twisted. That ring

cost twenty thousand dollars, he pleads, his breath wheezy. It's over, right? Well, I can't be paying twenty thousand dollars for two months of her time, now, can I?

I told you to let go of her, says Elray. This ain't tag-team wrestling, shithead. Let go before a judge sorts things out not to your liking.

You want this ring? asks the woman. She puts her ring finger into her mouth. She sucks for a moment, squeezes her eyes shut tight, then pulls the ring off her finger with her free hand and holds it out. Is this what you want?

Becca? Don't mess with me.

It's mine, she says. It's mine to do with what I want. She holds the diamond ring between her index finger and thumb. As if to assay its value. As if to offer it in auction. Or to hock at a pawnshop. For a brief moment. Then she smiles and moves to put the ring into her mouth.

Brown tries to grab her hand and snatch the ring but misses and stumbles, Elray still holding on to his ear.

Are you crazy? He tries to jam his fingers into her mouth. A confused struggle, his voice cursing her. Elray pins Brown by the neck against the rough wood siding of the motel wall. Brown's baseball cap cants sideways at a comical angle. Elray feels the flex of a windpipe. Brown's face goes purple.

Whoever you think you're dealing with here, says Elray, you are mistaken. I am a horse cop, yes. That's who I am. Who are you? You're the jailhound who just resisted arrest.

He thinks he knows everything and everyone, says the woman. He's walking poison is what he is.

Brown's gasps, his tongue visible in mouth agape. He seems to be shaking his head, grabbing at Elray's left arm with both hands. His hat falls and the woman catches it in the air, flings it backward over the railing. It lands brim down in an oily puddle. Brown continues to struggle. Elray pulls him forward a space and slams him back against the wall. His eyes bulge. He raises his hands.

That's probably good, now, says the woman. She touches Elray's arm. I don't want you making trouble for yourself. Come on, now.

I let you go, you going to touch this woman again?

Brown does the best head shake he can, his neck pinned and his face gone purple.

Elray loosens his hold and steps back, one hand held out as if to ward off a wild vengeance swing. Brown gasps and hunches over, wheezing, his lungs loosing a high-pitched hiss. He scrabbles on his knees for a moment, a squirming ball of faded western shirt and blue jeans, working the inhaler out of his pocket and into his mouth.

Oh, good Lord, says the woman. She kneels beside Jack Brown and strokes his forehead as he wheezes. Every time he tries to play the badass, his asthma acts up.

Elray watches crestfallen, afraid now that this little dustup is turning into something ugly and complicated. Domestics are always like this: One minute you think it's over, the next you're rushing a shirtless drunk to the St. Mary's ER or answering questions at a disciplinary hearing.

He going to be okay?

I think so. The woman helps Jack Brown sit up. He just can't breathe is all.

Elray asks for their names and an explanation of the dispute. Hers is Rebecca Cisneros, friends called her Becca. Long black hair like a show horse's mane and high cheekbones. She's the kind of woman who could be the mother of beautiful children or the teller of a First National Bank. Or end up broadcast on the Internet in a sex video shot in a no-tell motel like the Buffalo Head Inn, with bad lighting, shag carpet, a painting of elk and pines on the wall, and beneath her naked skin an ugly bedspread.

When he can talk Jack Brown says, My name is Smith. He stares at Becca as he says this.

Smith? Elray repeats. First name?

William. That's right. A vein pulses down the middle of Brown's pale forehead, and at each breath he grimaces. I'm guessing you've probably heard my name before.

Elray looks him straight in the eyes and does not blink. Sounds like an alias.

I'll get a lawyer, Brown says. Once this gets settled, you'll be sorry.

Elray has been holding the pepper-spray can at the ready, like it's an aerosol quick-draw contest. He tucks it back into a belt loop and says, Now I'm scared.

Jack Brown keeps wheezing. Yeah, well, you should be.

Becca wears the queasy smile of a woman who has swallowed a diamond ring worth twenty thousand dollars and now realizes the only way to retrieved it will be slow, painful, and unpleasant.

Most likely the only witness to its egress will be herself, in her mind the rightful owner of the pricey bijou and symbol of undying eternal affection.

Elray adjusts his hat and looks at the two of them. I tell you what. I hate domestics, you know? I don't like to get in the middle of other people's disagreements. Can we end this here?

He's not getting that ring, says Becca. Not now. Not a week, month, or year from now.

Forget it, says Brown. His face is blotchy and eyes bloodshot. He smooths his bushy hair with one hand. I can buy another one, he adds. And get another sweetheart. Same difference.

Let's hold off the insults, okay? says Elray.

Can I leave? Without you pulling a gun and plugging me in the back?

Go, says Elray. It will be my pleasure.

Brown walks away, wearing the look of a man who has lost a battle but is planning a war. The stairwell shudders under his boots and the weight of his body bounding down the steps. He goes to the parking lot and picks up his cap, brushes it off. Moments later a Jeep wheels out of the parking lot, squealing as it takes a right on the avenue.

You know how to make friends, don't you? says Becca.

I suppose, says Elray. He shrugs. Funny how people obey if you have them by the throat.

Becca touches his arm and tells him she appreciates his help, his standing up for her like that. She explains that Jack Brown gave him a fake name. You can't trust him. He gave me this engagement ring and then demanded it back. I said no way, she says. Then he got all huffy about it, insisted it was worth twenty thousand dollars.

Elray puts away his notebook. You're better off not married to any man who would ask for the ring back, what I'm thinking. You deserve better than that.

Becca smiles. You're sweet. Can I tell you a secret?

Does it involve lawbreaking?

She looks at him funny for a moment, wiggling her mouth and jaw, then reaches inside her lips with her fingertips. Bingo, she says and holds the diamond ring up in the air.

Elray grins. You're no dummy.

That's the truth. Problem is, Jack is. Just enough of a dummy not to let it go. I'm here hiding from him, but he found me. He's like a bloodhound. Dim and determined.

So what is this outlaw's real name?

I'll tell you on one condition. You interested in some dinner? I could fix us something. I'm not always involved in such seedy scenes, you know. Most of the time I'm downright civic-minded. I vote and pay taxes.

You don't, he says.

I do. She smiles. And I make a good plate of fried chicken. Sound good?

Elray says it does and he'll be glad to accept. They agree he'll show up later, after nine.

She gives him a kiss on the cheek and he feels the softness of her lips, smells her skin when she leans in close.

I'm looking forward to it, she says. You probably got the wrong idea about me earlier.

You're better off without that loser.

She nods and tucks her hands in her back pockets. I am.

Elray is love-headed on his way out the door, stifling a foolish grin, waving good-bye to her as she stands in the aura of the doorway. Half a mind to double back and ask if he can take her out somewhere nice. But then again, hard to refuse a woman who offers to cook for you. He keeps walking, his mind full of her smell and her softness. He moves on into the early evening, the sky a pure violet overhead, toward his horse, forgetful and enchanted, passing light-headed down the motel breezeway, down the stairs.

He's a mile toward home, sitting a bit chilled in the saddle, holding Apache's reins, when he realizes he's forgotten to get the real name of her abuser.

AFTER THE DOOR CLOSES Becca feels herself deflate. A depressing quiet settles like the hush of bad news. Her smile fades as she moves through the room, tuning the TV to the Weather Channel, pouring herself a glass of water. She's ashamed and realizes her engagement was nothing more than a pause at the intersection of Hope and Desperation. Forget marriage. She knows the reality likely will be her standing alone in line at a convenience store, trying to corral a two-year-old, buying tampons and a pack of Marlboro Lights.

She goes to brush her teeth and stares at her reflection in the mirror. A trace of wrinkles around her mouth and eyes and oh God she's thirty-one years old and getting older by the second.

Out the open window she can hear a couple arguing in the alley. She rinses her teeth and stares at the diamond ring on the counter beside her moisturizer and makeup. From the window she can hear a truck's loud engine throbbing and a burst of drunken laughter.

She rummages through her makeup kit and comes up with a small vinyl coin purse with the logo and address of First National Bank of Pueblo on it. She wads the engagement ring in several sheets of Kleenex until it's a puffy square, then wedges this inside the coin purse and squeezes it to make sure it fits securely.

With her palms sweating, Becca heads to the lobby. There the buffalo head looms over a sofa with cow-horn armrests. Before the sofa there's a coffee table covered with magazines and to the left a small table with a coffee pot, microwave, and creamer, sugar packets, and stir sticks.

Becca pours coffee into a white Styrofoam cup, facing the check-in counter, watching. She takes the coin purse from her pocket and crams it into the buffalo's mouth. She pushes it until she hears a woman talking on a phone, walking up to the front counter.

You need something, honey?

Becca wipes her hands on her jeans. No, I'm fine, she says. I was just looking for a magazine to read.

You want some company? They make a mean margarita in the lounge next door. Aside from the losers and degenerates, it's not half bad. They got free peanuts and pretzels too.

Becca smiles. I'll keep that in mind.

On the way back to her room, she stops at the soft-drink

vending machine, feeds a dollar into the metal mouth, her heart still beating wildly. She's reaching for a Pepsi can when a van pulls to a stop nearby and two goons step out, followed by Jack Brown, looking sheepish, calling out, Hey, Becca. We need to talk.

We don't need anything, she says, hurrying toward the stairs. Before she can reach them one of the goons clamps a hand over her mouth, dragging her backward. Becca's Pepsi can drops to the ground and fizzes. She flails as he pins her arms and the other goon grabs her feet. A car honks as she twists and squirms, shouting, until they slap a piece of duct tape over her mouth. Jack Brown follows behind, saying, Hey, go easy on her. She's my girlfriend. Or used to be.

The van is already moving before Jack is ready, and he has to run across the parking lot to hop inside, whatever he started already in motion and out of control.

PART TWO

Look out the window. And doesn't this remind you of when you were in the boat? And then later that night, you were lying, looking up at the ceiling, and the water in your head was not dissimilar from the landscape, and you think to yourself, "Why is it that the landscape is moving, but the boat is still?"

—*Jim Jarmusch,* Dead Man

The Painted Cliff Face

A HARRIED NURSE AT THE HOSPITAL
info booth tells officer James only immediate family members
are authorized to visit the young woman. Elray explains who he
is, how he found her in the manger.

When I called before I came, nobody said family only. I mean,
if the rules could be bent and not broken, I'd appreciate it.

Go on, says the nurse. I see why you'd be caring to know how
she is.

Could you tell me the name?

What name?

The girl. The sick girl.

Ruby Elizabeth Cole. Seventeen years old and a mother already. The young nurse in the info booth leans forward and whispers, Her father's a war vet, and a preacher to boot.

Elray wanders confused down several hallways before he finds
Ruby Cole. Her room is small and cramped, with two folding

chairs at the foot of the bed and barely enough room to cough without hitting your head on the ceiling.

In bed Ruby resembles a sick mermaid, her hair wet and bedraggled on the pillow, tendrils tangled and wave-tossed, breathing ragged, eyelids purple, nose pink. Her face looks cat-scratched, lips blushed and swollen. Elray watches the blue veins in her neck, the slight hollow of skin in the center of her collarbone. An IV stand holds liquids in clear plastic pouches, tubes from them to her arms. She's also hooked up to a monitoring contraption, a video screen that shows her vitals.

In the pale room, with its tiled floor and simple white walls, a single window presents a view of white sky and mountain silhouettes in the distance. Time seems to contract and withdraw, like an old-fashioned film in which the bright scene of the film's action—say, a farm in winter—appears in a circle surrounded by the blackest darkness until it contracts and all that's left is the mane of a horse, snow falling on a barn, a pitchfork upright in a hay bale.

Elray can't keep his eyes open. He dreams he's trying to swim but has no legs. He awakens with a crick in his neck. A nurse is checking the girl's pulse. She smiles at him and says he's a good man to watch over the girl. They're calling her the Miracle Girl, one of the few to recover from the fever after reaching stage three. They say she's blessed. Some visitors have even come to touch her, as if she possesses the healing powers of a saint.

Elray puts his hat in his lap and sits up. I only wanted to make sure she was okay. Looks like she's in good hands.

Ruby opens her eyes and blinks. She looks at Elray for a long moment, turns her head to the window and stares, reaches up to rub her face.

Well, look what the cat drug in, says the nurse.

Come again?

You're waking up, she says.

Ruby's bone-white face cringes. Where am I? Where's my baby?

The nurse tucks her sheets and straightens her IV attachment. Your family has your baby girl. She's doing fine. Don't you worry.

My family?

Your father is coming to visit. He can tell you everything.

Her eyes pink with tears. Does he have Lila?

Honey, now you just hush and don't worry.

I want my baby.

Elray stands to leave, cowboy hat in his hands. I hope you're feeling better, he says. I was the one picked you up.

Ruby rubs her face. I don't remember.

He nods. Maybe that's good. They say your heart quit beating.

She smiles weakly. People say all kinds of things.

That they do.

I guess you saved my life, then.

It's my job.

Saving people's lives?

He shrugs. Well, mostly I give parking tickets. The occasional drunk and disorderly.

Why are you here?

He picks at the brim of his hat. To see how you're doing.

Ruby's expression stiffens. She stares out the window. Behind him Elray feels a looming. He turns to find a tall, bearded man staring at him with a biblical squint and glower, standing too close. Elray can practically feel his body heat. He smells of wood smoke and soil, the reek of a farmer or a field worker. Elray extends his hand and offers his name.

Lord God does not accept the gesture. He's a good four inches taller than Elray and uses his height to bend him to his will. When he speaks his voice is hoarse and slow.

You know who I am?

I'm guessing you're Mr. Cole, Ruby's father?

Lord God only blinks and strokes his beard. I'm the man who fought for your freedom. I'm the man who went to war so you can eat your fried chicken and drink your beer. You look like a chicken-and-beer man to me.

I wouldn't turn it down, says Elray.

Tacos, too. Tamales. Lord God makes an exaggerated sniffing motion, like a hound trying to catch the trail of an outlaw. Perhaps the occasional enchilada with a margarita chaser.

I do like Mexican food. On the occasion of every chance I get.

It's written all over your face. That lazy hunger. A well-fed man is most likely a criminal, is what I believe. And if his fingers be slick with pork grease from tamales, he's most likely in league with the illegals. Taking payola is what I guess. And it's for you I fought in the desert overseas. For you and your ilk.

Elray wrinkles his brow. And we thank you kindly?

Do you see this leg? Cole lifts his pants leg to reveal his

prosthetic limb. I had my leg blown off, my eye put out. The Muslims put a bomb in the road as a welcome mat. All for my efforts to improve their world.

Elray believes that it's a mistake to occupy a foreign country and expect its people to welcome you with hugs and kisses, especially as a Christian man carrying weapons in a country that worships Allah. He looks at John Wesley Cole's leg and says, It looks to be they have you fixed right up.

Cole nods, his squint tightening. Is that what you call it? Fixed? I got one leg is what I got.

I should be going, says Elray. I was just here to hope she was feeling better.

Not so fast, Officer, says Cole. Let me ask you something. Am I right to assume you did not serve in the military?

Not me. Elray shakes his head.

And can you tell me why?

I guess I didn't think it was the right thing to do.

You guess.

An expression. I didn't join. Let's leave it at that.

You are an officer of the law, says Cole. I see this and I will give it what it's due. But please could you tell me what my daughter's hospital room has to do with any crime or criminal behavior?

He pauses. No one moves. The nurse has disappeared. Cole breathes loudly through his nose, as if Elray were an annoyance and he a giant. I was under the impression that she was to see direct family members only, he adds.

Elray tells who he is, what he's done. How he found her in

the manger, cold and sick in the snow. I just wanted to make sure she was okay. I heard she was better.

She's been here long enough, says her father. I'm taking her home. We thank you for your concern and ask that you now move your concern to other, more dangerous citizens of this county.

Daddy, where's Lila?

I got the Johnson woman down the road to come babysit for a few hours. She'll be fine.

Ruby glances at Elray and says, He didn't mean anything—

My daughter needs to dress and prepare herself. In the interests of modesty, you best be leaving.

Elray nods and backs away, bumping into the nurse.

She shoos both of them and tells Ruby's father to leave her be. She says Ruby can't be moved yet. This young lady is still running a fever, says the nurse. Plus the virus might still be contagious. She is not ready to be released. No way nohow.

Nonsense, says Cole. We'll care for her. She'll recover with her family, where she should be in the first place.

I'm going to get the physician in charge.

Do what you want. As will I. I'm her father and she does what I say.

Elray steps closer to Ruby, watching her face. I think the nurse is right, he says. She should stay a couple more days, till the fever's gone.

I don't need a yellowbelly to tell me what to do. You may wear a badge and carry a gun, but you are not telling me how to raise my daughter.

The girl is sick, says Elray, and she needs time and care to get better. It's not a matter of raising her.

Yes, it is. I'm raising her out of this bed and taking her home.

Cole reaches over the bed and tries to gather Ruby in his arms, but the IV tubes and stand are still connected at her wrists. They tangle as he lifts her to his chest, the stand flopping over onto the bed.

Put your daughter down, says Elray. I can arrest you and charge you with endangering the welfare of a child.

You wouldn't.

Try me.

She's a child no more, says Cole. My daughter has a child of her own. And her baby girl is in need of her attention.

The doctor comes and tells both of them to lower their voices. You can take her home, Mr. Cole, he says. In due time. First we're going to get some test results back and make sure she's good to travel. Just be sure to keep her warm and watch that temperature. Keep feeding her liquids. She might need to stay in bed a week or more.

I'll do that, says Lord God. She's my daughter and I'll lay down my life for her. He stares at Elray and adds, Now I think we've had enough law enforcement for the day.

WARD COSTELLO BEGINS his bird population study at a pullout near Lake Pueblo on a windy day, not a human in sight on the weedy dirt road, the only sound an invisible barking dog. Tumbleweeds cluster against the barbed-wire fence.

A Kestrel kites above the roadside ditch. Ward's head buzzes from insomnia, his mouth tastes like Band-Aids.

On his drive north through the panhandle of Texas and northeast New Mexico, Ward counted eighty-nine raptors, mostly Red-Tailed Hawks, with a number of Northern Harriers perched on low telephone poles or fence posts. Tasked with ascertaining the bird populations on the prairie, Ward estimates the number of birds based on a study of given areas, such as a ten-mile grid with clearly defined parameters. Seeing five Harriers in a five-mile stretch of highway is misleading: More Harriers linger near the highway, feeding off road kill, than in the open expanse of wind-ruffled grasslands. Five to two Harriers per five miles might extrapolate as some two hundred Harriers in a given two-hundred-mile stretch of highway, but that number is suspect.

The population of raptors—Harriers, Prairie Falcons, Red-Tailed Hawks, Ferruginous Hawks, and Golden Eagles—has dropped significantly in the last decade. Ward's scientific method compels him to stake out and define a particular region of prairie, such as BLM land west of Pueblo, Colorado, and do the difficult fieldwork of hiking the prairies and gulches, counting the number of apparent birds, verifying those numbers by numerous visits, and coming up with a rough approximation for the population.

Awakened late the night before by the flashing lights of squad cars in the Buffalo Head's parking lot, a radio barking static in the background as guests spoke to police, Ward's eyes sting and sag and he's bleary-brained. A Western Meadowlark trills from a fence post, liquid and lyrical. He records the sighting in a small spiral notebook, then follows mountain bike trails and finds himself wandering, counting candy-bar wrappers and plastic bags impaled on cactus and rabbit bush. Above him white vapor trails crisscross the pale winter sky.

In two hours he counts three Red-Tailed Hawks, eight female Lark Buntings, seven Horned Larks, a Brewer's Blackbird, a Winter Wren, a flock of thirty-odd European Starlings, and nine plastic bags. He clambers into a gulch that feeds Lake Pueblo and works back toward the highway, studying the mud nests of Bank Swallows. A Raven croaks and squawks as it struggles against the wind, landing in a cottonwood tree.

At one point a Great Horned Owl swoops from a cliff face and glides away. Spying the thicket of a large nest on a rock shelf above, Ward climbs the gulch walls and finds himself staring at a pair of fledgling owls, almost full grown, green eyes blinking, feathers fuzzy. One of the owlets beats its wings and opens its beak wide, hissing. Ward climbs down and crouches a few feet away, out of their line of vision, his heart beating wildly. After a while he takes a long climb out of the gulch to the upper rim across from the owl's nest, watches the owlets from a distance.

It's a good first day, but by the time he returns to his car he's exhausted and disheartened. Heading home, he loses focus and drives back two years into the past.

HE REMEMBERS THE NIGHT everything went bad. The beginning of the end of his little world. His wife and baby girl at the dinner table, green beans and carrots in a bowl.

His wife said she didn't feel right. I think I had better lie down, she said. I don't feel so good. She put her head in her hands.

Ward remembers staring at her hands, remembers how thin and withered they seemed, all veins and bones. She said she felt like all her blood had been sucked dry.

Before long he heard her vomiting in the bathroom. He crouched beside her and told her to get it out. She would feel better soon. Maybe it was food poisoning. Something inside that didn't sit well. He wet a washcloth and put it to her forehead. He held the plastic bowl and afterward, wiped her mouth with another washcloth. His daughter stood in the doorway and stared. Shocked and curious.

Six hours after his wife first fell sick, Ward began to worry in earnest. Her eyes sank into skull hollows. Her skin looked bloodless. She could not sit up. She lay in bed and breathed rapidly, her fever starting to make her skin burn. He called for an ambulance and first the fire department arrived. When he told them her symptoms they nodded and backed away, saying they'd best wait for the EMS.

The ambulance paramedics wore gloves and masks. They told Ward a lot of this was going around. It was contagious. Wash your hands, they said. Be careful not to let the baby touch anything that her mother has handled. Use sanitizers.

How can I do that? he wanted to ask. My wife touches everything in the house. It's her house. She should. She touched the baby just before she went to the bathroom and became sick. She fed her green beans with her hands, with her fingers.

He took his daughter to his mother-in-law's: He'd be back

in the morning, they would all be better. Nurses put his wife on a narrow hospital bed with an IV drip attached to her arm. She grimaced in pain, seized up with muscle spasms. The nurse said it was dehydration. Once we get enough fluids in her, she'll feel much better.

He slept on the floor of her hospital room, which had no door, only a curtain to the hallway full of bustling nurses and doctors and patients and visitors, a constant burble of noise. He sat in a plastic chair until his tailbone ached and he grew so tired he lay on the cold tile floor and tried to sleep. He woke up bleary with a nurse standing over him. She said he should go to the mercy room. It might be more comfortable.

It wasn't.

They said by morning she would be better. She would improve.

He awoke with a sore neck and gunk in his eyes, twisted up on a short sofa in the mercy room. A woman who looked as if she had been crying was sitting in the chair across from him, watching *Good Morning America*. He walked down the hall to his wife's room and it was empty. He had to find a nurse and ask for help.

Where's my wife? She was supposed to get out this morning.

She had been transferred in the night to another room, and had more equipment attached to her when he found her. Her fever was 105, and nothing they did seemed to help. They had her on fluids and anti-this and anti-that. They were giving her something to bring down the fever.

Is the fever worse? he asked.

The nurse did not answer. When the doctor came to give him

an update, he said it had climbed to 107 at one point. They had brought it down to 105. We're working on it, said the doctor. He had long blond hair and was short, heavyset. He looked like an old surfer. We're going to get this thing licked. Be patient.

Ward sat in the hospital room and read old magazines. TV stars from the past, from the time only a year before that seemed to reek of excess and vanity. Celebrity chefs. Reality-TV stars. Dancing contests. Hedge-fund billionaires. The world gone greedy, drunk, and stupid.

Without sleep or breakfast, his heart was racing. He kept rubbing his eyes to try to wake up. He checked on his wife again. She was asleep, her eyelids dusky purple, a frown creating a crease just between her eyebrows. He sat beside her and stared out the window. The hospital was expanding, a mammoth construction project with cement walls topped with steel bars. A giant crane sat in the middle of the project, a triangular yellow flag at its tip.

Ward could hear the muffled rumble of dump trucks and earth-moving equipment, could see a rotating concrete truck with a dozen men standing around it. The woman on the other side of the room awoke and started to moan in pain and call out, Nurse? Nurse? Where are you? Help me. Help, nurse.

Ward walked down the hallway to the nurses' station and told them of her calls. They nodded and said they were busy with an influx of flu cases. Someone would be there in a moment. He saw two nurses talking to each other and frowning. One of them said, Oh, good Lord.

He drove to his mother-in-law's and found his daughter

vomiting, her face pale and skin hot. She was crying and calling out for her mother. Mama's sick, baby, said Ward. She's in the hospital. But she'll be better soon and then she'll come home.

Mama, said his daughter. She held up her hands and said, Mama.

Ward drove his daughter to the same hospital that held his wife, with his mother-in-law in the backseat holding the child, trying to comfort her, a washcloth on her forehead. The emergency room seemed busier than before, with more people in the waiting room, watching television with worried looks on their faces. All the nurses and staff wore gauze masks over their noses and mouths. It muffled their speech and gave Ward a strange vibration in his chest. A tremor of fear.

The hospital put his daughter in the same room with his wife, moving their beds side by side. The older woman who had been calling for the nurse was gone. Ward stood beside his daughter in the hospital room and tried to calm her. She was crying so hard she hiccuped and had to be held down to put an IV tube in her arm. She looked into Ward's eyes and said, Go back home.

She didn't know how to say *I want to* yet.

Go back home, she said. Mama Mama Mama. Go back home.

I'm sorry, pumpkin, said Ward. You and Mama are sick and have to stay here until you get better.

Go back home, said his daughter. Now. Go back home.

Her lips were chapped and swollen. Her breath was ragged. When he put his hand on her back, he could feel each inhale, a rattling inside her. His hands were shaking as he tried to push the hair out of her eyes, as the nurse said, Please. You shouldn't be touching her. She's contagious.

Go back home, cried his daughter, stretching out her hands.

She never did.

He remembers returning to the empty house, how still and silent it seemed.

He didn't want to move a thing.

At first he was so exhausted from days without sleep and his body fighting the virus that he slept for twelve hours. He awoke groggy but with no fever. He half expected that he would come down with the virus, and every moment he felt queasy he thought he'd start vomiting and become weak.

He wanted to die, to get it over with. He didn't see the point in anything. He quit eating. He thought that maybe he would simply fade away, become too weak to get out of bed, close his eyes and sink into darkness.

But the days passed and he grew stronger. He starved himself until his body rebelled and he took to buying doughnuts and cheeseburgers. Food he had not eaten regularly since being married. He read constantly. About birds mainly, but other scientific works as well. Anything to ignore the hollowness of his world.

Months passed. He applied for grants to study the birds of the Colorado prairie, his specialty. One day a man from the Audubon Society left him a voice mail saying, Congratulations.

After he recovered from his weakness, he found that he could not fall asleep without his wife. When he was so tired he could no longer keep his focus on a book, he watched television until four o'clock in the morning and fell asleep on the couch. It became normal for him to watch the blue hour twilight before dawn. His wife's sister, Nisha, lost her job and came to his home, fixed meals for him, talked constantly, filled his house with cooking smells and sound. Late one night he found her weeping in his daughter's nursery. They hugged and kissed and told each other that they would watch out and care for each other. And then they were in bed.

At dawn he dressed and stole away, hands trembling as he packed a duffel bag and carried it to his car.

He left everything plus a note, asking Nisha to move into his home.

Pulling into the parking lot of the Buffalo Head Inn, he realizes this is home in his new life—a motel room with a toilet that won't stop running, bad cable TV, free beer at happy hour, and a Jacuzzi by the pool, closed for repairs.

RUBY WAKES in a dark room. A clock ticks somewhere nearby. She blinks, feeling unmoored, adrift in an oily black sea. The sound of high-pitched barking in the distance. The smell of wood smoke. Her skin burns and her mouth feels parched and raspy, her lips cracked and chapped. She's sweating, the sheets wet against her body. Her eyeballs burn and she can keep them open only for a moment. As her sight adjusts to the dimly lit room, she focuses on the wall across from the bed. The wallpaper looks familiar: cowgirls with buckskin skirts and lariats. Longhorn steers and prickly-pear cactus.

She comes to realize she's back in the house of Lord God, back in her old room, and feels a sense of drowning, of seeing the surface of the water high above her, a glimpse of sunlight she will never feel upon her face. Here the room is dark, only a thin blade of light at the base of a closed door.

In the musty-smelling bed she lies and listens to coyotes howling on the prairie that stretches beyond the broken fence, the stony fields of juniper and sagebrush. The coyotes yap and bark, high-pitched and playful. Yard dogs join in *el coro*, sounding more like wolf howls than barks, envious and mournful.

Beyond the closed door she hears Lila crying. Her nipples begin to leak, the wetness sudden as an adrenaline rush. She tries to raise herself out of bed. The sheets cling to her, sodden with sweat, the blankets heavy as a funeral pall.

She stands and wobbles, her skin tingling and tensing into goose bumps. She moves to the door and each step reverberates in her head, soft explosions in her skull. She makes it to her door and finds it locked. She struggles for the words, the words she needs to say. How to phrase them? What can she say? What can she call him now? Lord God? Sir? Daddy? Father? You bastard? She never knows what to call him anymore.

Lord God he is but you do not take the Lord's name in vain. Not in this house. One of the commandments. The numbered sins.

Papa? she calls. The door is locked. Let me out.

She pounds on the door, pleading for help in a weak voice. A wave of dizziness washes through her. After moments in which she feels as if she's falling, huddled against the doorjamb, she hears the thump and hiss of his prosthetic leg approaching. The click of the door. He opens it wide, his face like that of a prophet watching his predictions made real.

See? he says. I knew you'd be coming back. I knew you'd need me.

Please, she says, can I have something to eat? I'm hungry.

You still have the fever. Get back in bed.

I'm weak. I need something.

Do you want Lila to catch your sickness?

Where is she?

She's fine. No thanks to you. He shakes his head. You're shameless, you know that?

I want my baby.

He tells her again that she's sick, and her baby will die if she catches the infection. Doesn't she have any sense?

Look at you, he says. What kind of woman abandons her baby? And what kind of girl gets herself pregnant with no husband? I know what kind. I can't even say the word.

Ruby pounds her head against the doorjamb. I want my baby.

Lord God pushes her face away from the gap in the door, the smell of his palm against her nose. He pulls the door closed and tells her not to make a spectacle. Once again the room is dark and she alone. Through the door he tells her to get back in bed and sleep.

I'll bring you soup in a while, he adds. I've got other things to do. At the moment I don't have time for a girl who abandons her child. You want your baby now? You should have thought of that before.

I bet you thought it was funny, he says. Running away from a man with one leg? Who's laughing now?

Ruby awakens again, curled in a heap on the floor, the dusty smell of the wooden planks in her mouth and nose. The room is lighter now, a bluish tint of dawn light out the eight-paned windows. She becomes aware of her own smell, notices how dank and sour she's become. The door is still locked.

As soon as she moves, she feels intense cold, as if her body has been drained of all its blood. She shivers as she grabs at clothes in the closet, yanking a wool sweater over her head and over her flannel nightgown. She pulls off her underwear and dries her clammy, goose-pimpled skin with a flannel shirt from the closet, then hurries to her dresser to get a pair of jeans and wool socks, her hands shaking from the cold, her head pulsing with dizziness, eyes blurry from tears.

It's all she can do to stagger to the bed and crawl into it, smothering herself with the blankets. Outside, the wind sings against the low-looped power lines, a high-pitched chorus that mimics the keening of dust-bowl furies. It sings against the bleached slats tacked onto the staggered, crooked fence posts beyond the woodshed. It sings and buffets and thrums over the bunchgrass and juniper and aspens. Enough to drive a body out of her head.

Of weaker flesh and mind. You have to take it. To not think about it. To become accustomed to it. Like any pain. You get used to it.

She huddles there, grinding her teeth, trembling uncontrollably. In time she warms up, the blankets wrapped around her like a heated cocoon. She creeps far enough from the blankets to get a handful of Kleenex and blow her nose. When she can breathe again she lies back on the pillows and closes her eyes.

She wakes to noise in the room. Her mother carries a bowl of soup and crackers on a TV tray. Her face is drawn and careworn but she lights up when her daughter awakens. She smiles and strokes Ruby's cheek.

How's my girl?

Ruby blinks and tries to speak and can make no sound. She tries again, her voice breaking as she says, You're back.

Yes, I am. For now at least. I'll come every day to check on you and—

What about Papa?

John stays out of my way. He wants me to move back but I won't. He wouldn't hurt Lila for the world. He's a good man.

But he wants me to—

Hush. I know. That won't last, believe me. I won't let it. Okay?

Okay.

And now it's time to eat. You want to get strong again, don't you? You need to eat.

Papa said you didn't care.

Don't listen to him. I know he says a lot of hooey. I'm taking care of you and I say you need some soup.

Ruby leans forward and lets her mother spoon the soup into

her mouth, the hot metal touching her cracked, dried lips. The soup is salty and the chicken and noodles taste delicious. She feels the heat of the liquid as she swallows, filling her throat and passing like the warmth of sunlight into her belly.

That's good, she says. That tastes good.

The next day her mother brings a bacon sandwich. The smell of it dizzies Ruby. When she chews a mouthful of bacon and cheddar cheese, the flavor almost makes her swoon. She smiles then, as her mother watches her, urging her to slow down.

Don't chew too fast or you'll choke yourself to death. You don't want that, do you? You don't want little Pinky to grow up without a mother, do you?

Ruby smiles and shakes her head. She blinks away tears, her mother's image fuzzy through her damp lashes.

The bleached light of a dust-sky day. In the stretch of dried ranchland visible through her bedroom window, Ruby watches a shaggy steer rub its haunches against a crooked fence post, swing its tail. A Grief Bird perches atop the telephone pole beside the woodshed, croaking, its ruffled feathers shaggy and unkempt. Navajo Sparrows peck at a scattering of breadcrumbs in the grass. A ranch cat creeps in the grass beside the water trough, eyes on a rabbit near the fence.

Somewhere in the house Lila squeaks and babbles. Her voice sounds pure and clear and healthy. The bedroom door is still locked. Ruby's mother has already come and gone, has left a plate of bacon and eggs and a glass of orange juice.

Ruby raises the window and leans out. The sparrows scatter. The cat turns her head, her tail twitching as she watches the house. Ruby makes clucking sounds with her mouth and says, Donk? You leave that rabbit alone. I don't want to see another dead bunny.

Dressed in jeans and a pullover sweatshirt, she climbs out the window backward, dropping to the ground, her feet touching the outside world for the first time in many days. She feels the grit beneath her socks. Wind gusts wobble the woodshed door, its hinges squeaking.

She creeps along the house, its white paint peeling, scabbing off against the pressure of her fingers. At the back door she peers through the screen. Lord God holds Lila, sitting in a rocking chair in the kitchen, feeding her a bottle of formula. One pudgy hand stretches to grab his beard, its white tangle beyond her reach. He talks to her as he rocks. Ruby crouches beneath the window frame and closes her eyes. She listens to the faint sound of Lord God's voice.

You can tell the true worth of a man in war, he tells Lila. I heard that somewhere and it's true. You decide on which side you stand. The cowards turn tail and run. Some of them stay, only they close their eyes when they shoot. They don't hit anything but it looks like they're brave. Me, I aimed. I'm not proud of what I've done. Pride is one of the seven deadly sins. Neither am I ashamed.

It's a choice now between them or us and I'm on the side of the righteousness of the Lord. Mine eyes have seen the glory of the coming. There will come a time when we shall stand up and be counted. When we shall be taken away and dwell in the house of the Lord. Until then we need to be on our toes. What do you think of that, little girl? He smiles. You don't need to be on your toes yet. You can barely walk. He shakes his head. There's so much you have to learn. In so little time.

Lila says, Mama. Ruby hears it clearly, crouching beneath the window. Mama, her daughter says. Mama.

Mama's asleep, says Lord God. You'll see her soon enough. After a moment his voice continues: First you need a daddy is what you need. And don't you worry. Your mama, she'll come around. I'll see to it she does. And you won't have to worry about a thing. Like where your next dinner is coming from.

Ruby hears the shuffle and thump of his peg leg as he moves about the kitchen. Her lower back burns from crouching beneath the window. After a moment she hears Lord God say, Woe to the women who sew magic charms on their sleeves and make veils for the heads of people of every height to hunt souls! Behold, I am against your magic charms by which you hunt souls there like birds. I will tear them from your arms, and let the souls go, the souls you hunt like birds. But look at you. You're young yet and know nothing of the world. All that will come with time. You don't even know what a bird is, much less magic charms! You will learn, though. You will learn.

Ruby listens and squeezes her eyes shut tight, holding on to the house in a rush of dizziness. She feels the world turning, as if pinned by the weight of its centrifugal force. She looks across the prairie fields at the mountains in the distance like a castle wall over which she can never climb, and above them the brooding, cloudy sky. There's nowhere to run. The porcupine grass sharp as nails beneath her socks as she hobbles back to her window.

ISRAEL JAMES SITS slumped and half frozen in an old bulb-fendered pickup, rusted and broken-windowed, wheelless and a home for deer mice and packrats. On stakeout duty, he's glassing a rancher's back pastures. After guests at the Buffalo Head complained about a woman being abducted and other officers answered the call, he had to explain his role in adjudicating the domestic dustup between Rebecca Cisneros and "William Smith." He ended up looking the fool and having to pay for it. Worse yet, the crime was shelved as a "domestic disturbance," not a kidnapping at all, and the law washed its hands of the whole sordid affair.

He wears long johns beneath his jeans and a sheepskin-lined hat but still he's cold. Loose hay fills the cab and he can hear the mice scrabbling and burrowing. Elray crouches low to where he can see out the broken windshield for any signs of vehicles on the ranch road. Stakeout for cattle rustling is grunt work. Elray takes this demotion with quiet and vengeful anger.

He keeps a pair of night-vision 'nocs to his eyes. Three coyotes trot like ghost dogs out of the moonscape darkness of the prairie. The cattle herd grunts and shuffles. A cow nudges her yearling calf and maneuvers her body between the calf and the coyotes. One of the coyotes places its front paws on the water trough and laps quickly, drops back down, sniffs the dirt, hikes a leg.

When Elray sees headlights flash over the prairie, disappear in a swale and moments later rise up again, he gets out his wireless to call the dispatcher. He pulls off his gloves and trains the 'nocs on the small herd of cattle clustered around the water trough and feed tank. Half of the cattle stand and the others sit knees buckled and heads up. At the sound of the approaching trucks all start to move. The kneeling stand and the standing bump each other, yearlings cantering on the edge of the herd.

Four trucks come down the ranch road like they own the place until slamming brakes and skidding to a stop at the fence. Two of them haul cattle trailers, the other two have ATVs in their cargo beds. They stop and idle. A cloud of road dust follows the trucks, catches up and engulfs them, muffling the headlights in road fog.

A man in a cowboy hat emerges from the passenger-side door of the first truck and hurries to the gate, carrying bolt cutters. He wears a bandanna over his face. A big man, something familiar about him. A big man has a way of moving that marks his identity.

He works the bolt cutters into position, snaps the padlock, and yanks the chain free, dragging the swinging gate open wide for the trucks to pass through. The corrugated metal of the gate scrapes dirt, stirring up a cloud that grows thicker as the trucks move forward. The big man stands off to the side. He raises his hat and wipes his forehead, puts the hat back in place. He wears his thick black hair in a ponytail.

The cattle trailers head in first. Dust rises as they rumble over the cattle guards. As the trucks maneuver into place, strobes of the headlight beams splash the old pickup cab in which Elray sits crouched and watching through the night-vision binoculars. When the gig is in full swing, Elray calls the dispatcher again, suggesting they'd best bring backup, wait at the highway, expect nothing less than trouble, big time.

This looks like the Hole in the Wall gang with cell phones, he says.

The rustlers move both trailers into position and haul out the ramps. Soon the cattle thunder inside, balking and sidestepping, swatted and bullied. The hatted figures carry high-powered flashlights and cattle prods. A few hold automatic weapons and stand guard, watching the highway in the distance.

For a brief moment Elray catches a glimpse of a sentry looking his way through his own pair of night-vision 'nocs. Elray freezes. The herders slap the flanks of the cattle and send them running free, lift the ramps, and hurry them into place. Then they shut and bolt the back gates of the cattle trailers. The ATVs ride up the ramps into the pickup beds and the cowboys hop off and into the cabs. One vehicle is already moving before the cowboy has even shut the passenger-side door.

The first pickup rumbles over the cattle guard and out the gate, clouds of dust rising from the tires. The second truck is still loading when a stubborn steer bashes one of the rustlers into the side of the trailer. The two *vaqueros* at the rear of the trailer let the steer go, haul in the ramp, and bolt the door closed. The wounded man writhes in pain on the ground a few feet away, by the back passenger-side wheel of the trailer. The truck and trailer lurch away.

A second truck passes through the gate and flees down the

ranch road, a line of ruts in the prairie faint as the Oregon Trail. The wounded rustler still squirms in pain on the ground—left behind like a sinner after the rapture. Elray watches as the rustler tries to stand, falls again. He begins to crawl toward the fence, dragging his left leg.

Elray opens the old pickup's driver-side door as quietly as possible, steps out, his legs burning from being in a cramped position, the right one numb. He stretches and shuffles toward the rustler, keeping his eyes on him. The wounded man has no sidearm that Elray can see, but he might have a surprise wedged in his boot or the back of his jeans. The night air is cold as glass vapor, the Milky Way a river of stars in the blackness above.

When he nears the rustler Elray realizes why the big man opening the gate looked familiar. He recognizes George Armstrong Crowfoot, a full-blood Native, an ex-illicits dealer who stands scary tall and has a bad attitude to boot—abused as a child, distrusted as an adult, the usual. Elray likes him, has gotten stinking drunk in his company more than once.

Crowfoot is one tough hombre, half good at least. He's been known to bust a head now and then, but whenever he does, the victim deserves it. Crowfoot's anger carries its own homegrown justice. He never hurt a woman, and he never hit a man who didn't deserve it. If he commits a crime, Elray does his best to look the other way.

Crowfoot recognizes Elray as he nears, and stops crawling. He sits in the dirt, doing his best to keep a straight face. His leg's twisted funny, looks like it hurt.

What brings you here? he calls out.

Elray grins and shakes his head. George, George. Cattle rustling?

Crowfoot shrugs. I think the phrase was *easy money*. Next time a body tells me that, I'll jab a pig sticker in his knee.

Who's the genius here?

This between us?

Only.

Some hard-on Saint. Never heard a name, but it's somebody with funds.

Friend of a friend?

Crowfoot shakes his head. I don't know him. All I know is he's one of those Saints loves to have a harem of country-fried women, lives in that village of kooks out in Little Pueblo.

Listen, says Elray, I don't give a shit about all this. He waves a hand toward the herd of cattle, still standing and milling about near the water trough. This was punishment for me. Plus I called it in and where's the cavalry?

I wondered.

You help me crucify these Saints, I'll ignore this tampering-with-livestock infraction.

Crowfoot shifts his body, his arms propping him up. He grimaces and says, My pleasure. They do you wrong?

I met a woman who got stole right after she promised to fix me dinner. Made me look bad.

Stole?

Kidnapped you might say. Whatever you call it, I went hungry. I heard they had something to do with it.

I sense some disappointment.

Far as I can tell they think they're above the law.

Crowfoot smiles. They might be above it, but perhaps they need to look out for what comes from below.

GEORGE ARMSTRONG CROWFOOT pulls into the weedy parking lot of the Department of Nuisance Animal Control in his demolition-derby pickup, kills the engine, and waits. He's a half hour early, the first vehicle to show. He wears his long black hair loose. In his faded jeans and size thirteen cowboy boots with brass-plated tips, Crowfoot looks like Sitting Bull turned livestock rancher. Tucked in the crease of his cab's bench seat is a bowie knife. Under the seat a .45 sidearm wrapped in oilcloth. And Crowfoot is not comfortable. The gimp leg from the cattle-stomping incident hurts to move. It hurts to sit.

He bides his time for the boss man to show. He eats a pair of breakfast tacos, potatoes and eggs, hot sauce burning his lips when he wipes them on his sleeve.

As he waits, he listens to the steady hiss of traffic on Highway 50. After a time sirens wail and Doppler toward and away from him, fire trucks and a police cruiser. The sky is a dirty tan color. After the emergency vehicles pass, a hot rod races the other direction, bass throbbing, airbrushed flames licking down its side.

At the Department of Nuisance Animal Control the employees begin arriving, lumpy and misshapen, like a crew of carnies about to pitch a tent. When it comes time to punch the clock there are a dozen cars and trucks in the lot. Mosca is a no-show. Silas the boss man is last to arrive, parking in his designated space. When the heavy man climbs out of the hatch of his tiny China Doll, he looks like a rodeo clown there to distract a bull from the one true thing he wants to gore. He walks up to Crowfoot's pickup and bongs the hood. Crowfoot opens the door and eases himself to his feet, wincing. Silas asks how he's feeling.

Crowfoot shrugs. Crushed and broken. Otherwise, peachy.

What's the story?

You don't want to know.

Silas smiles. Could be worse. Could be your dick, right?

You got a point, says George. There's priorities involved.

Crowfoot follows Silas into the office and eats a glazed doughnut while he waits for the week's assignment. Silas sings the executioner's song on a group of crows that has been sighted off Highway 96, a murder that needs to be taken care of. Convince them to leave. By hook or crook.

Where's the fly?

El Señor Mosca is no longer with us. Silas shrugs. The screwball hasn't even shown to pick up his check.

You checked his home?

No answer. Silas shrugs. My guess he's on the lam. Must have crossed somebody. Like news at eleven, right? He probably sold somebody that head.

Crowfoot smiles. Maybe they truly believed it was Black Jack. Then the stupid wore off.

Silas says he's been thinking along those lines. And maybe they paid real money. For a fake head.

Crowfoot makes a few phone calls and gets nowhere. Mosca has vanished like the cartoon roadrunner, leaving only a puff of smoke behind, even if he more closely resembles Wile E. Coyote. No one seems to mourn his absence. In the alcoholic cave of a cocktail lounge, Crowfoot ends up talking to a barfly named Ramona. Body double for an Oompa-Loompa porn queen. Short and chubby, with thick mascara on her raccoon eyes, neck wrinkles galore. Mosca isn't exactly the discriminating type. Crowfoot buys Ramona a drink, feeling a pang of guilt. He doesn't usually encourage self-destruction. Then again, he doesn't usually get stomped while cattle rustling. Or cheated out of a thousand dollars.

A half hour and two drinks later, Ramona tells him where to look.

West of town, toward the Sierra Mojada, the prairie landscape undulates with foothills. George parks his pickup at the edge of a padlocked gate above a cattle guard and hoofs it across the desert. He follows a faint trail of tire tracks and beaten grass ruts. At the end of it a rusty freight boxcar sits stranded in this middle o' nowhere, with an old, low-slung Pontiac parked behind it. It's hidden from Highway 96. Crowfoot approaches from the blind side.

The wind gusts, yellowed grass trembling. Stick-people cactus don't move, as if to deny the wind. The sky is a tangerine color, dust and smoke filling the air from a fire in Huerfano County. It's said to be ten thousand acres wide, a mountain of smoke rising as if after a volcanic eruption. Crowfoot wears a mask over his nose and mouth, but his forehead is gritty with dust, and he has to squint his eyes to tiny slits just to see.

The walk is nearly two miles. By the time he reaches the

boxcar his left leg burns from his ankle to his hip. Each step jabs
a bolt of searing heat up his sciatic nerve, each step a hot re-
minder of betrayal. He struggles on, sucking air, his broken ribs
aching with his labored breath.

Trash litters the periphery of the boxcar. On its side a spray-
painted sign reads, SAY NO TO SOCIALISM! Crowfoot weaves past a
set of box springs rusting on a heap of cans and bottles. A mess of
shattered glass around a low wall of cinder blocks blinks in the
dull sun. Target-practice debris.

Twenty paces from the cinder-block wall for the target bottles
sits a tattered sofa. Cotton stuffing yellows in the sun like bad
teeth. A stack of porn magazines covers the cushions, once tooth-
some young maidens in shameless poses now bleached. Like a
science project of what time does to lust. Pages flutter in the
wind. Against the windward side of the boxcar clusters a jumble
of jaundiced tumbleweeds.

Crowfoot moves slowly and with no sound to the south end of
the boxcar, his faint shadow following. The entrance is a sliding
rusty metal door kept open, a wool blanket hanging over the
rectangular gap. At the foot of the rough curtain a black exten-
sion cord runs from the boxcar to a small generator propped on
a wooden pallet. Another stack of gray cinder blocks serves as a
porch.

Crowfoot swallows the pain as he gets a good footing on the
blocks. He inhales deeply, hauls himself up and inside the boxcar
in one quick jerk and step. The pale sunlight casts an amber glow
inside the darkened interior. Crowfoot blinks and steps to the
side, feeling something squish beneath his boot.

He looks down to see what it is, stepping sideways to get out of it. The opening of the wool curtain, hooked on his shoulder, briefly floods the room with light. In the guts of the boxcar, a packrat's mess. Clothes and pizza boxes and paper sacks. Empty bottles of Nyquil, tequila, and a pair of folding chairs. Before him a figure prone on another old sofa.

Cabron! hisses a voice. Close the fucking door.

Crowfoot lets the curtain fall back, though it catches on a box he knocked awry when he entered. The gap in the curtain lets a blade of yellow sunlight into the room.

It's you, says Mosca.

Crowfoot doesn't reply. He lets his eyes adjust to the dimmer light and notes the band of light falling on a folding chair, illuminating a rifle propped upon it. He reaches over and lifts it. As if he's in the market for such a weapon and might just offer a price. It's a bolt-action coyote killer. He checks and finds it loaded, then rests the rifle across his shoulder, barrel pointing to the wall.

Yeah, it's me all right. And I'm guessing I'm the last person you expected to see today.

Mosca tries to rise on the sofa. His breathing is raspy and he stinks. Jorge, *que tal?* he asks. *Estoy enferma.*

What's wrong with you?

What do you think?

The usual.

Mosca coughs, wet and ragged. More like the unusual, genius.

Crowfoot pulls his gauze mask into place over his mouth and nose. Mosca looses his hissing cackle and says something about an infection finding its home, no matter what you do.

You think you're immune, I bet, he adds. You'll see.

Crowfoot pulls the wool curtain farther back and hooks it on a metal ridge above the door slot. Let's shine some light in this pit.

It hurts my eyes.

Pobrecito, says Crowfoot. He lowers the rifle and uses the barrel as a tool to pick through the clutter and rubble in the room. In front of the sofa an old spiderweb-cracked windshield on milk crates serves as a coffee table. On it are tequila bottles, cough syrup, a small mirror with traces of white powder.

Crowfoot shakes his head. Look at all this shit, he says. What's the story? You come out here the middle of nowhere to die, is what I'm thinking.

I'm not dead yet.

Close to it.

And maybe you're closer than you think. *Claro, hombre?* Mosca laughs again, his gaunt face looking like a *calavera* from the Day of the Dead carnival toys.

Not as close as you, shithead.

Mosca snickers, devolves into a coughing jag. When he's finished he whispers hoarsely, Aren't you the lucky one.

On that rustling job I wasn't so lucky, was I, now?

Mosca raises his dark eyebrows and acts as if he's just remembered. Oh, right. Had a little spill, didn't we?

You could have given me a hand.

Mosca shrugs. What can I say? Cattle rustling isn't shooting crows from a pickup cab, is it, now?

You said it would be easy money.

Did I? So I was wrong. So sue me.

Crowfoot cocks his head as if considering the idea. The band of sunlight from the doorway illuminates half his body, the light falling on the back of his head, giving his long Indian hair a late-afternoon glow, like the aura of a badass saint.

It stinks in here, he says.

I like the smell. Reminds me I'm alive, says Mosca. He adds that he hasn't been out in days. He's living off crackers and cheese and peanut butter, when he can eat. Listen, full-of-bull. I'm sweating and chilled at the same time. Think you could close that curtain?

Crowfoot fits the rifle to his shoulder and takes aim at Mosca's face. The sick man blinks and licks his lips.

If you want to pull that trigger, be my guest. Put me out of my misery.

I did, says Crowfoot. Before I came here, the whole fucking way I limped here across those fields of nothing, I was planning on ways to make you bleed and squirm. Now look at you.

Mosca closes his eyes. Whatever.

I'll make you a deal. Tell me the whereabouts of the head honcho on that rustling gig. Do that and I'll walk away.

I do that and I'm fucked anyway.

Maybe so. But in the meantime, you can enjoy your place among the living, right?

I don't think you'd do it, says Mosca. He musters the closest he can come to defiance. I think you're so disgusted with me you don't see the point in hanging my scalp on your belt.

Crowfoot allows there's some truth to that. Only thing is, he adds, I don't plan on killing you. He pulls his bowie knife from its sheath and lets it catch the sunlight, sparkle and wink. Remember I said you could have given me a hand?

Mosca shrugs. I done so much crank, my memory's shot.

You could have given me a hand before. You didn't. Now you make a choice. Either you give me that name or I'm taking your hand right here, right now.

Mosca coughs painfully. Crowfoot winces just hearing it. Finally, when Mosca can breathe again, he croaks, Page. Hiram Page. Happy now?

Where does he live?

I don't know. Check the phone book, genius.

I'm asking you.

And I'm telling you. I don't know. Now, leave me alone.

I'll leave you all right. Same way you left me.

Mosca pulls a serape tighter about his shoulders and, with trembling hands, takes a sip from a bottle of cough medicine. I was one of a dozen, he says. Just one of the braves.

Crowfoot gestures with the knife. Put out your hand.

Like hell.

I said put out your hand.

You got to be kidding.

Do I look like I'm kidding?

George? Don't do this to me. Mosca's bottom lip quivers. I'm begging you, George. Don't do it. It wasn't my fault.

I'm not going to do anything. Crowfoot places the knife on the table. You do the honors.

It wasn't my fault. You trying to get back at someone? It was those fucking Saints, that's who. They're the ones who said to ditch you. You want to find Page? Go see Gata. He's got a pawn-shop right down the street from her. Maybe she knows. Or you could just follow him like a stalker.

Gata de la Luna?

One and the same.

Without reply Crowfoot eases his gimp leg down from the boxcar, holding fast to a vertical iron bar as he climbs down, and limps away. Still in earshot, he hears laughter behind him and turns to see Mosca standing there, grinning, holding wide the curtain door.

I'm not that sick! shouts Rodriguez. I was just plucking your heartstrings so's you wouldn't hurt me.

Crowfoot nods, grins back. Yeah, well, I wasn't going to cut you anyway.

Mosca does a little fandango jig. I'm feeling better already!

IN CHURCH, RUBY COLE leans against her mother's shoulder and suffers the rants of Lord God. He says the one true prophet believed it was the duty of right men to prop-agate the earth, and to preach the word of the one true church.

We are bidden to bring forth the flowers of children to this desert. And we shall! The prophet did not die in vain! Brother Joseph was martyred by nonbelievers but his blood yet flows like cold mountain water in all his descendants and all the children of the Latter-Day Saints who know he lives on as the second true martyr.

Lord God glares at the small group assembled before him as

if they are both to blame for Joseph Smith's murder and sympathetic to the greater cause. He holds his anger like the very plates of gold at his chest and looks from one individual to the next, striding back and forth on his prosthetic leg, his hoary beard great and disgusting, his coarse breath loud and almost painful to hear. He thunders on, stretching out the moment long enough for all to be made uncomfortable, looking into each of their faces as if he knows some dirt on every one of them and will use it if he must.

I have spilt the blood of Muslims and a time will come when all the faithful, all true Christians and Saints, will have to do the same. We are blessed in this the land of Eden and we must defend it with our blood and with our muscle and sinew. We must take unto each of us many wives and propagate so that we as a people do not die out. We are the true sons and daughters of Israel. The bloodline of the chosen people. The Lord would curse us for our failure if we are so weak as to fail and fall.

Ruby tunes out his words. She sees through the tales of suffering, the noble banishment in the Great American Desert and the construction of the New Jerusalem, and beneath the table she smells a ripe bucket of hooey.

What kind of church is this? No stained glass. No stone statuettes of the beatific Virgin bearing their sorrows in her bosom. This is more like a drop-off station for Goodwill Industries junk. In one corner stands a half-dozen rolls of pink Johns-Manville fiberglass wall insulation and a jumble of paint cans. The altar is a cardboard refrigerator box covered with a stained tablecloth.

Ruby endures it, holding sleeping Lila to her chest, feeling the sweet rhythm of her breathing, the limpness of her little arms like the softest blessing touch of an angel. She sits still as the Virgin Mary and stares at the metal ripples in the corrugated walls and listens to the voice in her head. It's not of a Christian or Saintly cast, this she knows, but you can only take so much Jesus and Brother Joseph Smith propaganda before you wanted to trip the Son of God down the stairs and poke the prophet in the eye with a pitchfork. She listens to the voice in her head and she plots.

She vows to crush Lord God and free herself of his yoke. To lie in wait like the whipped dog she is, obedient and twitchy, waiting till the master sleeps, till she can catch him upside the head with an ax handle or perhaps the blade itself and lay him low. She will do this if she can.

In her heart she knows she can't.

Juliet squeezes her tight and without a word urges her to persevere, to lie in wait, to have patience. She comes to Sunday service only for Ruby's sake and suffers the scowls and opprobrium of all who know she no longer chooses to live under the same roof as Brother Cole or sleep in his sanctioned bed.

At sermon's end she leaves as the lumpy congregation filters into the parking lot to mingle with pleasantries or exchange new omens of the apocalypse many believe is knocking at the door and about to come true. Ruby follows Juliet to her car, carrying Lila, who has awakened and is now beginning to squirm and fuss. Ruby wants to get in the passenger-side door but knows Lord God is watching from the front steps of the ridiculous tin-can temple and will come limping if she so much as reaches for the handle.

Ruby leans down to take a kiss on the cheek and holds out

Lila for the same, smiling as Juliet says, Now, listen, baby girl. You be good for your mama. She needs you.

The middle of night and Lord God awakens, his heart beating so hard his neck veins pop against the pillow. The pulse-touch sounds like tiny cymbals ringing. The only other noise is the whistle and seep of wind against the windows. He lies in bed, his one good eye open wide in the inky darkness, its pupil swollen wide as a giant squid's in the depths of the sea. He hears a thump on the roof. As if something has landed on it. An owl? An angel? A creaking of the timbers and asphalt shingles, the footfalls of a body walking upon the roof.

Lord God lifts his head and strains to follow the sound. The creaking approaches nearer and nearer still until it comes to a stop above his head. Lord God thinks to rise from bed and rush outside, to catch a glimpse of the beast, the thing, whatever it is. But the air is cold and the sheets and blankets a warm cocoon. It would take time to attach his leg and by then perhaps whatever it is would have fled. The room smells of dust and dirty socks. It's nothing. Things that go bump in the night. Only the house settling.

His eye stings from being stretched wide so long, and then he has a vision. The ceiling and the walls vanish and it is as if he is naked to the heavens. No stars or moon or clouds. Only a yawning vastness sucking him up like a vacuum into the very eye of God. It feels as if he is hurtling, stomach in his mouth, wind in his face.

He rises above the earth and is looking down on it from above. It is neither day nor night but a sooty twilight. The land is afire. The mountains to the west flare and sizzle, the forests like towers of pine flame. In town to the east flames curve and gutter out the windows of courthouse, hospital, home. A voice calm and low begins to speak in his ear.

Wed Ruby to the righteous man, says the voice. Your days in this world are numbered and will end soon. Marry your daughter to a man who will protect her in the trouble to come. You cannot save her, but you can help another to watch out for her after you are gone. Your time is ending, but hers is just beginning. You must protect her. You must.

The voice goes silent. The vision fades like campfire embers. Lord God comes to in his own bed, the same smells in the room, his heart beating wildly, no more sound of weight upon the roof. He lies there in the silence until the grayness of dawn breaks the spell.

He wakes late and Ruby has already fed Lila. She stares at him curiously, with tenderness and reserve. She does not know what vision he has seen. She should not know. She would not believe him. It is his knowledge. His knowing will make a difference.

This is not the first time Lord God has heard voices and seen visions. In the past he's glimpsed prophecies of a world to come, like pages from the Book of Revelations. Glowing white horses galloping across the prairie behind the house. A horned owl with eyes like polished rubies in the aspen near the woodshed. Stars that formed circles in the heavens and spun like a Ferris wheel. Herds of glowing antelope that stretched to the foothills of the Sierra Mojada.

Once he saw a naked woman with the head of a donkey. She came toward him through the cactus fields, weaving her way through the yucca and the cholla. Her skin was cinnamon-colored, like Lila's, her hair black as onyx. She seemed to float above the parched prairie grass and tumbleweeds. She faced the house and Lord God knew it was he whom she was seeking, though he held back, edging his face to the window only just far enough to look out, afraid she would see him and snag his soul.

She passed behind a juniper and when she emerged on the other side he clearly saw temptress nakedness—nipples large and stiff as pumpkin stems, tangle of pubis dark and V-shaped, hips wide, and belly round. But as she moved out of the shadow of the juniper he saw that her head was not human but sported a long snout and tall ears. He'd heard of the Donkey Woman before and reckoned her to be a servant of the devil. He slammed his door and crouched behind it, his heart beating so fiercely it made him weak. After some time he stood up and peered out the window to find the vision gone.

Mostly he keeps to himself these gifts from the Lord and temptations from the devil. His soul is a conduit, a link between the world of the ordinary and the spiritual, the unearthly. He fears Ruby shares his talent and curse and will not tell him. He recognizes the look in her eyes. The wrinkle of her brows. The sense of her knowing more than she will say.

.   .   .

Another night Lord God wakes to the house burning and his throat and nose constrict with the acrid smell, the cinders stabbing his eye. Flames lick and gutter up the ghost curtains in his bedroom as he hurries to attach his leg and pull on his pants, his hands trembling. A gush of heat envelops his neck and back as he lurches forward. The room is dark with smoke.

His prosthesis is not attached well and wobbles as he puts weight on it. He cannot move fast enough to save his family. The roof will collapse and trap them in the flames. He coughs from the fumes and his throat burns. He trips on a plastic dinosaur in the hallway. He bellows for his daughter, fallen and helpless, seeing the meaninglessness of his life rush upon him.

Ruby appears at his side and crouches down.

What's the matter, Papa?

Hurry, he says. Throw on some clothes and get Lila. Come quick.

Come where?

The house is afire! We have no time to waste!

Fire?

Can't you smell it?

Ruby stands up and blinks, rubbing her eyes. She wears a white nightgown. Lord God looks down the hall, expecting to see flames funneling out her bedroom door.

I don't smell anything, she says.

She helps him to his feet and they make their way down the dark hallway to her room, where she turns on the overhead light.

All seems normal and in place. Lila squirms in her crib and raises her head to look at them, her black hair a curly cloud around her head and face.

Mama? she asks.

I'm right here, pumpkin. Go back to sleep.

She frowns and drops her head back on the pillow, her diapered butt in the air.

AT THE POST OFFICE, holding Lila in her arms, Ruby kills time, waiting for her turn to be called, listening to a college girl in front of her blab blab blab on a cell phone, all about how she borrowed her roommate's credit card to buy a new dress and the bitch had the nerve to say she was going to call the police if she didn't get the money pronto. Ruby bounces Lila and tries to keep her entertained, staring at help-wanted ads on the bulletin board. One ad reads, *Person needed to count birds. Ornithological knowledge useful but not required. Will train. Enthusiasm a must. Generous pay. Flexible hours.*

She calls the number. A man with a soft voice answers, tells her how much he can pay. The work sounds good to Ruby. She says she likes birds and that she's an accurate counter.

I count them on my own, anyway, she adds. There's not as many as there used to be.

That's why we count. To see how many there are now. Compare that to past populations, project the future viability of species in peril.

Ruby says she counted eighteen Navajos by the train trestle

near her house. Six Grief Birds off Highway 96. A trio of Nodding Owls on the prairie west of her house. I mark the days by counting birds, she says.

Grief Birds? he asks. Navajos? Nodding Owls? There's a long pause at the other end of the line. I've never heard of these before.

Those are my names for them, says Ruby. I make up special names for all the birds I see. I know the real names, actually. Most of them.

Can you give me an example?

I saw a pair of Audubon's Warblers in the aspens near our house. I call them Yellow Flitchets.

Why?

They flitter and twitch in the branches of the trees. Flitchets, see? Ravens I call Grief Birds, because they always seem to be in mourning, dressed in black feathers.

What do you call crows?

Crows.

What are Navajos?

Vesper Sparrows. I call them Navajos because the pattern on their wings reminds me of a Navajo rug. Like, Sparrow Hawks? Why do they call them Kestrels, anyway? That doesn't mean anything to me.

It's just a name, says the man. It's a word we use so we know what we're talking about when we say Kestrel.

What about *Turdus migratorius*?

The American Robin, yes.

It sounds ugly.

Well, yes. I suppose it does.

I like Robins. Why would anyone who likes birds call them a turd?

You know Latin genus and species names for all these birds you name?

Not all. Some.

What's a White-Crowned Sparrow?

A Snowcap.

What about the Latin name?

I don't know. What is it?

Zonotrichia leucophrys.

I like Snowcap better.

So do I. But we need a common language. Scientists share their findings. We can't make up our own names for things. Unless we discover a new species.

I know that.

Then we wouldn't know what we were talking about when we described a thing.

I said I know. I'm not stupid.

I didn't say you were.

Anyway, you should hire me. You won't find anyone else who can count birds like me.

I never meant to imply you were stupid. I don't know you. I don't think someone is stupid when I don't know them.

Okay. I didn't mean anything by it. Maybe we can meet later today? I could get a ride into town.

You don't have a car?

No, I don't. I'm still in high school. Or I was, until recently.

Ruby waits for his reply, long in coming.

Finally the man says, I'm sorry. I need someone who can get around on their own, to meet me out of town. My test area is west of here, mostly.

I can do that.

No, well, I mean. I need someone with his or her own transportation. I'm sorry.

What are you sorry about? Pick me up. I live west of town. It's not out of your way.

I don't know.

What don't you know? You can come get me. I'll walk down Red Creek Road to the highway. It's only two miles. That's a thirty-minute walk. Maybe twenty. I can do it. I walk everywhere I go.

I'm sorry, Miss Cole. I just don't think it's going to work out.

You think I'm simple, don't you? Because of my special names for the birds? I'm not. I'm complex. Only I come from a simple family.

I don't think you're simple. I don't know you. It's just that I think it's probably smart of me to talk to other people first before I decide whom to hire.

No, you shouldn't. They will cloud your eyes. I'm here and now. And I know birds, Mr. Costello. I'd be perfect for this. You have to hire me. Her voice quavers. You have to, she says again. It's my destiny and it's yours too. I count birds, you know? It was fate I saw your ad. There's no denying that.

I've got other people to interview, says Ward. Let's say I'll get back to you and we'll see what happens after I talk to the others.

Listen, says Ruby. Listen to me. You can't turn away from this.

I'll talk to you soon. I promise. Now, I have to get going.

Where are you? she asks.

Ward pauses a moment, then tells her where he's staying.

I know exactly where that is. My mother works not far from there. I'll come see you later today, all right?

There's a long silence at the other end of the line.

Okay, says Ward. If you make it here we'll talk.

Are you sure?

Yes, I'm sure. I'll be glad to meet you, okay?

Okay. I mean, thank you. You won't regret it.

You want the job?

Yes, says Ruby. Yes, I do.

Well, I certainly do need somebody.

I do too, says Ruby. I mean, I need the work.

I know what you meant.

I'll be good at this, she adds. I promise.

Ward meets Ruby in the lobby of the Buffalo Head Inn. Usually field biologists with research grants use college students as interns in the field, most of them coming from a few schools like Cornell, the University of Michigan, or Auburn. Not Ward. He wants a local, someone who knows the landscape, someone who won't ask so many annoying questions, someone he can learn from. Someone who knows the prairies, the foothills, the nesting sites, the canyon walls and creek beds.

Ruby convinces her mother to take care of Lila at her place in town.

I need to make money, she says. I have to get started somewhere. Lila's getting easier to handle. She's on formula full
time now.

In the lobby, Ward sits on a cracked leather sofa beneath
the buffalo head, looking like a camp counselor at a dude ranch.
He's easy to recognize because of the glossy bird book in his lap.
He wears wire-rim glasses, a plaid western shirt, and jeans. He
shakes her hand and tells her to call him Ward when she says,
Mr. Costello.

On the coffee table he spreads out the bird book. Ruby
watches as he moves aside the bronco-silhouette napkin holder,
the cactus salt-and-pepper shakers, the Colorful Colorado! place
mats. He says the book is a classic published in 1933, complete
with illustrations by Louis Agassiz Fuertes. She asks who that was.

A famous illustrator and ornithologist, says Ward. He worked
from the real thing, often dead birds, like John James Audubon. I
know that seems odd but that's how they did it in those days.

They painted illustrations of dead birds? How did they
find them?

Usually they shot them.

So they killed the birds and later tried to save them?

That's about the gist of it.

The what?

The gist of it.

What does that mean?

That's the truth. More or less.

The gist, she says.

The main facts about something, adds Ward.

She smiles. I learned a new word.

Ward turns the book to the illustrations of Ivory-Billed Wood-peckers.

They started to realize, back then, that some of these birds would be hunted to their end. Many of the birds Agassiz illus-trated no longer exist. In another century they'll become legends. If not sooner. The forests west of here used to be filled with Blue Grouse, and now I've heard you're lucky to see even a pair.

Ruby turns the large, heavy pages of the book, beautiful color illustrations. Ward shows her the pages he has marked, birds that are listed as either rare or on the brink of extinction. Some of these were common only a few decades ago.

I saw one of these in the spring, says Ruby, pointing at a light-green warbler. It's not gone. I call it a Hide-About. She looks up at Ward and grins. It's not easy to see, seems to like to hide about on the ground, pecking at leaves, or flitting about in the aspen leaves.

The Orange-Crowned Warbler. *Vermivora celata.* Used to be one of the most common warblers in the west.

I've seen it.

Could you find it for me? If we went on a search?

Ruby purses her lips, staring down at the illustration. Usually don't see that orange cap on the Hide-Abouts.

Right, you don't. Only in mating season. Or when it's afraid.

When it's trying to show off, she says. My father shoots them from our porch.

Warblers?

No. Crows. Ravens, too. He says black birds carry evil spirits.

Ward keeps his face averted. He's staring at an illustration of a White-Faced Ibis. He says her father isn't the only one.

It's like they want something to blame. Birds are an easy target.

That's partly why I want this job.

What is?

My father. I have to get loose of him.

May I ask a rude question?

I guess.

How old are you?

Seventeen.

So you still live at home?

Me and my baby girl. Lila. My father helps take care of her. He keeps a roof over my head and food on the table. He says he fought the war for me. Which he reminds me of twenty-four seven.

Then why do you want to leave?

He wants to marry me off to a man I don't even know or like and who already has two wives. It's a Saint thing.

Ward blinks and frowns. Ruby can tell he doesn't understand, but doesn't want to say anything to hurt her feelings or make her seem an oddball. A Saint thing?

The FLDS. Fundamentalist Latter-Day Saints. We just call them Saints. You're not from around here, you don't know. You're lucky. Everyone else does, and it's embarrassing. Most people think they're scum.

You must get picked on.

Ruby shrugs. Some. Dad preaches at an FLDS temple. It's not much of a temple, really. More like a bunch of kooks. But don't tell him that. They're polygamists. Or polygs for short.

Ward stares at her for a moment, turns his attention back to the bird book. He flips through to a glossy photograph of a Bobolink.

I've heard of these people, he says. But I don't understand it. Not really.

Think clan. That's what it's like. They don't work much but the ones that do pay for the freeloaders. They help each other out. Do each other favors. Like, I'll scratch your back if you scratch mine. Only far as I can tell, I'll be the one doing the scratching. Plus this guy he wants me to marry? He owns a pawnshop. Which is pretty low, if you ask me. So I'll be scratching the back of a man who cheats people for a living.

Ward makes a face. He sounds like a catch.

Don't I know it. Trouble is, he's got money.

Business must be good.

It's boom time for him. He's basically buying me. And Lord God will get a good price.

Lord God?

My father. That's what I call him. He acts like he's Lord God, the one true believer.

I know some Mormons in Texas, says Ward. They seem squeaky clean.

He doesn't like mainstream Mormons. He says FLDS are the true believers. But sure, he's gold plate to the bone. In his head he's the third in line, direct from the Prophet Joseph to Brigham Young to Lord God. He wanted to take a celestial wife but Mom wouldn't let him. She was so mad she moved out. Plus he lost a leg in the war. Ruby shakes her head. He's a mess, you want the truth.

I'm sorry to hear that. It must make his life hard.

Ruby shrugs. At first I felt sorry for him. After a while it gets old. He milks it, you know? This war-veteran hooey. Plus he wants me to do what he says. To obey. And I can't take that.

In the breakfast-bar area, the coffee maker gurgles. Ward says, Some birds are polygamous. Bobolinks, for instance. Have you ever seen them on the prairie?

Sometimes. She stirs her tea. They're rare. I call them Yellow Necks. They're pretty.

They're on my list, says Ward.

The endangered ones?

He nods. He sips his coffee, then tells her they haven't been counted reliably for several years. They may be gone, he adds.

Guess that polygamist angle didn't help them.

I guess not, he says.

It sure works for these gold platers. People call them the American Taliban. That's probably about half right, far as I can tell. Kooky but persistent. Fervent. I like that word. That's what they are. Fervent. And they're breeding like rabbits.

GEORGE ARMSTRONG CROWFOOT stares out at the desert sunrise, the eastern sky pink as his bloodshot eyes.

A trapped fly buzzes against the window, whining like a harmonica. He regards it for a moment, feeling a headache pulse in his temples, getting his bearings. Gata de la Luna lies naked beside him, sleeping as if drugged by a love potion. He gets to his feet and gulps a glass of cold water, his throat smarting.

Crowfoot's trailer is perched atop Wild Horse Mesa, as remote as you can get without being an all-out survivalist. There's a crooked gate at the base of the mesa and one narrow, rutted road up. No one can surprise him with an impromptu and unwanted drop-in. The way he likes it.

Crowfoot is left staring groggy and uncoffeed at the drought-chapped yard with its sad, rusted swing set, a stack of bald truck tires tumbled in the dust, and a barbecue grill made from a sawed-in-half fifty-five-gallon drum. He makes coffee and washes the dishes, rationing the water. He gets what water he has from a two-hundred-gallon plastic tank, shuttled in the back of his pickup. He stands there moody and hungry, listening to the echo of Johnny Cash stuck in his head. A flock of Grackles flies to the juniper near the mesa cliff edge. The crows have all been shot or driven out and the smaller black birds are taking over.

He moves slowly and quietly. Gata de la Luna isn't one to face if she rises on the wrong side of the bed. At the moment her naked body fills his single-wide trailer like a suitcase bomb. A stripe of morning sunlight illuminates the wrinkles of her Navajo sole. The lines of her footprint seem cryptic and deliberate.

Crowfoot believes that if he were skilled in that way he could read her future while she sleeps. He isn't so sure he can't. The same bar of light snakes up her leg and makes her left butt cheek glow bold as a Russ Meyer audition. She's a latter-day rustic shepherdess, has her own palm-reading shop, her fingers in every pie.

She filled him in on Señor Hiram Page and his crooked ways. What she knows could put the man in prison, but she's not one to testify.

As he notches the tongue of his death's-head buckle into its tooled leather belt, Gata stirs, rolls over, pushes the darkness of her hair from her face. She stretches and the foot on the coffee table upends a tray of weed and an ashtray. Both thump to the floor in a small, ashy cloud.

Oops, she says.

Crowfoot steps over the mess and leans down, kisses her instep. You're forgiven.

Where's the fire, jackrabbit?

I tried not to wake you. I was a mouse.

She grins. I doubt that. If you were, cats be running scared.

I thought I'd look for that gold plater. Maybe catch them at prayer time. Feeling holy and all.

I'm warning you.

I know. I heard you.

And you're going to go after him anyways.

Did I tell you how beautiful you are in the morning?

She throws a pillow at him. Don't change the subject. I'm on to you.

All I need is that address, he says. You know you're going to tell me, so just quit dancing around the obvious.

What's in it for me?

He leans over again, this time kissing higher up her leg. What about a good time?

Later, with Gata de la Luna's *molé* yet lingering on his lips, Crowfoot heads west on Highway 50, toward the zombie subdivisions of Little Pueblo. A developer's dream before the Big Fall. Since then the banks have foreclosed on most of the homes, and anyone with a job and money has cleared out, afraid of zealots and squatters.

He trolls down side streets where most of the homes sport graffiti tattoos. A few are burned, baring charred walls, garages gaping open like hospital cadavers, their insides full of cardboard boxes, washer-dryer sets, toppled trash bins. Old cars sit jacked up and tireless on cinder blocks. Plastic bags drift across the vacant lots or are impaled in cactus gardens. On a nearby ridge looms an abandoned line of ranch homes halfway built, some with scaffolding still in place, like a shabby Easter Island.

To reach the FLDS compound strangers have to pass a roadblock manned by rifle-toting Saints. Crowfoot avoids that, parks his pickup in a dry gulch behind the neighborhood. He creeps through a no-man's-land, what was once an off-road shooting range, picking his way through tumbleweeds, yucca, and spent rifle casings.

Beyond the shooting range twist the trails of a motor-sports park, where back in the day kids rode motocross bikes for the sheer mayhem of it, whining across the desert like mutant mosquitoes. Now it's silent as a nuclear test site in Nevada. Drifts from the dust storms cover the old motocross trails.

Crowfoot recognizes the tracks of turkey, deer, and coyote in the deep sand. He scares up a long-eared jackrabbit, a gray blur on the brown prairie, weaving past pale green clumps of sage and the tall white blooms of yucca. A stray horse watches from the top of one of the motocross hills, unmoving. Crowfoot carries a lever-action .30-.30 wrapped in a serape. The Saints think themselves superior, holding M-16s, but truth be told, the rapid fire makes them cross-eyed shots.

The first house he nears reminds him of Mosca's boxcar fortress of solitude. Naked fence posts mark a border. A spool of barbed wire sits near one of the posts. It could have been left there years ago, another project abandoned. The wire is rusted now and the posts half covered in sand. Closer to the house, a jumble of lost toys litters the dead grass—armless dolls, a G.I. Joe with a melted head, a plastic Wiffle-ball bat with a dent in it, a kiddie pool full of sand.

Crowfoot approaches at a fast walk, head down, hands in pockets, as if his car has run out of gas and he's just hiking to a station. At the house corner he flattens his body close to a wall, stops at the first window he reaches. Behind the glass he glimpses a cluttered bedroom, a mess of clothes on the floor. A middle-aged woman rummaging in a cardboard box. She doesn't see him. She sighs and shakes her head, grabs an armful of clothes, and stuffs them back in the box.

The next window is the kitchen. There he sees another woman feeding a baby, trying to coax it to open its mouth. A pot steaming on the stove.

At the second house he watches a woman working bread

dough on a wooden table. When he opens the door and steps in, she looks up with annoyance, her hands covered with flour, a white streak on one cheek. Before she can speak he asks, Are you Rebecca Cisneros?

She wipes a bang of hair from her forehead with the back of one hand. Who's asking?

He tells her who he is. That an old friend of his, Israel James, said she might need help.

Don't be teasing me. I'm in hell and I don't need another devil to poke me.

I'm not.

I don't know what to tell you. She looks down at her ankles. I'm a hostage. More like a slave. You got something to cut me free, go at it.

On her ankles are shackles looped through a ring bolted to the floor. About an eighteen-inch span of chain.

I can't run, she adds. I tried once and they caught me. Her eyes go pink and liquid. After that, they chained me. To teach me a lesson. She shakes her head. But I'll try again.

I can bust these, says Crowfoot. We'll manage somehow. Plus I got the law on my side.

Don't get the law involved, she says. They're in cahoots. Otherwise I'm game. She looks out the window with glazed eyes. Sure, let's do it. Much more of this and I'm eating rat poison. She unties her apron and then stops. He's back, she says.

They hear the sound of gravel crunching in the driveway, the hum of an engine coming to a stop. A door slams.

Crowfoot holds a finger to his lips. He points to his chest and shakes his head, then makes a flapping motion with his hand. Becca nods and shoos him. He backpedals to a shadowed spot against the far kitchen wall, behind a washing machine topped with a laundry basket. With one twist of his hand he unfurls the serape and flips it over his head, making a cowl.

The faint whoosh of a door opening. Hey! a voice calls. Where you at? I got you something.

I'm back here, calls Becca.

He wears a washed-out T-shirt and has short dark hair parted on the side. A skinny young guy. Fuzzy white puppy in his arms. With the dog licking his face, he says, Check this out. You said I never bring you nothing, and you said you got no friends. What about two stones with one dog?

Becca wipes her sweating hands on her apron, goes back to kneading the bread dough. That's nice, she says. I always wanted a puppy.

What's the matter? I thought you'd be happy.

What do you want me to say? I'm baking bread. You're so happy you go play with him.

There's just no pleasing you, goddamnit. I'm telling my uncle I've had enough. You can work your debt off with someone rougher than me, that's for damn sure.

I don't owe anyone a thing.

Right. Keep telling yourself that. The man shakes his head, making kissing faces at the white puppy. Just give up that ring, all will be hunky-dory.

Maybe the chains around her ankles put a crimp on her feelings, you think?

The man freezes. The puppy keeps licking at his face. He stares at Crowfoot crouched by the washer-dryer, covered with the serape, aiming a rifle. As the young Saint stares, Crowfoot seems as if he's shimmered into being, an apparition out of time. Like an Arapaho ghost come to right the wrongs of centuries past.

The man licks his lips and blinks. He looks at Becca and sets the puppy on the floor. Where'd you come from?

Don't matter.

With the rifle still aimed at the man's chest, Crowfoot raises himself to his full height of six feet four inches and shrugs the serape off his shoulders. Looking at the dude in the T-shirt, he can't help but feel contempt. The man has no chin to speak of and a huge, hillbilly Adam's apple. Acne scars pock his cheeks like the surface of an ugly moon. He resembles nothing more than a weakling with moneyed friends. Which he is. Which makes him all the more loathsome to Crowfoot, who is all about muscle and no cash in the pocket but what he earns.

Take those chains off that woman, ugly.

The man raises a hand slowly. Wait a minute. We're not alone here. You give this a thought, Tonto.

Crowfoot moves across the room. Tonto? You want your brains splattered, is that it?

Listen. What I think is—

He smacks the man in the face with the rifle butt. The weak-chinned Saint falls back and whimpers, squealing high-pitched and hurt.

I said get those chains off her. Now.

She owes us eight thousand dollars, he whines. I got signed

papers saying she agrees to pay it off in three years' labor. It's all legal. You take her and I'll get the law on you. She owes me big time and I think—

Crowfoot kicks him in the ribs. He scrabbles backward and Crowfoot comes on, angling for another boot. Listen, stupid and pathetic. You know what I think? I think you don't deserve to breathe. I think you—

He keeps the key on a chain around his neck, says Becca.

Crowfoot bends over the man, who now whines how he'll get even, yes, he will, you bet your fuckin' life on it. Crowfoot gets a hand on the chain and, once he has the key in his fist, rips it free.

She's our ward, hisses the weak chin. You know who Hiram Page is? He gave me her as domestic help. And the law will back him up. We keep her chained so she don't run off.

Crowfoot unlocks the jerry-rigged shackles. Becca thanks him and rubs her ankles, says, We should go, quick. His cousins live next door, and his dad is two houses down. We don't want to mess with them. We'll be lucky to get away with them not seeing us as it is.

The weak chin wipes a smear of blood from his mouth and curses Crowfoot. You got no right to treat a white man like this, he says. I've got friends, shithead. I'm part of something bigger than you and you'll find it out and you'll be sorry. You just wait. I'll cut your balls off and use 'em for a purse.

Crowfoot pulls a roll of duct tape from his back pocket and peels off a strip a foot wide. Weak chin keeps talking. I'll get you stomped, he whines. Stomped and beaten and shot and take you to court and have you thrown in jail. Mark my words. You'll regret—

Crowfoot slaps the duct tape over the man's bloody mouth. He tells Becca to step outside and look around. If you see anybody, come tell me. If not, chill.

We have to hurry, she says. They catch you here they'll hurt me bad and you they'll—

Comprende, says Crowfoot.

She smiles. Okay, she says. I'll go but you hurry.

After she closes the door Crowfoot pulls out the long knife from his hip sheath. He holds it in front of weak chin's face. Tonto? he says. The man's eyes go wide as Crowfoot grabs his dark hair and yanks up his head. Here's something to remember me by, ugly. He cuts a quick gash at the top of the man's forehead. Blood streams down his face as the man squeals and twists.

Crowfoot says, Who's Tonto now, ugly?

Outside the back door, Becca peers at the blood on Crowfoot's hand for a moment before realizing what it is. He notices her looking. I gave him a haircut, he says. That will make them blink twice.

Oh, Lord. They're going to be after you.

Crowfoot puts his hand on her back and tells her he doesn't care. It's history now, he says.

L o r d   G o d   c o m m a n d s   Ruby to quit counting birds. You are like the starving man eating his boot, he says. Next you will consume the newly dead. I cannot abide such foolishness. Standing beside the woodstove, stirring Lila's oatmeal, he commands the very sun to rise and shine. His back stooped, he wears a face like a jump-start mummy. Morning light floods the cracked windowpanes and shines upon his wrinkles and glass eye. His wiry gray beard casts its own oblong shadow upon the faded wallpaper roses.

You've got a daughter to care for, he adds. I can't be your baby-sitter all the time. I have the Lord's work as well.

Ruby watches him and does not reply. She has a diaper bag packed and when Ward's car pulls into the driveway, she grabs Lila, rushes out barefooted, and jumps in the passenger side breathless.

Go, she says. Hurry!

Ward blinks and puts the car into gear, hesitates. But you forgot your shoes.

No, I didn't. She raises her day pack in the air. Got some sandals in here. But hurry or Lord God's going to come out here and yell at us.

Ward can see the front door opening as he eases forward. Why would he yell?

I told you. He doesn't want me leaving the house. He doesn't want me doing anything except what he has in plans for me. And I'm not doing that.

Ward pulls away as Lord God's shadowy form lurches onto the porch. Ruby refuses to look back. Lila is supposed to be in a car seat, she says. But we can't do normal things around this house. I'm going to hold her.

I'm sorry, says Ward. I don't want to get you in trouble with your father.

It's not your fault. It's his. He doesn't want me to work with you.

Ruby brushes her face with the sleeve of one arm. Her eyes are pink and shiny. I hate him. I wish he'd die in a car wreck so I could laugh at his funeral.

Now, come on, says Ward. He probably means well.

No, he doesn't. He just means to protect himself and his clan. He wants to marry me off to some weirdo and make me wear prairie dresses and have ten more kids and I'm not going to let him.

Okay, now, says Ward. Everything's going to be all right.

No, it isn't, says Ruby. You're just saying that to make me feel better.

Ward drives to a Wal-Mart and gets out, tells Ruby he'll be back in a few minutes. He returns carrying a car seat. She's changing Lila's diaper. When he sees the naked squirming legs on his backseat, he stops and waits in the hot sun. She finishes and glances up, then smiles.

You didn't have to do that.

Well. We can't be driving around like barbarians, now, can we?

They return to the prairie west of Lake Pueblo to count birds in the shadow of a water pipeline and along several ravines. In the first hour they see a Sage Thrasher, which Ruby calls a Hookbeak, several Western Meadowlarks, and a Burrowing Owl. By noon they sight eight Horned Larks and five Lark Sparrows. Both species are dwindling across the Great Plains, with most of the land converted to industrial agriculture years ago, and now that the drought has settled on Eastern Colorado, Kansas, and Nebraska, many of the bird populations have all but vanished. Pueblo is west of the depopulated zones: Here most of the land is too arid for farming.

Ward uses a small spiral notebook to record his sightings of the Horned Larks. He has his own system of species identification and record, with lines like a prisoner recording his days scratched upon a cell wall with chalk. Beside the numbers he adds the circle-arrow and circle-cross symbols for male and female. He has given Ruby her own notebook and kids her that she always sees the birds first, which is true.

You're better at this than I am, he says. You should be the ornithologist.

Maybe I will be, says Ruby. She sees Ward smile. He wears a different face here on the prairie. In a side canyon they come upon the Great Horned Owl nest in a cliff Ward had discovered earlier. He shows her the midden below it, a litter of bird bones and owl droppings. She finds a Raven skull bleached white by the wind and sun. She keeps it in honor of the bird. Smooth and white and graceful, with large eye sockets and the white upper beak part of the skull itself, it's a natural piece of art.

In a deep gulch she shows him a mammoth cottonwood where a pair of Western Screech Owls live. She likes the deep gray bark of the tree. Ward wonders how many owls live in that gulch alone, several miles long. Ruby guesses three pair. She's heard the soft dwindling call of a pair near her house. It's like the whinny of a little feathered horse, she says.

As Ward stands there, pensive and watchful, Ruby is struck by how different he is from all the other men she knows. And the way he looks at her is unlike any face of Lord God.

You're a strange one, you know that? You don't drink but you say nary a word about Jesus. Every man I know is either a drinker and a gambler or quotes the Lord every time he burps.

Ward shrugs. God is an idea that people want to believe.

Lord God says the Muslims will take over the world and make good Christian folk their slaves if we don't stop them. He says we must rise and smite them before we are lost and wandering in the desert like the Israelites. Myself, I don't know. I've never seen or met a Muslim as far as I can remember. I don't believe what I hear from Lord God. But he believes. And that's what matters.

Ruby and Ward take turns carrying Lila. She accepts Ward's arms as if that's where she's supposed to be. She reaches up and takes his glasses.

Oh, no, he says. Don't take my glasses, sugarplum. That's how I see.

Ruby has to pry them from her fingers.

They stop for lunch in a wind cave. Ward says it's the kind where you can find petroglyphs.

What kind of rock this is, I don't know. Sandstone, I guess? He takes a bite from his sandwich and stares at the cliffs above them, looming almost pink, with strata like rippled reflections of water. Maybe it's metamorphic. I don't know.

Oh, come on, says Ruby. I thought you knew everything.

Ward shakes his head. Not rocks. I'm not a geologist. He plucks an elk thistle from his jeans. I only know birds.

I was just kidding, says Ruby.

Ward keeps chewing. You know, I used to have research assistants working for me, college kids. Or university students, if you want to get fancy. He paused and squinted at Ruby. You're better than them. More focused. Less self-conscious or obsessed.

What about smarter? asks Ruby.

That too.

She smiles. You're just saying that, I know. But that's okay. You're being nice.

He tells her the sandwich is good and that he's thankful she brought them. You're lucky, he says. You have a baby and a mother and father and you're not alone.

That's not what it seems to me. My mother lives in town and my father wants to auction me off to the highest bidder.

I'm sure he loves you still.

Like you said, you don't know everything.

Ward is quiet until he finishes his sandwich. He folds up the foil it was wrapped in and puts it in his back pocket like it's something precious. Some people like to be alone, he says. Single people. They like to do things their own way and not have to compromise.

Ward says this as if it were a foolish idea, like crossing the Atlantic on a Jet Ski.

I never wanted to be alone, he adds. After my wife and baby were gone, I didn't know what to do. The house was so quiet and at night I was scared of every sound. Birds saved me. Something to focus on. Birds are easier than people. That's why I count them. They matter. More than most people know. When all the birds are gone, the world will end. That's what I think.

Lila begins to fuss. She pulls Ruby's hat and tries to take it off her head, and when Ruby says no, stop, she cries.

She's getting tired, says Ruby. She'll probably fall asleep soon as we start moving again.

A horsefly lands on Lila's neck and Ruby shoos it away. She cradles Lila in her arms and swings her side to side, cooing and saying, It's all right, baby girl. It's all right. I shooed that mean old fly away. I won't let him bite you.

Lila grabs a corkscrew curl of Ruby's hair and pulls on it, says, Bird, Mama. Bird.

Ward smiles and touches her cheek. I wish I could be like Lila. Not a care in the world.

What are you always worried about?

He puts the binoculars to his eyes and scans the opposite side of the canyon. Birds, for one thing. And the weather. The drought.

Ruby nods. We still get rain here sometimes, though. When the storms come quickly and make the prairie wet, I call it wild-flower rain, she says. The flowers start to bloom after a good rain.

Through the binoculars Ward spies a plain gray bird. He shows it to Ruby and asks her what it is. She takes a moment to answer. A female Cowbird?

I don't think so, says Ward. Brown-Capped Rosy Finch? Without the reddish colorations on its primaries? Probably not. Maybe it's an immature female Cowbird and will always be plain gray, with a bit of mottled black flecks in its plumage.

Is that what you think I am? asks Ruby. An immature female?

Ward keeps his binoculars trained on the Rosy Finch. You have Lila, he says.

Yes, I do. And why do you say that?

For that reason alone, you're no immature female. You're a mother.

I guess I'm a little young for that, aren't I? She strokes Lila's cheek. Sometimes I wonder if I'm too young to be a mother. Sometimes I think she's the best thing that ever happened to me.

You're a mother because you're supposed to be a mother. Things happen for a reason, don't they?

Do you believe that's true?

He smiles and says, It's an idea that people want to believe.

Ward watches Ruby coddle Lila and can't help but feel a pang. Tender and sad and wistful all at once. The sky turns darker. He stands up and steps to the jumbled stones at the edge of the wind cave and stares out to check on the approach of a thunderstorm.

The dusty smell of rain. The crackling sound of thunder as if an enormous sheet of glass were breaking. Fat raindrops fall to splat against the stones at the cave's mouth. We're going to get wet, says Ruby.

Across the canyon a Northern Harrier glides along the rocky ledge, a few feet over the ground of the canyon ledge. The prairie hawk gleams pale, almost ghostly white, framed against the dark blue storm clouds above. Its back is dark but the breast and belly are white, giving it almost the appearance of a Snowy Owl, but the tips of its primary feathers are black, splayed like fingers to catch and feel and hold the air. Harriers were rare even before the decline of the prairie and grasslands—more so now, a raptor that lives in the plains, that hovers and glides above the prairie floor to pounce on rodents.

A flash of lightning strobes the landscape. Ward follows the Harrier with his binoculars, holding his breath, and has to think deliberately, to tell himself, Breathe, breathe. And as he watches, the Harrier veers away from the gulch, flaps its wings, and vanishes out of his line of sight.

Bird, says Lila, pointing.

Ruby holds out a graham cracker for her. That's right, Lila girl. That's a bird. A hawk or harrier, actually. She smiles at Ward and adds, I'm starting to teach her the names of specific birds. I don't know if she gets it yet, but what the heck. It's a start.

Ward nods and takes a bite of his sandwich. The wide prairie opens up before them, a violet landscape in the shadow of the rain clouds. The spring rain signals hope for the drought's end. Alone here on the prairie, with the Sierra Mojada in the distance, with the summer monsoons coming on, it feels like all will not be sand and dust. There's something about the chance coincidence of seeing the Harrier gliding, the rainstorm, and Lila's calling what she sees *bird* that electrifies the moment. Ward feels as if he'll remember this event, this particular moment, the rest of his life. Bird, baby, storm. The world in a moment.

SHE COMES TO HIM on a windy day, the sky a dirty mix of wildfire soot and dust storm. She pulls up in his driveway, her ex-driveway, and is slow as second thoughts in getting out of the car. The wind gusts try to blow her back inside. She pushes and heaves against her driver's-side door and the wind and the force of difficult decisions that have made her leave and made her return to do some good in the world, the wind an invisible force to assure her it won't be easy. John Cole sees the cloud of dust rise along the driveway and sweep upon the house. He heads toward the front door, curious and hopeful in the claptrap of his domain.

Juliet opens the rear driver's-side door and collects her things—a diaper bag, chocolate treats and toys for Lila, a book to read, her glasses. A patina of resolve coats her face of perpetual worry. When she turns the cinnamon cloud has swept over the front porch and curtained it. As if by a magician's trick or miracle divine, when the dust settles there stands her husband, John Wesley Cole, the man to whom she has given her life and the man upon whom she has turned her back.

She tries to hold her hair, swirled by the wind into her eyes. Her movement up the stone walkway is like wading in muddy remorse, against the wind, against the current of how his and her lives have flowed off course, an oxbow of heartache. She rubs the dust in her eyes and the cinnamon gusts ripple and roar. She squints to survey the peeling paint on the porch rail, the cracked wood, and an old clay flowerpot full of dry dirt.

Well, this is getting to be a regular event, says John. He nods and smiles, his windburned skin a mask of wrinkles, weathered like the woodshed walls. You're looking good, he adds. Single life must be treating you well.

Thank you, she says. She shrugs. I don't know.

What don't you know?

If single life is treating me well. It's hard. She steps up close to him before she stops moving. I get by, she says. Sometimes that's the best to hope for.

You look better than getting by. You look ten years younger from where I stand.

She blinks and nods. Maybe it's your eyes.

Eye, he says.

I'm sorry. That's stupid of me. I didn't mean anything by it. It's just what people say.

I know, he says. That's okay. I'm glad to see you. Say whatever you want.

Well, aren't you agreeable.

Absence makes a man lonely, I guess. I'd say it's the work of the Lord but you'd roll your eyes.

I'm here to help with Lila. Ruby has to work today and I promised her I'd come.

Work? Is that what she's calling it?

Work it is, John. She's a research assistant, whether you approve or not.

I don't. And I think what she's researching is just how sad that poor bird man is without a woman. Or how happy he is to find a new one.

You haven't even talked to him, have you? He's giving Ruby some confidence in herself, which she needs.

Anybody who counts birds for a living got to be an egghead, you ask me.

What? she asks. You'd prefer a righteous dropout who campaigns for Jesus instead of a man with an education and a good job?

The world's full of educated idiots, says John. He rubs his upper thigh, where the prosthetic leg attaches to his stump.

I'm sure the doctors who fixed me up had plenty of education, but it still hurts like I'm walking on a broomstick.

Well, at least you're walking. Juliet moves past John into the living room, where she hears him shuffle and thump through the doorway, following her. The morning sun beams in trapezoidal blocks onto the hardwood floor and backlights a falling snowscape of dust motes in its light.

Don't you ever vacuum anymore?

I do, he says. Ever' chance I get.

Looks like you don't get many chances.

Take off your shoes, John says. Lila's asleep.

Juliet removes her huaraches while looking around the room, noting dust on the television screen, streaks on the dingy curtains. Plastic toys litter the floor—square and rectangular blocks of Legos colored blue and yellow and green, a plastic triceratops and allosaurus, a polka-dotted horse. A pair of Teletubbies figures perch on a windowsill. Juliet tiptoes to the back bedroom and finds Lila in her crib, angelic and peaceful. She's lying on her back, her hands tucked under her head, her striped shirt hiked up to show the soft plumpness of her belly. Her eyelashes are long and dark, like feathers of a delicate bird.

Juliet reaches down to stroke her face. She brushes the bangs off Lila's forehead and tucks the blanket above her waist. She notices milk stains on the crib sheets and tells herself she will have to pull them off and wash them as soon as Lila wakes. She senses John come up behind her, the hiss and the lisp of his prosthetic shoe on the floor. She feels a force field of anger welling up behind her, a force field of the past, all the moments of silent fury and things gone wrong in her life yoked with his. And yet this child makes the pain bearable.

She can feel John breathing behind her and knows that he is standing there looking at Lila, mute and proud and defensive.

She's so precious, whispers Juliet.

I worry about her, says John. She needs a father and Ruby's so hardheaded she won't admit it.

Ruby seems to be doing okay. She's a good mother.

A good mother doesn't run off and abandon her child. A good mother sticks it out. What would she do without me? She wouldn't have a roof over her head.

Soon as possible I'll move to a bigger place. They could come live with me.

They could but they won't. You left your daughter and that's how it stands.

I left you. There's plenty of house for the two of you here.

The three of us, he says.

I know you'll do the right thing about Ruby and Lila.

If you know that, why did you leave?

Juliet backs away from Lila's crib and leaves John standing in the shadows. In the kitchen she puts the kettle on for tea. She stands at the window, looking out at the trio of aspens, her favorites. The leaves are shaped like green hearts, casting lovely shadows on the woodshed. A Robin perches in the upper branches, and as Juliet stands there lost in thought, a Flycatcher swoops out of the lower branches to feed off insects that hover around the wet patch of earth beside the water faucet.

Beyond the aspens and woodshed stretch the reddish prairie

fields with parched grass and yucca. It's a landscape she has seen many years of her life, as she stood here washing dishes. She misses it. The view out the kitchenette window of her apartment in town looks out on a liquor-store parking lot. Here beyond the prairie loom the gentle ridges of the Sierra Mojada. The presence of mountains in the distance has always felt like the promise of things to come, a sense of hope.

John shuffles down the hall and into the kitchen. She knows this without turning, his presence always behind her, a part of her life left behind.

I said why did you leave?

John? Why are you doing this?

Doing what?

Dredging up all the past?

Because I want to know. Because it's not the past.

It is. I don't live here anymore.

Tell me what to do, he pleads. Tell me what I did wrong. Tell me how to make it right.

Don't play stupid. You know. I left because I couldn't stand living here any longer.

You act like there's only one way. Like I can't change.

Can you?

I don't know. If I thought it was the right thing. If I needed to.

You don't think you need to.

Maybe you can change my mind?

Don't start that. I'll leave if you don't give me some peace. And I mean here. Right now.

Calm down.

Don't tell me to calm down.

From the hallway comes the sound of Lila crying. Juliet goes toward her first without a word. John follows. Lila is standing in her crib, tears in her eyes, her black hair matted on one side where she has slept.

What's the matter, angel? asks Juliet. Did you have a bad dream?

Lila whimpers and holds her arms out. Juliet lifts her in her arms and kisses her cheek. Oh, there, there, she says. It's not that bad, is it?

Lila nods and burrows her face against Juliet's neck.

What do you have to give you bad dreams? It wasn't the Donkey Woman come to take you away from Grandmommy, was it?

Lila stops crying and gives a half smile. She shakes her head.

I didn't think so. Was it a coyote wearing cowboy boots? Juliet nibbles at Lila's ear. Did he try to bite your ear like this?

Lila giggles and squirms. She shakes her head again.

Juliet smiles at John, who has come to stand beside them. He ruffles Lila's hair and tugs on her other ear.

Well, then, says Juliet. If it's not the Donkey Woman or a coyote in cowboy boots, I think you're going to live.

Cookie, says Lila. Cookie duck duck.

She wants one of the Nilla Wafers in the duck cookie jar, says John. She's crazy for those things.

Then let's go find a cookie duck duck, says Juliet.

She carries Lila to the kitchen, where the lighting seems to have dimmed. The back door shudders and a fine spray of dust sifts through the cracks of the doorjamb. Out the window a clay-brown cloud of dust roils across the prairie toward them. Juliet finds the Daffy Duck cookie jar and takes a handful of Nilla Wafers. Lila yelps with delight. As soon as Juliet hands her a cookie, she smiles and her eyes go wide and electric with joy.

I hope Ruby isn't out counting birds in this duster, says John.

Lila makes a face and reaches into her mouth, removes a masticated lump of wafer, and drops it on the floor. She reaches her hands into the air and starts to whine.

What is it, baby? asks Juliet. I don't know what you want.

Lila continues to whine, drops her head, and huddles into Juliet's thighs, whimpering.

She wants her pacifier, says John. She can't go five minutes without having that thing in her mouth. She's still teething. It makes her feel better.

Juliet finds a pacifier beside the kitchen sink and waves it in front of Lila's face. Look here, look here. Is this what you want?

Lila smiles when she sees it, grabs the pacifier, and plops it into her mouth.

That's what I do all day, says John. He smiles. It beats getting your head shot at in the desert. Or playing Ping-Pong on one leg.

I clean up dog crap is what I do. Juliet rubs the back of her neck. Not all the time, of course. But maybe too often.

John puts a teakettle on the stove. I thought you were the one who wanted to work. You were the one who thought working for a vet would be fun.

I didn't say fun.

What'd you say? Rewarding?

It is. Sometimes.

Juliet? The word out of John's voice sounds odd, off-kilter. As if he were trying to speak another language. Juliet? What can I do? Tell me what is and I'll do it. In a heartbeat.

What do you mean?

You know what I mean. What can I do to bring you back? I don't want to live this way. We've been married for eighteen years. And you know I love you. Doesn't that count for anything?

Juliet doesn't reply. She watches the teakettle boil and puts an animal cracker in Lila's mouth. You want a cup of tea?

I can do that.

They sit down at the table and both smile at Lila and stroke her face, giving her animal crackers, hiding the pacifier behind the sugar bowl.

Isn't she the prettiest thing ever? says Juliet.

She is. John rubs the spot where his prosthesis connects to his thigh. She's a little angel is what she is.

AFTER CROWFOOT RESCUES Becca Cisneros from the Saints, he takes her to his trailer, leaves her there alone, and explains nothing.

Hang loose, he says. I've got errands to run, but I'll be back.

What am I supposed to do? she asks.

Nothing, he says. Relax. I'll be back with something for dinner.

I can cook, she says.

He frowns. That sounds like work, right? You've been working enough. I think you'll be safe here for a few days. There's no lock and key. You want to leave, it's your choice.

That's an improvement, then, she says. Maybe I'll just lay low here for a few days, you think?

He nods. I think.

She watches him leave, his beaten truck bouncing over the rocky driveway, disappearing behind a ridgeline of junipers as it switchbacks down the mesa. Becca senses he's a badass but a good man, the kind who gets misunderstood, easy-like. She's heard his name before, and placed him in her mind as something of a legend, like the blind circus knife thrower El Ciego or the Donkey Woman.

Turkey vultures float by the windows, catching updrafts out of the valley below, their raggedy black wings and ugly red heads stark against the blue sky. Alone in his trailer, she doesn't know what to do with herself. Liberated from a work camp into a hermit's nest.

She cleans his kitchen and straightens his living room. She finds a pile of oil-stained rags and wipes the sandstone dust from everything and sweeps the floor. She scrapes old bacon grease off his stove. She doesn't go near his bedroom.

Early evening he comes home and looks around. What the heck? he asks. I seem to have misplaced some coffee stains and dirt clods.

I take that as a thank you very much, says Becca. If not I'll beat you with a broom.

She sits in a folding chair and watches clouds roil out of the Sangre de Cristo mountains. The metal chairs perch beside a wooden cable spool used as a table. Everything is makeshift and functional. Atop Wild Horse Mesa, the trailer sits in the shadow of a cliff face above Cañon City. There's no running water. She has to hike a short ways to the outhouse perched above a shallow rock pit.

He has no electricity except a sheet of solar panels on the roof hooked to a pair of truck batteries, plus an arc of solar lawn lights in front of the trailer. I've been off the grid for years, he tells her. They say the oil is going to run out and the power plants close. Okay, then. He smiles. Bring it on. I'm ready.

At dusk Crowfoot builds a fire in a pit of blackened stones at the foot of the cliff face where the trailer is tucked. Soon the solar lights leak their blue glow into the air and flames of the campfire toss their shadows against the sandstone cliff face. It seems they're living in a time beyond work shortages and immigration wars.

Lightning zigzags over the plains, over the old Arapaho lands now full of cattle ranchland and dry crops, all of it parched with drought. Crowfoot cuts an onion and takes a pound of ground meat from the ice chest that serves as his refrigerator, puts the onion and meat in a cast-iron skillet on the fire, stirs it with a rough-hewn wooden spoon he carved himself.

Can I help? asks Becca.

At first he doesn't respond. She's about to repeat the offer when he says, What say you clean up after.

It's a deal, she says. What are you making?

Sloppy joes. He offers her a rare smile. You ever had buffalo?

He places a foil-wrapped bundle of tortillas on the hot stones at the fire's edge. After a few minutes he flips them with his bare hands, wincing and waving his fingers in the air. Then he yanks them from the stone and opens the foil, rubs a stick of butter on one, rolls it up, and hands it to her.

Appetizer, he says.

She eats a half-dozen tortillas like this, licking the butter from her fingers. The moonless night opens before them like a black hole. There's a sharp drop-off at the cliff edge not twenty paces from the pit.

When Becca steps away from the flames' glow she looks up at the black velvet sky. Above her the Milky Way flows like a powdered-sugar river of other suns. After two months as a polygamist captive, she feels the cool air on her face, the stars in her hair, like proof of the world's wheeling.

You're welcome to sleep on the sofa, says Crowfoot. It might be a bit dusty. But I got a spare pillow and a good wool serape. He grins. Actually, it's a horse blanket.

Do I look like a horse? she asks.

He squints one eye and cocks his head. What about a pony? Graceful and high-spirited?

You're a sweet talker, says Becca. And yes, she adds. The sofa will be fine. Besides, I can't thank you enough. You saved me. I won't forget that. Ever.

Crowfoot shrugs. Whenever you save a person, it doesn't end there. It's like you're tied together the rest of your life.

I'll pay you back somehow.

You make dinner tomorrow night, he says. We'll call it even.

Okay, she says. We won't be even. But we can pretend.

After dinner a gibbous moon rises, swollen and bright above the eastern plain. Crowfoot says, Come here a sec. I got something I bet you never seen the likes of.

He leads her away from the trailer, along the sandstone cliff face on an ever-narrowing ledge. They find their way in the moonlight. He leads the way and she follows. At one point he turns and says, It gets kind of tight here. You best hold on.

He hooks her hands to his wide leather belt and slows for a moment. In the pale blue moonlight Becca sees they're on a cliff edge no more than four feet wide, with a good forty-foot drop to a jumbled talus slope below. They shuffle on.

You scared? he asks.

A little.

Don't be. I wouldn't let you fall.

I know.

I saved you, remember? He says this with a hint of humor in his voice. Wouldn't make sense to tumble off a cliff after all that, would it?

I guess not, she whispers.

The ledge widens. After what seems a long passage they reach a hollow in the cliff face. Crowfoot removes a wooden pole jammed into a crevice, takes a butane lighter from his pocket, and lights the end of it. The torch burns fitfully for a moment, but he rolls it this way and that until it burns smoothly and casts a smoky flame.

A little art project of mine, he says, holding the torch against the cliff face.

Becca stands for a moment, spellbound, until she realizes her mouth is open and her eyes sting from being kept wide.

What in the world, she says. I mean, amazing. You did all this?

No big deal, says Crowfoot. Like I said, it's a project. Been working on it three years now.

On the cliff face before them, illuminated by the smoking torch, stretches a tableau of petroglyphs. The figures are palm-sized or bigger, in arching rows, rough but recognizable figures of cars and planes and trains and explosions. In the lowest left corner is a figure of stylized towers in flame, into which two planes crash. Beside it a giant wave. Farther down the wall a circle with a long tail to symbolize the great comet.

It's the twenty-first century, says Crowfoot. A history of it. I started with the towers and I don't know what I'll end with.

Who's this devil figure?

Take your pick.

Fields of crosses. Hordes of running figures. Cactus and slanted lines and stylized suns to symbolize the drought. Kachinas shaped like angry machines. Hooded executioner figures.

Crowfoot points to faded figures repeated here and there—coyotes and elk, human hands, weird turtles and birds—telling her that these are original, ancient Native art. The entire cliff is a palimpsest of petroglyphs past, the smoking torch illuminating a cliff from a thousand years before, a reckoning of ways past meeting ways future.

Becca feels her eyes burning but she can't blink. Crowfoot's torch luffs and looses a steady swirl of black smoke. She feels sucked inside the history of the world. There are oil wars and riots and the comet that frightened everyone blazing through the night sky, the omen of the first great oil shortage. She's seen handprints inside caves in New Mexico. She never thought much of them, crude art in a crude world. This is something greater.

Her skin fizzes like a shaken can of soda. She wonders what George Armstrong Crowfoot has in his heart that gives him the confidence to offer his own depiction of the history of the world. There's a daring quality to it. A bravery against the wind and sun.

This is amazing, says Becca, and immediately regrets it. The words are weak and meaningless. She can't express her thoughts clearly and knows if she gushes too much Crowfoot will think her a phony.

He shrugs. It kills the time, he says. I don't have TV, right?

That's a good thing.

If you say so.

He steps back and holds the torch high, the flickering flames casting ripple shadows on the painted wall like light reflections from burning water. He says it's something he believes in. A body has to find a thing worth doing, and then do it, he says. I get so mad sometimes I could kill someone, like the Saint with the weak chin. I could have slit his throat, easy. Crowfoot shakes his head. But then I'd be smelling that blood the rest of my life. As it is, he's just one scar uglier.

He'll get over it, says Becca.

Check this out. Crowfoot plays the torchlight upon the end of a row of figures—horses, a ring, a death's-head face. I got a place for pretty boy at the end of that line. I'll show you when I'm done.

But it's a shame it's out here so far from everything. I mean, you should share this with the world.

Crowfoot keeps the torch held high. It's where it should be.

Who's going to see it? she asks.

You.

Becca feels that same buzzing, this time like an alarm clock smothered by a pillow. Without another word or warning Crowfoot pushes the burning torch into a pile of sand at the base of the rock face. All goes dark. Becca puts her hand on his arm to steady herself in the pitch blackness, the sharp tang of smoke in her nose. When he moves to head back, she grabs a handful of his shirt and holds tight.

On the cliff ledge not much wider than twice Crowfoot's shoulders they short-step back to the world of the living. Becca lets her fingernails dig just a tad into Crowfoot's skin to remind him she's there. Clouds now blanket the Arkansas River valley and shut out the moon and stars. She can see nothing but the rough black wall of cliff on her right, her only link between the past and future being the tall, hard body of the legendary George Armstrong Crowfoot, the kind of man who cuts his enemy for the rough scrape of retribution.

Her heart pulses in her throat the whole way and when she thinks she can't take it anymore she sees the brightest blue-white constellation so low on the horizon she fears they'll step on it. She wonders if she's hallucinating. Any minute Crowfoot could shapeshift into a Raven and flap away. Then she smells wood smoke. The ledge widens and they're back at the trailer. The constellation she sees is nothing more than the arc of solar lights.

Crowfoot opens the trailer door and after a moment has a pair of candles burning, filling the aluminum-sided box with an amber glow. He folds out the sofa and gives Becca a flat pillow and a dusty-smelling serape. It's not the Waldorf, he says. Then again, what is the Waldorf? I never been there.

Becca thanks him and says she'll be happy to sleep on rocks if it comes to that.

She lies in bed and listens to the wind in the canyon. The pillow and serape hold the smell of dust and mice but the cool night air carries a sweet tang of juniper and pine through the open window.

She can't sleep. At one point she gets up and walks out the front door, wrapped in the serape, and watches the stars through ragged holes in the clouds. She finds a smooth stone near the fire and it warms her rump. A Great Horned Owl hoots somewhere in the cliffs below. Its call is poignant and lonesome and when she thinks her heart will turn to wax and melt, the moon comes out and she sees George Armstrong Crowfoot standing beside her.

I couldn't sleep, she says.

I figured as much.

Crowfoot sits down cross-legged near the fire. Clouds cover the moon and hide his face. Beside her he is no more than a black silhouette. He says nothing. He stirs the coals until he has a cluster of orange embers pulsing. He breaks a handful of kindling and carefully places it on the embers. The twigs begin to smoke and soon burst into flame. The moon rips free from clouds and shines on their cliff face. It's clearing, he says. Soon we'll see the Milky Way again.

It's nice here. I love it.

But you can't sleep.

Becca nods. I don't know. I might not sleep all night.

They sit by the flames for a while without speaking. Crowfoot stands and stretches. You can have my bed if you want.

I couldn't do that. Where would you sleep?

He takes a moment to answer. I'm not going anywhere.

She looks at him and can only see a hint of expression on his face.

A half hour later she creeps into his bed. He's awake, lying on his back, his head resting on his hands.

I'm glad you came, he says. I don't like to sleep alone.

Me neither, she whispers.

Becca wakes naked in Crowfoot's bed. He's gone and a woman is standing in the doorway, staring at her. She has short black hair and wears an onyx necklace.

Where's Sonny? she asks.

You mean George?

The woman steps to the window and peeks through a gap in the curtains, looking outside. We call him Sonny. I thought he'd be here.

Becca sits up, holding the serape to her chest. She blinks and tries to look alive. I don't know, she says. I just woke up.

You want some coffee? asks the woman. I know how Sonny makes it here, on a little white gas stove. It's crude but it makes a good pot o' java.

Becca nods. Sure. That would be great.

The woman smiles and leans forward, holding out her hand. I'm sorry. I'm Joy, Sonny's sister.

Oh. Becca shakes her hand. You must think I'm some kind of skeevy woman.

Skeevy?

A floozy. A tart.

Joy shrugs. Sonny is a good man, so why not? I've opened my eyes in a few strange places myself.

I'm not a tramp. It was just, you know.

Joy waves her hand like Becca should forget it. She walks away, down the hall. From the kitchen she calls out, How long have you known Sonny?

Becca pushes her hair out of her face. I just met him, actually.

What?

Becca gets out of bed and pulls on her clothes. She shouts this time. I just met him.

As Joy moves in the kitchen, making the coffee, Becca hears her laughing.

Okay. You're not a floozy, she calls back. But you must be easy.

HIRAM PAGE MEETS an unsavory acquaintance at a highway pull-off near Lake Pueblo, a windswept half moon of beaten-down prairie from which a body can see for miles in every direction. It's late in the day and the sky is hazy blue with summer heat. Their only company is a pair of mountain bikers who ride up and dismount, stand there chugging Gatorade, wearing sports sunglasses and helmets. Page leaves his diesel engine running and the windows rolled up. The cyclists give the pickup dirty looks as they load their bikes.

Hiram's friend runs a lucrative chop shop, goes by the name of Porter. Long hair and sideburns, a windburned face. He's the one who arranged the cattle-rustling caper, the one whose brother works for the Pueblo County sheriff's department.

I'm sure it's risky, says Porter, but it just might be worth the trouble. BP must have insurance out the wazoo. Look at what's going on with all those pirates in Africa? All the companies do is write off the losses and keep on truckin'.

What about tracking devices? asks Page. Some kind of GPS gizmo? They probably have something on each and every rig to know where it is.

My friend says he knows where it is, how to unhook it.

How are we going to sell this black gold? All the stations must keep records.

I've got that covered. We slap fake plates on it and haul the rig to Utah, and some locals there will do all the paperwork and sell to a few independent stations in Colorado City. We give them a discount and still make a bundle.

Hiram Page sits and stares west. The dried prairie grasses look burnt orange in the late-afternoon light.

Who do you plan on taking with you on this caper? he asks.

Well, I think Ezra for one. He's got a pair of balls and needs the money. We'll need three, four guys besides me. I'm sure I can find somebody. Probably Ezra can scare up a couple of his buddies who know enough to keep their mouths shut should something go wrong.

Which it better not.

Agreed. Which it better not. But if it does, we want some of our own on this.

What about the driver?

We drug him, says Porter, mimicking an injection in his neck.

He wakes a few hours later and hitches a ride home. You're long gone?

That's what I'm thinking. You like the idea? asks Porter.

Page purses his lips and nods. One condition. I want a cousin of mine to ride along, a kid named Jack Brown. He's a cheap date. We'll pay him enough to keep him happy, which won't have to be much.

Is he up for this kind of work?

Hiram makes a face. He's young, dumb, and full of cum.

I don't like the dumb part. Dumb gets people hurt.

Tell him what to do and he'll do it.

Porter watches another Jeep pull in and skid to a stop, raising a cloud of dust that drifts onto Page's pickup. Teenagers in Lycra bike outfits get out, laughing. Okay, then, he says. I'll nursemaid your cousin, long as he doesn't get a dime from my cut.

Deal, says Page.

Sounds like we've got a plan.

Page nods. As the great ear-biting boxer Mike Tyson once said, Everybody's got plans, until they get hit.

When the day comes Porter meets his motley crew at a scenic pull-off in the Bighorn Canyon, beside the legendary Arkansas River, former boundary of the Louisiana Purchase, former dividing line of Arapaho and Comanche territories. Now it's a hot spot for commercial float trips, whole families bobbing along in orange life vests, taking pictures with digital cameras as the water splashes and they squeal.

Porter is in a bad mood, glaring as Mosca and Ezra Page stand jawing beside a red pickup. In the cab are crammed three polyg flunkies, with Jack Brown sitting bitch in the middle, looking squashed and put out. Porter looks the chop-shop mechanic that he is, with a pit-bull face and sideburns, long hair in a ponytail.

A red pickup? I thought I told you to be low key?

I told them you wouldn't like it, says Ezra Page, Hiram's blood nephew.

Porter shakes his head and sighs. Well, goddamnit, you might as well put up a sign that says, Remember Me. But whatever. We're here now and we got a job to do.

We're cool, says Ezra. No one will see a thing.

You better hope they don't. Meanwhile, listen up. I'm going to hang back and get behind the tanker once it passes. Ezra, you get in place in front and block the road with the trailer once I give the word. I'll call and tell you when he's headed your way. You, he says, pointing at Jack Brown, try not to wet your pants or stutter too much.

I don't stutter, says Brown. I mean, sometimes I can stumble on a word or two like anyone else, but that's normal, isn't it? I mean—

Better yet, don't open your goddamn trap. We don't need chatty patties on this job.

I'm not—

Are you stupid or what? Just shut your fucking mouth, okay?

Okay.

No use putting a trucker in his grave without he deserves it. Now if he goes and tries something funny, all bets are off. Rodriguez, you ride with Ezra.

Why me? asks Ezra. I thought I'd be riding with you.

You're second in charge. I want you to keep an eye on Mosca. In my book, a loose-lip Mexican can't be trusted 100 percent.

Ezra frowns but takes out his keys and points Mosca toward his dirty white pickup hitched to a flatbed trailer stacked with hay bales. Ezra Page is thin as Ichabod Crane, with small eyes and huge Adam's apple. He wears a cowboy hat with a short, straight brim. Mosca smirks. He thinks it looks old-timey, like this is a Saint who fancies himself living in an Old West comic book. While they're talking Ezra takes off his hat to adjust it. Just above his hairline is an awkward gauze bandage the size of a man's palm.

You always wear a new hat to a bushwhacking?

Ezra frowns and settles the hat back in place. It's not new.

Right, says Mosca. I bet you've had it at least two weeks.

They climb into the cab without another word. Ezra drives. He looks to be no older than nineteen or twenty. You sure you're old enough for this? says Mosca. I mean, you do have a valid driver's license, don't you?

I'm old enough, don't you worry, says Ezra.

Mosca stares out the window, his pinched face stiff, eyes squinting out at the rocky canyon walls. A half mile down the road he says, Fucker better watch who he calls a Mexican.

Ezra grins. You're the one who should watch what you say.

That's Porter you're talking about. I wouldn't fuck with him, no way nohow.

I'm just saying—

I know. Just leave me out of it. Let's just do this and make a ton of money, okay?

The sky fades to violet and lavender, then deep purple, with a stencil silhouette of the Sangre de Cristo mountains to the south. Mosca watches the taillights of the pickup ahead and imagines bushwhacking Porter, having George Armstrong Crowfoot hold him down as he cuts out his tongue. That would be hard to do, to grab a squirmy thing like that and cut it free. Maybe his ears would be a better target. Smug sumbitch. He thinks he can make fun of *mi familia* he's got another thing coming.

Mosca chatters to pass the time. He says he's heard some ski resorts might close this year. Frankly, I don't give a shit. I mean, what's the point in skiing? A sport for rich assholes. Sliding down a mountain on a couple skinny boards? Sounds pretty damn silly if you ask me.

The Lord is punishing the rich for their hedonism and profligate ways, says Ezra. That's why the cost of everything is so high. It's a great reckoning. It is. You mark my words. This is just the beginning.

If this is just the beginning I'd hate to see the fiery *adios*.

You will. A time will come when the one true prophet will emerge and all the evils and sins of the world will be made right.

Except for this fuel appropriation, right? Mosca grins.

It's not a sin to take what doesn't belong to anyone to begin

with. It's our right and ability. The oil lay below the holy land, oc-
cupied by sand monkeys.

The headlights shine on jagged cliff faces that loom over the
road. Highway 50 follows the Arkansas River like an asphalt
shadow. Mosca says this is a famous stretch of road. Stagecoaches
had regular routes here in the 1880s. I'm a history buff, he adds.
I like to know where we been and where we're going. I won the
head of Black Jack Ketchum in a card game. I might auction it off
to the highest bidder sometime, if you know anyone might be interested. Aren't you Saints keen on the past, Brigham Young's
wives' petticoats and all that?

Don't blaspheme the worthy.

I was just saying.

Some things you don't kid about.

On State Highway 69 south of Texas Creek they wait at a
tight bend on an uphill slope. Porter calls on his cell to tell them
the turkey is on its way.

Mosca rolls his window down and smokes a cigarette. The
night air is cool and smells of pine and juniper. He says he loves
this country and can't imagine living anywhere else. He doesn't
blame the other Mexican migrants for wanting to come north. I
mean, there's work here for them. Everybody wants to make a
living, no matter where they might be born.

That head you say is Black Jack Ketchum's. You say you won
it in a card game, right?

It's the Lord's truth. I had two aces buried in a hand of Texas
Hold 'Em. I was sweating it all the way till the last man called. I
figured someone might have a full house.

When was that?

Two months back.

Had a big mustache, didn't it? Funny because I knew of a Saint by the name of Morris Dinwoody who had a bad car wreck about a year ago. Decapitated, he was. Ezra smiles. Can't get any worse than that.

Mosca jabs out his cigarette. And the point is?

I'm willing to bet more money than you won at the card table the head was Morris Dinwoody's, formerly of Florence, Colorado.

Goddamnit. No one believes me. When Black Jack Ketchum was hanged in 1901 his head popped clean off. The man I won it from said he knew some archaeologist types who dug up the coffin to do some kind of DNA test and—

You weren't playing a man named Curtis, were you? Red-haired son of a bitch? With a high voice?

Mosca doesn't answer. He flicks his cigarette out the window. Fucking DNA test proved it was Ketchum, he says. I don't give a shit what you say. I know what I got and that head is worth some money.

Curtis works for the mortuary that handled Dinwoody's corpse. He didn't have any people who cared for him and he was a turncoat polyg, so they'd just as soon spit on his grave. I heard Curtis had the head dried and cured as a joke.

Mosca says, That trucker should be coming soon.

Well, not a joke, adds Ezra. More like a curiosity object I suppose.

Long as we're shooting the shit, what happened to *your* head?

Ezra takes his time answering. What happened is not the question. Or the issue, you might say. What's going to happen when I catch that redskin motherfucker, that's the issue.

In the dark he can't see the smirk on Mosca's face.

A cell phone buzzes on the dashboard. Ezra answers it and listens. Okay, we're ready, he says. He folds it shut and digs under his seat for a machine pistol. Lock and load, *amigo*. It's showtime.

They pull the truck into the middle of the road and cut the wheels hard to the left, getting the front wheels just off the edge of the shoulder, blocking the way of both lanes with the hay trailer. Mosca jumps out of the cab and climbs onto the flatbed, kicks off a stack of hay bales. A few minutes later they see the headlight beams of the fuel tanker shining on the pines and junipers. Ezra tells Mosca to stay on the flatbed trailer and don't do anything stupid. They pretend to be reloading the hay as the tanker approaches.

Remember, says Ezra, I'm in charge here. Got it?

No problema, says Mosca. You the man.

From their spot in the middle of the road all they can see of the tanker are two bright headlights. Ezra waves his hands for it to stop, a machine pistol tucked into the back of his jeans. He smiles as he walks up to the cab, the diesel engine throbbing above him, and as he steps in closer he realizes he's forgotten to grab his flashlight. He can't see the trucker behind the wheel. He stands there ready to give his spiel about it being just a minute while they load the hay back onto their trailer. The cab door does not open.

The semi's diesel engine throbs and rattles. The headlights shine on Mosca in the flatbed of the hay trailer. He holds his hands up to block the blinding light.

Knock on his door! yells Mosca. He sees Ezra lean in to bang on the side of the cab door, and in the same moment it swings open. Ezra snaps back and falls to the shoulder of the road.

The gears shift and the engine throb drops to a deeper growl. The truck starts to reverse.

Mosca jumps down from the trailer and lands badly, feeling a lightning bolt of pain shoot up his ankle. He cusses and limps forward. Ezra is getting to his knees now, his machine pistol in his hands. Behind the truck are two pair of headlights, blinding Mosca. He limps forward a few feet, stops, and takes a shot at the receding truck headlights. He misses. In the red glare he sees the two pickups park sideways. The truck doesn't stop or slow, smashing the passenger-side door of the first truck and knocking it backward.

Ezra runs and shoots at the cab windows. The bullets spiderweb glass. He keeps shooting and black holes of broken windshield appear, sparks flying where bullets hit metal. The truck slows and jackknifes. The cab door opens, the driver jumps down, backlit by the pickup headlights. He runs for the pines beyond the road shoulder, tumbles into the ditch, scrabbles up the rocky embankment.

Stray bullets kick up dust around him. He slips and grabs at his back, flinches, and stumbles. He turns and in the headlights his face is clearly visible, looking back. Mosca and Ezra come up with their guns drawn and pointed.

The trucker is a heavy man with a beard and black-framed glasses. You had no cause to shoot me, he says. You did that just out of meanness, didn't you?

You started it, says Ezra. You're the one who smashed that door into me. I bet you anything I'm having a black eye and bruises in the morning.

The trucker coughs raggedly and struggles to breathe. Mosca tells Ezra it looks like he's lung-shot. If he don't get to a doctor fast he's a goner, he says.

Shut your trap, hisses Ezra.

The trucker inhales raggedly to speak, spits up blood.

Porter and the others approach, casting long shadows across the embankment as they pass before the headlights. They wear hats and bandannas. Porter walks up to Ezra and stands close. Who did the shooting? he asks.

Boy genius here, says Mosca.

Who are you sonsabitches? wheezes the trucker. I didn't do anything to you. I'm just driving a goddamn truck and you fucking shoot me.

Ezra shakes his head and says, You started it. All I was trying to do was—

Porter cuffs his ear. Goddamn you. That man's blood's on your hands.

Listen, says the trucker, I'm getting cold here. Just take me—

He stops in midsentence and slumps, his body settling into the dead grass.

Goddamnit to hell, says Porter. He cuffs Ezra again. You stupid, stupid son of a bitch.

Jack Brown is busy tossing the hay bales off the road. He shouts that they need to get a move on, cars could come by any minute.

Ezra stands dumb, staring down at the dead trucker and wiping his hands on his jeans. Porter turns and jabs a finger against his chest. Enough of this, he says. You drag his body into the woods, then drive the flatbed home. And don't you say a fucking word to a soul, you got that?

Ezra nods, stumbling as he climbs up to the road, falling to his hands and knees for a moment, then getting up and brushing himself off.

Porter points at Mosca. You, drive the rig and follow me.

Okay, boss.

Mosca climbs into the cab of the big rig. Taped to the dash is a photograph of a baby wearing a cowboy hat several sizes too big, smiling and holding on to the brim, one eye obscured by the shadow of the hat. A plastic tray near the shifter holds a thermos of hot coffee. Mosca shakes his head and puts it into gear, moves slowly through the litter of hay where they had blocked the road. The night air is cool but he can feel himself sweating. Now that the rig is on the move, he doesn't like the idea of stopping anywhere the Saints want. They have just killed a man and there's going to be hell to pay.

OFFICER ISRAEL JAMES has no jurisdiction in Fremont or Custer county but when he hears of a fuel tanker hijacked and a body discovered he drives to the site south of Texas

Creek. The road through Bighorn Canyon snakes beside the Arkansas River, undercutting sandstone and granite cliffs. It's summer monsoon season. By the time Elray nears the crime scene, it's afternoon and the sky darkens with cloud shadows. The jagged sierra horizon turns black over the Sangre de Cristos.

The road turns in a sharp uphill curve and he pulls off on the rocky shoulder to park behind two state patrol cars. Lightning cracks overhead and it thunders so loud he can feel it in the dash. Hail rockets off his windshield. He waits it out, wind rocking the tiny car and pea-sized hail coating the black asphalt with a crust of white. After a while it dwindles. He's waiting in the driver's seat when both state troopers get out of their cars and come back to tap on his window and ask to see some identification.

He shows the Mounties his badge. I've got a gut feeling this is the work of polyg squatters in Little Pueblo, he says.

The troopers frown like he's speaking Russian. One of them is young and blond and has the air of a fool who thinks he knows everything. You're telling me Christians did this?

The other one grins. Or is that your gut doing the talking?

Well, they're not Christians like most people think of. You know, with all these nutcase Saints moving in, seems like Colorado has become Utah's prettier sister.

Saints? The blond one grins in an ugly way. I'm Mormon, he adds. It's the Church of Latter-Day Saints. We believe in Jesus Christ. Much like any Baptist.

And we enforce the laws, says the other. We don't break them.

I know, I know.

Sounds like we got a case of religious discrimination here to me.

Listen, I'm not trying to argue over God here. These aren't your average Mormons. They're a low-life splinter group of fundamentalist types who see this as the end times. As far as they go all bets are off, and anything that has to do with the government or big business is ripe for picking. They're scam artists mainly.

And you think scam artists shot this man in the back? And stole an entire fuel tanker?

Elray shrugs. They make up their own rules as they go along. They're not church ladies, that's for sure.

He walks away from the troopers and approaches the dead man. Flies buzz the corpse covered with a blue plastic tarp.

One bullet wound in the side and a smaller wound in the back. The embankment is muddy and goldenrod grows knee-high in the ditch. Elray can hear the state troopers talking into the radio behind him. The blond one says it looks to him to be the work of Mexican drug gangs. Maybe they're targeting fuel tankers now. Maybe the money is better than drugs. I don't know. Illegals are taking over the southern half of the state, says the trooper. It's getting to be a white man can't drive the road without a gun and the will to use it.

Elray returns to the road and squats down low, the asphalt still covered with hail. He finds broken glass from both headlights and turn-signal plastic covers amid the strewn hay. Where'd the illegals get all this hay? he asks the troopers.

They stare at him. Same place they got the semiautomatic weapons, says the blond. Retail most likely.

Where would you buy hay around here?

I don't know. Farm-supply place?

Ranchers make their own hay in this valley. Leastways when they have enough rain.

You saying ranchers did it?

I'm saying it was someone or a group of someones who knows a rancher who has access to hay. By the size of these tire tracks they had a big flatbed here. Elray squats again to get a look at the tread pattern. I just don't see a Mexican gang getting easy access to a flatbed full of hay. Without we'd hear about it.

Mex drug gangs do whatever they want, whenever. And kill when they want too.

Elray stands to leave. Well, then. I guess you two got things covered and figured out. He smiles like he's giving them the finger. I thank you for all your help. Maybe I'll be seeing you in church sometime.

I don't see how this is any business of yours, says the blond trooper. Aren't there enough crimes in Pueblo to keep you busy?

Oh, we make out.

That's what I hear. The cop smirks. In fact, what I hear, it's a hellhole.

B E C C A W E A R S a corduroy jacket that belongs to Crowfoot and her dark hair spills over the collar, down her back. She brushes it away from her face and cheeks, showing off a pair of silver crucifix earrings. By the campfire she tells him the whole story. Why she ended up in Little Pueblo, shackled to a kitchen counter, kneading bread and swatting flies. She gets excited as she talks, waving her hands in the air and mimicking Jack Brown's weakness, complaining how they were treating his "girlfriend" rough.

Crowfoot doesn't comment except to laugh when she tells about mock-swallowing the ring. It is a cloudless June night. The tang of piñon and sage in the nearby gullies. On the eastern plains below the mesa city lights shine and shimmer, while Crowfoot and Becca face the north star, with the Big Dipper pointing toward it on one side and the witch's signature of Cassiopeia on the other.

And when he gave you to the Saints and kept you hostage, you never gave up the ring?

No way, says Becca. He threatened me with all kinds of things, but I wouldn't give in. That's how I ended up at the compound. They said I owed them eight thousand dollars plus interest, so they wrote up this contract and made me sign it, saying I'd work off the debt.

I thought it was supposedly worth twenty thousand?

Even Saints aren't that stupid.

Crowfoot adds a juniper branch to the fire. What happened to it then?

The ring? I hid it. It's in an undisclosed location near the motel where I was staying. I was lucky to squirrel it away. Two minutes after I did it, Jack Brown showed up with a couple of his goon friends and grabbed me in the parking lot.

Crowfoot stands and walks over to a pyramid of split wood stacked near the trailer porch. He collects a handful of white aspen pieces and returns to the fire, adds a couple to the smoldering branches. After a moment the aspen begins to crackle and flame, casting an orange glow on Becca's face. The smoke swirls and shifts direction, heading her way. She stands and steps back from the smoke, her shadow oversized and dramatic against the walls of the trailer.

You should give it back, says Crowfoot.

Becca steps farther away from the campfire and her shadow shrinks against the trailer wall. She rubs her eyes and walks in a wide circle around the fire, staying behind Crowfoot. She watches as he gathers his long black hair to loop a hair tie around it.

People are always telling me what to do. Especially men.

Crowfoot finishes putting his hair in a ponytail. She watches his slow, careful movements and waits for him to say something. He picks up another piece of split aspen and pokes at the fire, says, My eyes are burning. This fire's too smoky.

Everything smells like smoke. My hair, my clothes, my skin, says Becca. Here I am holed up in the mountains like an outlaw and I smell bad and I have some Indian guru telling me I should give up the only thing I own that's worth anything.

Medicine man, says Crowfoot.

What?

Medicine man is what I should be called. He turns to her and smiles, the campfire glow casting his wide face and sharp nose in shadow and light, like the features of a carved talisman. I'm a licensed Arapaho medicine man.

And you think I should give back that ring? After all the trouble I've gone through because of it.

Crowfoot shrugs. It's just my opinion. Don't worry yourself. People have opinions.

Well, yes, they do. And maybe they should keep them to themselves.

He looks at her and smiles again. After all this time? I thought you wanted some feedback.

You thought wrong, she says.

He nods. The fire burns brighter, the split aspen aflame and the branches no longer smoldering. You hungry?

Maybe.

Think you could eat elk?

Becca laughs and shakes her head. I smell like smoke and sweat and juniper and bacon grease. I'm using the bathroom in a lime pit on a cliff face. And I think I missed my period. Can I eat elk? I don't see why the hell not.

Crowfoot looks at her for a long time, a softening expression on his shadowed face. I like the way you smell, he says. You smell like a woman who has more on her mind than shopping.

I don't even know what that word means, she says.

He stands up and heads toward the trailer. One elk steak coming up, he says.

Becca sits by the fire, watching the embers pulse and glow like stars in another galaxy. In a minute Crowfoot is back with meat wrapped in wax paper.

And what was that about you missing a period? he asks.

I'm three weeks late, she says. I don't know. Maybe it's just a scare.

I'm not scared, he says. He leans down and kisses her forehead. I've always wanted to be called Daddy.

She keeps her head down but can't help but smile. You might just get that wish, hot stuff.

The next morning Becca lies alone in bed, feeling peckish and put out. A russet glow is visible outside her window. Just after dawn. She hears Crowfoot rattling around outside, but she stays in bed, sulking. She tells herself that today she's going to leave, that she's not going to have anything more to do with George Armstrong Crowfoot, no matter how charming and New Age sexy he can be. If she's with child, she'll go to a clinic and never look back.

George is getting on her nerves. Waking her at dawn, telling her what to do, making enough noise to wake the dead. The bedroom of his tin-can trailer smells like horse and he doesn't even own one. The outhouse is a hike and when you get there, you have to hold your nose.

She lies in his horse-smelling bed for a good fifteen minutes, trying to get back to sleep, trying to deny her hunger, trying to pretend that the day has not yet begun. Outside her window there's a sound of chopping. Rhythmic and quick.

When she can't take it anymore, Becca pulls on a sweater and crouches on the bed to look out the window. George has his hair down, an ax in his hand, facing the other direction. She feels as if she's spying on an untamed animal. Like a nature program on PBS. It must be 40 degrees out there and he's wearing a western shirt and jeans.

There's a thin line between brute strength and brute. Crowfoot is so strong he's scary. She notices how he can wield that long ax one-handed. Living with him all alone on this cliffside, she gets a spooky feeling now and then, knowing he could split her head like a watermelon with that ax and no one would be the wiser.

Crowfoot's movements are unhurried, graceful, exact. He places a bucked log of aspen on his chopping block, spreads his legs wide, and swings the ax in a quick and fluid arc. The log splits, and he calmly picks up the pieces and splits them as well until the pieces are thin white staves. When he's done with the first log, he grabs another and starts on it.

She watches, half fascinated and half disgusted. He looks like the kind of man who would chop off a chicken's head like it was nothing. He gets a pile together and squats over his campfire, stirring the coals. He adds a handful of tinder from a coffee can and places it in the center, leans forward to blow on the embers, and soon has a flame. The other day he told her that using paper and lighter fluid was cheating. He doesn't cheat. He's so competent it irks her.

Becca gets up and puts on her clothes, keeping her eye on Crowfoot through the window. She half wants him to come inside and apologize, then beg her to get back into bed. He doesn't do that. He squats beside the fire and nurses it, and she sees that he has a skillet and a pound of bacon in a wax-paper bundle on a rock nearby. She walks into the kitchen, makes a pot of coffee on the Coleman stove.

Crowfoot comes in and smiles at her as she hands him a cup.

You're an angel, he says, then reaches into his Igloo ice chest for his creamer.

He has his back to her, stirring his cup of coffee, when she says, I want to thank you for everything, but I'm starting to feel kind of stir-crazy. I've thought about this over and over. So I've decided I don't care anymore about what the Saints might do, I'd like to head down the mountain today. I mean, if you could give me a ride to Pueblo, I'd appreciate it. It's time I get on with my life.

No problem, says Crowfoot. But you think you could do me a favor?

What? she asks. You want me to give you the ring and let you sell it? For rent?

Crowfoot laughs. I was hoping you'd help me carry some things to the cliff face. I haven't done any work on it in a couple weeks and I've got the itch.

Oh, sure, she says. I'm sorry. I was just kidding.

He nods and ambles outside. She follows and finds him staring at the flames, a half smile on his lips. Let's have a little breakfast first.

I'm starving, says Becca.

Good. I like a starving woman.

Why? Because they're desperate?

He grins. Desperate, thankful. What's the difference?

Good manners, she says. Plus a kiss on the cheek.

Crowfoot nods. Now you're talking. He lays out strips of bacon in the skillet. It starts to sizzle, filling the fire smoke with the bacon smell. Get a little food in your belly and you'll be a whole new wonderful.

Becca huddles in her sweater and shakes her head, unable to hide a smile.

What? asks Crowfoot.

Don't you go trying to get on my good side.

After breakfast Crowfoot mixes three pails of clay with red, black, and yellow pigment. It has the texture of watery mud. In an old paint can he carries a half-dozen brushes. He hands one of the pails to Becca and heads toward the painted face without a word. She follows behind him, watching his footsteps, his long hair blowing in the cold wind. The ledge that looked narrow and nightmarish is safer than it seemed that first night and is wide as a decent footpath.

It's still unnerving: To the north there's a hundred-foot drop broken only by buffalo-sized boulders and jagged cliff spires. In the tight spots Becca keeps her eyes on her feet and follows Crowfoot until the ledge opens up to the width of a road, and on the left is the low-ceilinged wind cave with Crowfoot's petroglyphs in a row above it.

He heads to the end of the forty-foot-long mural and arranges the pails of clay, explaining that he's putting them where both of them can reach all the colors.

You can mix the colors together if you want, he adds. He picks up a plywood scrap that has dried clay on it. I've used this before to make a purple.

Becca puts her hands on her hips and walks up and down the mural. I don't know, she says. It's your project. What if I screw it up?

You can't screw it up.

You don't know that.

Yes, I do. Besides, I don't think of it as my project. It's a mural, a painted cliff. I shouldn't be the only one working on it. It's kind of hollow and lonely that way, isn't it?

I don't know. Maybe.

Crowfoot dips a brush into the pail. So quit your yappin' and get to work.

What do you want me to paint? asks Becca.

It's not a matter of what I want you to paint. It's what you want.

That's a lot of pressure.

Oh, Jesus. Crowfoot makes a wide arc of red, daubs a series of dots below it. He adds more swirls that look like wind.

The pink snowstorm, says Becca.

Crowfoot keeps working, his back to her. By his silence, Becca thinks she's guessed right. That he thinks they should not talk, only work.

After a while she gets to it, doing her best to draw a buffalo head—in profile, with great black horns and clouds of smoke puffing out its nose. Inside the lines of the buffalo's head she places a yellow ring with rays shooting off it to convey its brightness. She doesn't have any white to show the diamond, but at least the yellow represents the gold band. Halfway through it she calls out to Crowfoot, Why do you say I should give the ring back?

He keeps his eyes on his work but shrugs. That rock is worthless. It's got bad energy. All it's good for is greed.

But I'm broke and he gave it to me.

Crowfoot shakes his head. A gift given in bad faith is worth nothing.

That's easy for you to say. At least you have a home.

Crowfoot puts down his brushes and takes out a bandanna. He stares into the distance, to the mountains in the north. He blows his nose and asks Becca if she's ever been up Phantom Canyon. She says she hasn't.

It's in that direction, he says, nodding with his chin toward the north. Everything is wild and rocky. Way cool.

Maybe you'll have to take me there.

Maybe. I could take you a lot of places, he adds. But it would all be easier if you didn't have this Jack Brown and his Saint friends hunting you for that stupid rock.

They'll be hunting you too, she says.

I can handle myself.

I can too.

But if we take the ring back and return it to this yahoo, maybe both of us will be able to sleep a little easier.

Will you help me?

Crowfoot doesn't reply, but he nods. He's finishing the touches on a black house with a stick-figure couple running away from it, chains on the woman's ankles. I'll be right beside you, he says, staring at the mural. I think they'll notice my shadow.

When they've used most of the pigmented clay in the pails, Crowfoot takes the leavings and slings them off a pinnacle of the cliff face to splatter on the rocks below. The yellow, red, and black splatter together to resemble the guano of a colorful bird colony.

The morning dew sends dark rivulets down the red cliffs. The air is fresh and Becca feels lighthearted and special as she follows Crowfoot back along the narrow ledge to his trailer. It's a day of change and renewal. The whole of Colorado opens to the north of them—miles away the sound of trucks on Highway 50 shifting into low gear as they head out of Cañon City toward Bighorn Canyon.

You think you can give me a ride to the Buffalo Head? she asks.

I don't see why not.

You do and I'll get that ring, says Becca. We'll take it to Jack Brown and be done with it.

Smart girl, says Crowfoot. That rock is bad news. It's like a dead skunk around your neck.

Don't you mean an albatross?

I've never seen an albatross. Not even sure I'd recognize one if I did. A dead skunk? I've seen one. Smelled it too.

AT THE BUFFALO HEAD INN, the parking lot is spotty with cars and fast-food wrappers from the burger place next door, a pile of French fries and ketchup on the sidewalk. Crowfoot parks his pickup and sits in the cab as if he doesn't want to intrude, but Becca give his long hair a tug and says, You come along with me and ride shotgun. I figure no matter what I do, nobody's going to say squat to us.

Crowfoot nods and gets out of the truck. If they do, I'll lift their hair.

Becca laughs and heads toward the lobby. It's quiet inside but for the burble of a television in the back office. She hesitates for a moment, then quickly walks over to the buffalo head and reaches into its mouth.

Can I help you? Fufu, the dirty-blond hotel manager, leans over the counter to give Becca a what-the-hell-you-doing look. She glances at Crowfoot, who has come to stand just inside the lobby entrance, his hands crossed on his chest, a look on his face that is close to a glower.

No, I'm okay, says Becca without turning around. She panics for a moment, not feeling anything inside the buffalo's mouth.

Excuse me? says Fufu. What the hell you doing?

I left something here. Becca maneuvers her body to get closer, to get her hand as far inside the mouth as possible.

Fufu comes out from behind the counter. Her boy starts crying in the back office. She pauses, staring back at Crowfoot now as if challenging him to open his mouth. Don't I know you? she asks.

He nods. You used to wait tables at Jorgé's Café, right?

I did.

You serve a good puffy taco.

I remember now. You'd come in with Mosca?

I work with him. Crowfoot smiles. He's a scruffy one, isn't he?

Oh, thank God. Becca pulls her arm out of the buffalo's mouth and turns toward Crowfoot, holding a plastic coin purse in the air.

Girl? Fufu frowns. What in the world are you doing with my buffalo?

Becca hurries toward the door. Never you mind, she says. I just had to retrieve something I left there, that's all.

The crying from the back office gets louder. Fufu lets Becca pass, shaking her head. I'll be right there, Diego! she calls out.

Crowfoot holds the door open for Becca and winks at Fufu. Trust me. You don't even want to know.

Becca gives directions to Jack Brown's house in east Pueblo, an industrial barrio of warehouses, auto-supply stores, and one-story wooden houses on the edge of town. Here lies the boundary of the Great Plains. Dry-mouth desert with yards full of dead brown grass, junky cars, and on every other corner Mexican *farmacias* and eateries. Crowfoot drives and tells Becca he knows the neighborhood.

I used to live on Montevista Drive, he says, a mile from the coal-burning power plant. I could see the smokestack out my back window. I kind of liked it. There's something hopeful about a smokestack belching that tells you people are working. It's closed now.

There goes the hope, says Becca.

Adios, esperanza.

Jack Brown's house stands next door to a discount-tire warehouse. The warehouse has 50% OFF! stickers on its windows, a banner that reads, TRUCKERS AND BIKERS WELCOME! A black column of knobby truck tires towers on the other side of Jack Brown's chain-link fence. In the driveway, a Jeep with a flat tire. On the front porch, an old futon in a bleached wooden frame next to a *chiminea* with burned wood and ashes in its mouth. A bicycle padlocked to one of the porch columns. Dust drifts against the steps.

Oh, great, says Becca. I was hoping he'd be gone and we could just leave it with a note. You're coming in with me, aren't you?

You used to live here? asks Crowfoot.

Are you kidding? Not in a million years.

Crowfoot parks his truck on the street and kills the engine. But weren't you two an item?

We were engaged. But I wouldn't spend more than an hour in this rathole. Becca gets out and wrinkles her nose. This neighborhood is *muy malo*, you know what I mean? If I went for a walk, I'd have to take Monster with me. And a baseball bat.

Monster?

His German shepherd.

Crowfoot frowns. I'm not so wild about dogs. Especially the kind that bite.

He's not a biter. But he can scare the shit out of a body, that's for sure.

They walk up the sidewalk slowly. He's probably playing video games, says Becca. He's addicted to the Country Star game. He thinks he's Randy Travis.

They reach the door and knock. Up close, everything on the porch looks dirty and unkempt. Dog hair covers the futon. As soon as they knock they hear Monster barking and his claws clattering against the floor inside. After a few moments the door opens and there stands Jack Brown, his short hair spiky and a surprised look on his face. He has hold of Monster's collar. The shepherd whines as Becca coos at him and says, Hey, Monster. How's my boy doing?

Well, I'll be a monkey's uncle, says Jack Brown. All my sins come home to roost.

What are you doing home the middle of the day? she asks. Quit your job after I left you?

I got laid off.

Surprise, surprise.

A lot of people are out of work, Becca. You wouldn't know because you never worked to begin with. Your whole game is livin' off your looks. Monster! Get back! He yanks on Monster's collar and pushes the dog behind him, then steps out onto the porch and closes the door.

Here, Jack, says Becca. She reaches out and opens her hand. I've got a present for you.

Jack Brown stares at the engagement-ring box. He starts to reach for it and stops. He looks over her shoulder at George Armstrong Crowfoot. Is this a trick?

Crowfoot gives him a long, cold look and says nothing. He looms in all his height and muscle, wearing faded jeans and a T-shirt with a bloody tomahawk and the legend CUSTER HAD IT COMING.

No trick, says Becca. When he goes to grab the ring, she closes her hand and yanks it back quickly, putting it behind her back. One condition. I never want to hear from you again, and I don't want any Saints coming after me either.

Jack Brown steps onto the porch and glances at the street, as if seeing whether the coast is clear. A tow truck cruises by with a wreck hooked onto its rear, spiderwebbed windshield flashing in the sun. Jack Brown has half a smile on his face as he says, Now, I can't speak for all those polygs you pissed off, but I'll say this. You give me that ring back free and clear and for damn sure you won't hear from me again.

You promise?

Jack Brown puts his hands in his pockets and nods vigorously. Cross my heart and hope to die.

Okay, then.

Becca reaches out and hands him the ring in its red velvet jewelry box. Jack Brown takes it with a certain degree of awe, opens the box, lifts the ring out, and squints at it.

You tell your Saint friends that if they come looking for me, they'll end up looking at the inside of a coffin, says Crowfoot. Got that?

Jack Brown keeps his eyes on Becca. I don't have any Saint friends to speak of. But yeah, sure. I'll pass along the info. No word to the law about this?

This is just between us, says Becca. I don't want to hear, see, or smell you again.

You have my word, says Jack Brown. But if you don't mind my asking, what gives with the change of heart?

Becca turns her back on him and puts her hand against Crowfoot's chest, gives him a little shove to get going. Without turning around she calls out, That ring is dirty. Be my guest.

Jack Brown makes a face and sniffs the ring.

Back in the pickup, George squeezes Becca's thigh as he drives away, says, *Adios, amigos.*

I don't know how you talked me into that. She sighs. That ring was worth something.

It's time for us to go the straight and narrow. We've got a baby on board, right?

I don't know. I think.

Driving past a Walgreens, he slows and looks her way. Maybe we should find that out.

One of those do-it-yourself things? asks Becca.

Before I get all excited about a name, we ought to be sure, right?

Oh, my Lord, she says. Okay. I've been thinking about it.

Crowfoot pulls into the parking lot, a slight smile on his dead-pan face. We'll just see, he says.

LORD GOD HOPES for Juliet's car to come bumping up the driveway again and again stir up a cloud of dust and a torrent of hope in his heart. His beard has grown ragged, unkempt. His fingernails are dark-lined half moons long as claws. His leg stump aches and without Juliet the pains seems sharper and relentless.

His one good eye looks upon his small and dusty house with suspicion and remorse. He can't muster the energy to sweep and mop so he walks about with a cherry-picker gizmo collecting Lila's toys and rinsing them in the kitchen sink. The water runs a faint pink color like blood hosed from a sidewalk or in a bathtub.

His whole day revolves around caring for Lila when Ruby is out pretending to work. Without the child he knows he would have no reason to live or wake in the morning. The warmth and woman smell of Juliet in the morning and Juliet at night and Juliet in the afternoon come back to him so strong and sharp he fights the impulse to weep. There's no use feeling sorry for yourself. The Lord gives a vision and lets the man decide to accept or deny his truth. Still the bitterness of a life alone haunts him in everything he does. No plan but to go on, keep moving, let the hand of providence guide his daily ministrations.

The wind picks up and with it the heat. The sky turns a pale yellow shade from noon until dusk. So much grit in the clouds that the sun is a hazy label behind a shimmer of fish-scale clouds. Traffic on the highway west of Pueblo trickles to the odd pickup loaded with fuel and cardboard boxes of canned goods, headed toward survivalist enclaves or compounds in the Sierra Mojada, places where people are holed up with their own beliefs and own laws. They drive with rifles propped out the passenger windows, a warning to anyone who might try to waylay or ambush them.

The post office doesn't deliver to rural routes anymore. Once a week Lord God drives into town to pick up the mail. On this day he waits in a queue for a half hour to pick up a package. It's addressed to Ruby Cole, shoebox size. The return label is Optics Etc. He can guess what it is. Binoculars most likely. She said something about her bird-counter friend sending her something in the mail, to keep an eye out for it. Like this is something she needs.

Lord God shakes his head as he returns to his truck, his good knee aching. The world is going to hell and his daughter spends her time numbering birds on power lines.

He returns from town to find a pickup black as oil parked in his driveway. Lord God squirms in his seat and rifles through the glove compartment, damning the conglomeration of ballpoint pens, plastic straws in white paper wrappers, coins, and Lotto tickets. Beneath the mess is a handgun he keeps for just such surprises.

He's stuffing it into his pocket when he eases his prosthesis down from the cab and manages to get balanced. A man sits on his front porch and gives a wave. Lord God's good eye is cloudy with dust and all he sees is a fuzzy image of a stranger at his house. He doesn't wave back and keeps a poker frown as he walks up his path and steps onto the porch.

It's Hiram Page with two red jerry cans at his feet. His face is like a visage in a dream, a fog-enshrouded grinning figure. He calls out, Good day, Reverend!

You been waiting here long?

No, sir, says Page. Just long enough to relax the sore muscles in my back.

What can I do ya for?

Nothing. Nothing at all. I just happened to come upon a windfall of some good fuel. I thought you might could find a use for it. Hiram Page nudges one of the jerry cans with the tip of his boot. You need any more, I can get it.

And to what do I owe this favor?

To nothing. To being neighborly. Page smiles with all his white teeth.

Lord God stares at the jerry cans and then looks Page square in the eye. I find that hard to believe.

A pulse of hot wind rattles loose asphalt shingles on the roof. They make a flapping sound. The dust gets in Page's face and he sits there, squinting and rubbing his eyes. You wouldn't be looking a gift horse in the mouth, now, would you?

There's no free lunch. I like to know why.

Why what?

Why are you giving this to me?

Not just to you but to all of you. You, your daughter, Ruby, and her baby girl.

We got no need for handouts.

It's no handout. The Lord tells good people to share and especially to share among the righteous. No strings attached. You don't want two containers of good fuel, fine with me. I'm sure someone else will find a use for it.

Well, I'm sure I could use it too. But I could use a lot of things I won't accept someone giving me for nothing.

Maybe you ought to open up a bit. Not be so suspicious.

You don't get something for nothing. That's one of the basic laws of the universe.

I never was one to accept laws, basic or not.

Your choice. Me, I pay attention to the laws.

It's a new world order, Mr. Cole. Laws? They're going out of fashion. Fast.

Lord God pins Page with a stare that goes through him and beyond. He's a man who prides himself on being able to read people. He believes he can look into a man's soul by the way he holds his face, by the way he moves his hands, by the way he stands. And here's this Saint with two wives already, showing up at his doorstep with a king's ransom of gasoline, smiling like an insurance salesman.

He wears new blue jeans with fancy stitching like he's about to do a two-step on the stage of the Grand Ole Opry. His hair is white and combed slick with some kind of goop and he looks like he bleaches his teeth. He opens his mouth wide when he talks to show them off.

You don't like to be beholden to any man, says Page. I understand that. But that's not a reason to turn down a gift. Something your daughter and her daughter could well use.

Lord God does not invite him into the house. He sits down on an old wooden bench beside the front door and stares out at the prairie, grit in his eyes. The corner of the house protects them from the worst wind. They watch the dust clouds roil like herds of ghost buffalo across the fields.

There's a right and wrong to everything. The world is full of choices. The Lord offers us goodness, and Satan tempts us to the wicked.

Hiram Page nods. I admire a man of strong convictions.

That may be, says Lord God. But do you follow those convictions your own self?

I have my own ideas about the world, Mr. Cole. Hiram Page squints into the dusty vision of the mountains in the west. I look out here and I see a simple world. I look there—he nods toward the east, toward town—and I see complexity.

A thing is either right or wrong, says Lord God. Always. Gray is the color of mice. A weak and inferior creature. Something to keep out of your house. Something to set a trap for. Gray is for the professors and doctors, the people who say, Money is no object. For the rest of us, it's an object and it's one that's hard to get.

Maybe harder than ever. For a while we had lots of it. Now we don't. Get used to it.

I couldn't agree with you more, Mr. Cole. That's why I'm here to help.

Lord God turns away from Hiram and spits. I've never been one to be needing help.

You don't trust me, do you? I'm sorry to hear that.

A man has to earn trust. Isn't that what they say?

They say a lot of things. They say it's wrong for a man to have more than one wife. What if he keeps all his wives safe and sound? I remember a sermon you preached a couple months back about this poor gal who forgot her child in the car and left the windows rolled up as she worked at a restaurant. The little boy died of heat prostration and his mother, well, you can imagine how she felt.

I remember that story. She's a single mother with too much on her plate. Running around trying to raise a baby boy and make ends meet at the same time. She was supposed to drop the boy off at day care. But she was late. She forgot he was in the car.

You know if she had a husband who treated her right, that boy would be alive today. So what if he had another wife? What if he provides for both of them, gives them warm clothes, a roof over their heads, food on the table? Cares for their children? We're coming down from a time when we were gluttons. Fat and sassy is over. The world is turning.

Lord God nods. There's still a right and wrong to things.

There's an art to having more than one wife. It's not always easy.

How many you got?

Two.

So where would Ruby fit in?

She'd be the third. I don't count them up that way, but I suppose they do now and then.

I've got one wife, says Lord God. He pauses, staring into Hiram Page's eyes with a look of scorn and pain. And she won't have me around anymore.

We all hurt somehow.

That's easy for you to say, with two wives at home. Juliet waited for me all that time I was in the Arab desert. She was a good woman all that time. It wasn't until I got back that she decided she couldn't take me anymore.

People say it's unnatural, having two wives. Or three. But you know the worst thing, don't you?

I don't know. A lot of things are bad. I wouldn't put a word to the worst amongst them.

You live it every day, Brother Cole.

I live my life is what I live.

The worst thing is being alone. And a man with two wives, he's never alone.

I'm not alone. My granddaughter here fills my house like a bright light. She's like a comet to my night. She's more than I can say.

That's the joy of children.

And if you take Ruby as a wife, what then? She'll be just another wife to you? And my daughter and my granddaughter will be living with you. And me alone.

I'll look after both of them. Times are hard and I'll protect them.

That's what I do.

Hiram Page says, You think I'm trying to buy your daughter, don't you?

I didn't say that.

A man's words have meaning, Mr. Cole. I'm not stupid. I heard that explanation of right and wrong and I sense you're saying that what this gasoline here is is a bribe of some sort.

Back in the day the Cheyenne would buy their brides with horses. This isn't too far from that now, is it?

You could say that. If you ask me, a man deserves a gift for giving up his daughter in marriage. And it's not me alone, either. This kind of thing has been going on for thousands of years. Probably back to fires in caves, hides of fur and flint knives. Maybe this is a taste of the past in the future.

Lord God sits on the bench and watches the wind strip the dust off the prairie. The aspens by the woodshed whip and sway in the wind, their leaves now dusted and abused-looking. Maybe all things are coming around to the old ways, he says.

You're right about that. How many wives did Abraham have?

Lord God scratches his good leg. Refresh my memory.

He had more than one, I know that, say Hiram.

Two, says Lord God. Sarah and Keturah. He lived to be one hundred and seventy-five years old, he did. And Sarah passed away before he took another wife.

Hiram stands and brushes the dust off his hands. He looks a bit put out. And then there's King Solomon, he says. But I won't waste any more of your time, Mr. Cole. Let me tell you this: People say I'm not to be trusted. As you might imagine I find that insulting. I know that people say it and think it. The reality is none say it to my face. And if they do they live to regret it. Myself I don't have many regrets expect perhaps the women I was not able to help and provide for a better life. That is in terms of both physical comfort and spiritual well-being. A good woman not only enjoys a certain degree of physical comfort but she both expects and deserves it.

There's more to life than comfort, says Lord God.

That there is. Hiram Page lifts his chin and stands to go. Now, I come from Custer County and we have the strongest and loveliest women in the world but they don't always get to enjoy the comfort they deserve. It's cold in the winter and windy in the summer. Some winters the best you can do is shovel a canyon out your front door. Come summertime the wind will blow so hard you can't hear yourself think.

I've been there, says Lord God. The wind is a bother, that's for sure.

One year the wind blew a woman's mind clean away so she tore off her clothes and ran naked and screaming across the prairie. It was a sad thing to see. But we weren't surprised. It fills your ears with an unholy roar like you got a seashell cupped up against your ears constant-like. So people ask me why I have two wives. Me, I wonder why I have so few. I do get along with women quite well and I'm not ashamed to admit that I know how to keep a woman happy. Thank her for what she's cooked you for dinner and show her a good time now and then. Make sure she has plenty of work to do to discourage any foolishness. Tell her how nice she looks but don't let her get a big head about it.

Amen, says Lord God.

The prophet Joseph said it's the duty of every man to propagate the world. You don't do that by sitting around a bar, polluting your body with drink and whining about how some filly broke your heart. You get out amongst them. You find a woman who is glad to have your attention. You make her happy and keep her safe. The world is a dangerous place. Women know it and want to be protected. That's where I come in.

That's all fine and dandy, says Lord God. But I still got a daughter with a mind of her own. I'll tell you what. I'll take that offer of gasoline and thank you kindly. But there's no guarantee of anything. The best I can do for you is set up a how-do. I'll do my best but if you want her for a wife, it's going to be her choice, not mine.

I respect that, says Page. Winston Churchill put it right: We make a living by what we get. We make a life by what we give.

Lord God rises stiffly and limps to the front door. He pauses there for a minute, still watching the wind whipping the aspen branches into a state. I'll talk to her about a meeting here. I might could set that up.

Hiram Page dusts off his hat. That sounds good to me. He sticks out his hand and shakes Lord God's hard and fast. We'll be in touch, okay?

Lord God nods. I'll make sure that's good with Ruby. Then I'll give you a call.

He stands inside the screen door and watches Page drive

away. The dust clouds cast a milky reflection in Lord God's pale eyes. After a moment, he drags the jerry cans through the yard, back to the woodshed.

J A C K B R O W N V I S I T S the pawnshop three times before he catches Hiram page behind the counter, busy with customers. Brown's hands are sweating and he wipes them on his jeans as he stands there, waiting his turn. He's silently rehearsing his argument of how much money he's owed for his role in the hijacking, how much the ring might be worth. He knows Page is a shrewd customer. One not likely to open his wallet out of the goodness of his heart.

Finally Hiram comes to him and says, in his rich voice, So the prodigal cousin returneth, bearing his hat in hand.

Brown hitches up his pants and puts his hat back on his head. The first thing you'll learn about me is I'm a man of my word.

Maybe not the first thing, but let's not quibble. Words are men's daughters, but God's sons are things.

What's that supposed to mean?

In the vernacular? Put up or shut up.

Jack Brown puts the jewelry box on the counter and taps the glass with it twice. This is a carat and a half of top-quality diamond, set in white gold, over a hundred years old too. So it's no bloody diamond, for what that's worth.

Hiram Page says nothing and opens the jewelry box as if it may contain a bomb. He takes the ring and looks it over closely. And how did you manage to retrieve this piece of ice? he asks.

Last I heard your ex-Mex sweetheart absconded from my nephew's house with an Apache. Hiram raises his eyebrows and adds, Who left him with a rough-cut scalp.

You might not believe this but they just up and gave it back. Dropped it off at my house like a lawn mower they borrowed. The damnedest thing.

You saw this Indian?

Jack Brown nods and laughs. Scary-looking sumbitch he is.

He and I aren't finished, says Hiram. I can't let a man like that make a fool of me and get away with it.

They gave me the ring and far as I'm concerned, end of story. Here it is.

Hiram Page stands for a moment in thought. A dachshund waddles down the aisle of the pawnshop, approaches Jack Brown, and sniffs at his boots.

Hey, pooch, says Brown.

Hiram Page smiles at the dog and walks around the counter, takes a bone-shaped dog treat from a glass jar, then offers it. Weenie here is a favorite of mine.

I love a good dog, says Jack. He watches your back, right?

Hiram scratches Weenie's ears for a moment, then says, Would you mind if I get my gem loupe to make a more professional assessment of its commercial quality?

Your what?

Loupe. A magnifying glass.

You go right ahead.

Hiram Page stands up, takes the ring and the jewelry box, and heads to his office. Jack Brown shifts his feet and sighs, staring at the oddities and curios on the shelf behind the counter: A pair of velvet handcuffs. A porcelain cookie jar made in the likeness of a grinning red-faced cartoon Indian with a tall feather headdress. He wonders what Becca's friend Cochise would think of that little number. He can hear Hiram Page laughing and joking with a Mexican woman in the back office. He seems in no hurry. It's like a goddamn bank in here, is what it is. They make you wait just to mess with your head. Bank or car dealership. Same difference.

After a moment Hiram returns and holds the diamond up to the light, peering at it through the loupe. Well well well, he says. That's a nice stone you have there. I might be able to make you an offer.

That's what I want to hear, says Jack.

Let me ask this first: Did you tell me you were planning on buying a new truck?

I hope so. Of course I'm owed some money here already, right?

That you are. Page steps away to open his cash register and returns with a white envelope. Now, you can take this, or we can talk about that truck you need.

Jack Brown opens the envelope, counts out two thousand dollars in hundred-dollar bills. Well, that's a start. But what do you mean, we can talk about a truck?

Hiram holds the diamond ring delicately and peers through the loupe. The color is a bit milkier than what we'd like, he says. Not the best-case scenario, mind you. And there are a couple of rough spots and tiny fractures, almost like spiderwebs. But they don't ruin the gem. You say this was your grandmother's ring?

It's been in our family for three generations. I hate to sell it but money is hard to come by these days. I got laid off from my contracting job and my Jeep's always broke down, one thing or another. So I guess I have no choice.

Hiram sets the ring and loupe down on the counter and purses his lips. Well, I'm not sure that's the end of the story. Maybe you do have a choice. You've done me favors now and that counts for something. Come with me, he says, and passes from behind the counter to the front door.

They step out into the parking lot and Hiram points to a Ford pickup. How would you like to be driving that?

Jack Brown looks at him askance. You're shittin' me? That truck looks new.

It's not two years old yet. But I might be persuaded to give you a deal on it. You won't even have to let that heirloom ring leave your family.

Hiram Page explains that he'll take the two thousand dollars in the envelope as down payment, the ring as collateral and sell Jack Brown the truck, doing the financing himself, so Jack'll owe him a monthly payment and if he doesn't make it, he'll lose the ring.

But as long as you keep making those payments, the ring stays in your family, says Page.

Jack Brown walks around the truck and peers into the tinted windows. What is this, eight-cylinder? Four-wheel drive?

Sure is. You know your way around a vehicle, don't you?

You bet I do. Jack squats low and checks out the underside. Skid plate, tow hitch, the works. He stands up and peeks in the passenger-side window. Looks like it has a nice sound system too.

The best, says Hiram. It'll blow your ears out if that's what you want.

Jack Brown squats again and looks at the knobby tires. What's the blue book on this baby?

It's worth twenty-eight thousand. But I'll cut you a deal. I got it from a dealer and didn't have to pay full cost. I think I could let it go for eighteen K.

Eighteen thousand dollars?

With five thousand dollars' collateral on the ring.

So I'll owe you eleven?

No, thirteen. Or just north of that. I've already figured in a discount for deeds done. But I think we can get those monthlies down to be pretty reasonable.

Jack Brown smiles. That sounds like a mighty sweet deal to me. He sticks out his hand and shakes Hiram's. When can we do it?

I'll get the papers drawn up this week.

I knew it was going to work out between us. That man is one smart SOB, I said that to myself, soon as I met you.

I'm not so smart, just His vessel. Or as was once said, Unless the Lord builds the house, its builders labor in vain.

Well, shit. You know the Bible by heart?

Not the whole thing. Hiram winks and takes Jack's shoulder to steer him toward the cab for a closer look. Only the good parts.

He doesn't mention that the truck has been burning oil for months now, that it's a chop-shop special with dubious parts and patronage. The boy is a fool and the surprising thing about young fools is how many survive to become old fools.

RUBY FINDS HERSELF listening to the liquid melody of a Western Meadowlark. She realizes that in her mind she no longer calls it a Yellowbib but by its common name, Meadowlark. The genus and species even crop into her brain and sit on their own barbed-wire fence, singing like their namesake, *Sturnella neglecta*. It bothers her at first that her habits are changing, that she's becoming Ward's shadow. He never ordered her to call birds by their accepted names, but after a time his way just made horse sense.

Still she doesn't like the idea of being under Ward's thumb, under anyone's thumb. She's changing. Is she giving up a piece of her personality? Of her specialness? The reason for this preference of Meadowlark over Yellowbib is simple: She's now witnessed a Common Yellowthroat in cattails near the Arkansas River, and Yellowbib is too close to Yellowthroat.

Now she's begun to see her special names as just another quirk of a backwoods mentality. Even backward. Hick names, she thinks. And she doesn't want to be hick. She may have been born a hick, but she wants to live as something entirely different. Ward insists she should finish high school and go to college, maybe become a biologist.

She thinks he's right. The tightened focus of another world, one beyond Lord God. A higher level, she hopes. She used to lump similar birds together and not worry about their variations, but now she feels rather foolish not to have recognized the difference between the White-Breasted Nuthatch, her Tuxedo Bird, the Red-Breasted Nuthatch, smaller, with a cinnamon belly and an eye stripe, and the Pygmy Nuthatch, smaller yet, with a gray cap. She finds herself swollen with learning, watching the Mourning Doves fly across the afternoon blue sky and alight on the telephone line, and wonders if the White Pelicans have arrived at the mountain lakes yet.

Lord God told her the day before, Don't get cocky. Remember that pride is the worst of the seven deadly sins. You're setting yourself up for a fall.

What? she asked. By learning something? By being useful to the world?

Useful? Counting birds? Lord God shook his head. It's foolishness is what it is.

It's science. It's knowledge.

Those scientists don't know nothing. It's all a bunch of hooey.

Ruby went silent.

After a moment he said, The world's going to take you down a notch, you can bet on that. Soon as you think you're something, you'll regret it.

But I am something. So are you. So are we all.

Lord God stared at her as if at a halfwit child. The late-afternoon light caught the deep lines in his face, the tangled gray wires of his heavy beard. He looked like the ancient mariner himself and said, What you don't know would fill the Grand Canyon.

Thanks, Papa. I love being told how stupid I am.

Not stupid, no. But too young to know. Someday you'll realize what's important.

I know what's important. Lila, you, Mama.

But there's so much you don't remember. It breaks my heart. All those years and all those moments. Remember your little ceramic bunny, Bonnie the Bunny, the one we found in the forest? You would wake up after a nap and immediately give her an Eskimo kiss. You would rub your nose against hers and it was the cutest thing in the world.

I don't remember that, said Ruby.

Juliet and I were happy then. Look at me now, cursed and broken. Lord God shook his head. But what's done is done.

I remember there was a stack of concrete pipes at the pipe factory down the road, said Ruby. You would take me there after closing hours to crawl through them.

You loved those silly pipes. I never really wanted to go because it was trespassing, but there was an easy way down the back alley where we used to live. I met the security guard and he said he didn't care. Besides, I had to. If I didn't take you, you'd cry and scream.

I liked the tunnels. It was like another world inside those pipes. They weren't pipes. They were portals to another world.

That's what you called it. The Tunnels. I took you there every Sunday after church. It was the only way I could get you to get dressed up for church. You'd ask, Can we go to the Tunnels afterward? And I'd say, Yes, of course we can.

I don't remember Mom ever being with us.

She didn't go. She didn't like to stoop over inside those tunnels. And she wouldn't have let you crawl around inside them in the first place because of bugs.

She's got this thing about spiders, doesn't she?

Half your childhood she thought you'd die of a spider bite.

Lord God reached out to touch Ruby's hand. She stared down at his outsized, scratchy hand, the knuckles so wide they seemed swollen, the nails dark with oil grit from working.

He believes in an absurd God who visits him frequently and gives him visions colored by anger, jealousy, and paranoia. If she can steer him toward the way out, will he listen? She doesn't think so. But he's a good man and her father, and he's in need.

She couldn't turn away. All she could do was stare at his hand and squeeze it.

She raised her face to the kitchen window and wiped her eyes. Outside, the warm autumn wind swept furiously across the prairie, tousling the branches of the aspens by the woodshed. From one branch hung the bird feeder full of black oil seed. Black-headed Grosbeaks and White-Breasted Nuthatches bucked the wind to light on the metal cylinder of the bird feeder and peck seeds through its cage.

Lord God stood and shuffled away. He seemed to be moving slower than ever. His hand grazed the top of Ruby's head. I'll go check on Lila, he said. Maybe you should grab something to eat. You've been working too hard.

Later Ruby lies in bed and stares at the watermarks on the ceiling, remembering when they had first moved into this house, when she imagined the shapes to be bears and owls. They were her favorite childhood creatures, real and close at hand, not mythical. A Great Horned Owl had lived in the cottonwood tree in the gulch behind their house. Years ago, when enough rain fell that a small creek still flowed down the center of the canyon.

She remembers green frogs she caught in the brackish pools, frogs that slipped through her fingers when she tried to catch them. Once she had sat quiet and still by the creek, watching late-afternoon shadows rise up the cliff walls of the gulch canyon, as if the dark were a river rising, as if it were being flooded with inky blueness. And then a shadow seemed to come to life in the branches of the cottonwood across the creek from her, a sudden unfolding of wings and a silent, graceful swoop toward the rock pool of the creek near her, the inky wings crossing into the silver reflection of the pool as, with a quick jab and thrust of talons, the owl snared a fat frog sitting in the reeds, pinning it to mud.

Ruby loosed a yelp and the owl swiveled its head to look at her, blinked both its feline eyes twice as if wondering what creature this was sitting so still and silent, then dipped its head to bite the frog. Ruby marveled at its feathers, intricately layered with leaf browns and mouse grays, a splash of white at its throat. It ruffled its feathers and flapped its wings as it repositioned its hold on the squirming frog, then leaped into the air and flew soundlessly away to a perch in the cliffs.

It all seemed to take place in the split second of a special moment. When Ruby stood and stretched and wiped the sand from the bottom of her shorts, the sunlight had passed below the mountains. All the gulch bathed in a royal blue wash of twilight. She could see up to the prairie, to the pale yellow world above.

She didn't want to leave. Still she had to. She knew she would be in trouble with her mother and father if she came home in darkness. She crept home slowly, trying to stretch out the moment she was alone in the wild, just another animal at dusk. By the time she reached the crooked fence that marked her yard, her father stood at the back door, shouting her name.

She lies in bed and hears Lila saying, Papa, Papa, Papa. It's her new word. She learned it from Ruby herself, from her calling out to Lord God, her father. Lila now calls Lord God her Papa. She does not know who her real father is, will never know. Lord God has become her father. Her other new word is Hi! Now, when she meets Lord God in the morning, she's learned to say, Hi, Papa!

Lila smiles wide and loving when she says this. She knows this man as nothing but good in the small window of her life. She's a beautiful girl and it hurts Ruby to see this, to remember her childhood, to realize there will come a change, a time when it will not be enough to be beautiful and sweet. A time when those things will become a burden. When beauty and sweetness will become a curse.

Maybe Lord God is right after all. Ruby hates to admit it. Lila needs a father, a man to look after her, to stand up for her and make sure the doors are locked at night. A man to toss her into the air and hear her squeal with delight.

She hears Lila's voice from the kitchen, calling, Papa, Papa, Papa. She hears the deeper, rough voice of Lord God answer. Ruby can hear the cupboard cabinet doors being opened and shut and the creak and squeak of the hardwood floors as Lord God shuffles about. He must be getting Lila something. He cares for her with patience and kindness. He wants nothing but the best for her.

When Lila begins to cry, Ruby pulls on a robe and goes down the hallway to the kitchen, where she finds Lord God bouncing Lila on his lap, trying to calm her.

I took away her pacifier, he says. It's time she gave it up. She keeps it in her mouth all day long and it's not good for her.

Lila cries harder and reaches her hands out for Ruby to take her. Tears wet her cheeks and she says, Mama!

I think she's teething, says Ruby. Her teeth and gums hurt. That's why she wants the pacifier.

Ruby gives Lila the pacifier. She can feel the heat and pressure of Lord God's disapproval as if she's at the bottom of a swimming pool and his presence is the weight of water. The room is so quiet she hears the drip of the kitchen faucet, the whistle of the wind against the windowpanes. She picks up Lila and kisses her neck. My God, this girl is getting too big for me.

She's a healthy thing, isn't she?

Ruby carries her to the living room and sets her in the playpen in front of the picture window. The cottonwoods bend and sway in the dusty wind. There's so much smoke in the air from the wildfires that you can't see the mountains in the west. A rust-colored haze stains the sky, making Ruby feel claustrophobic, cut off from the rest of the world. Lila throws her dolly from the pen and reaches out to be picked up.

Ruby groans and lifts her from the playpen, takes a seat on the sofa, then bounces Lila on her lap, staring out the window at the dirty world unfolding before her. Before long Lila falls asleep with the passy in her mouth. After waiting until she's completely limp, Ruby lays Lila down in the playpen and adjusts a blanket around her legs. She returns to the kitchen, where Lord God is reading the paper.

Go ahead and set it up, says Ruby.

For a moment Lord God hesitates, then he asks, Are you sure?

No, not at all. But I'll meet this Mr. Page. You set it up and I'll be there.

Are you doing this just for me?

Well, yes. You. And Lila maybe.

Okay, then. I'll give him a call.

I'm not promising anything. Don't get your heart set on getting me out of the house.

Is that what you think this is about?

Lord God sounds hurt. Ruby looks at him and gives him a little smile. No. I don't think that.

If you leave here, I don't know what I'll do.

She comes up behind and him and gives him a hug. It's the first time they've touched in weeks. He stiffens at first, then gives in to it.

I'm not going anywhere, says Ruby. I think you're stuck with me, Papa.

His voice comes hoarse and trembling. He says, I wouldn't want it any other way.

EZRA PAGE VISITS his uncle in the backyard of his home in Little Pueblo, where Hiram is overseeing the building of a gazebo. Two Mexicans are carrying a stack of two-by-twelves from the back of a pickup to the center of Page's prairie landscape. Ezra walks up wearing his short-brimmed cowboy hat. Hiram sees him and nods, makes him wait.

He's explaining to one of the workers how he wants the gazebo positioned, the entrance facing the house due north and the inside benches facing east and west. The gusty wind blows grit in Ezra's eyes and as he's rubbing them, his hat flies off his head. He takes off running to catch it, and when he returns, Hiram looks at him and says, Nothing as foolish as a man chasing his hat.

I'm sorry, Uncle Hiram. I know I let you down and I mean to make it right.

Hiram cocks his head. You mean by losing your hat? No skin off my nose.

No, I meant, you know. My trouble.

Not sure what you're talking about.

Well, you know I didn't mean to—

Stop right there, kid. I don't want to hear it. I don't even want to know what you might be apologizing about. That's your business.

Okay, then. I get it.

You get it? Really? You do?

I do.

Then shut your mouth and listen. I want you to come work for me.

Ezra grins. I like the sound of that. Doing what?

Security.

Security?

Right, genius. At my business. I'll set up a station for you inside and out, to watch who comes and goes. We've got closed-circuit TVs on the front and back door, but no one's been watching them. That's going to change. You'll be in charge. If anyone shows up who looks like they're trouble, I'll want you to talk to them first. Can you handle that?

I think so.

You think so?

Okay. Sure. I know so.

You start tomorrow. The pay won't be much at first but you do a good job, it will get better. Wear a white shirt, clean jeans, boots. And see if you can keep that hat on your head. Though I like the scar. It gives you some gravitas.

Ezra puts the hat in place, holding it by the brim against the wind. It itches, he says. The scar I mean. Helps me to remember it's there.

That's a good thing, says Hiram. I want you to remember everything. Keeps a person on his toes. Which you'll need to be. Now go.

Hiram offers his hand to Ezra, who starts to step away and then sees it, stumbles back to grab it, squeezes too hard. Hiram watches him cross the yard and turn the corner of the house, holding on to his hat, a figure not exactly inspiring confidence. His brother's boy, who takes too much after his mother, a woman whose forebears may have dipped into the same gene pool once too often. A plain Jane whose every notion comes from a garbled reading of scripture. Now her boy has a mortal sin on his soul like a discount sticker.

His first week Ezra makes a point to show up before Hiram every morning, to prove he's on the ball, that he can be trusted. His uncle tends to ignore him, and he's gone most of the time anyway, so Ezra is often alone there with Gracie, Hiram's clerk/manager, or her daughter, who often comes by to visit. They ignore Ezra too, and he senses the daughter doesn't like him. He's bored, sitting on a stool before the three security cameras when he's not walking the aisles. And the pawnshop hardly ever seems busy, so he waits, peevish and restless.

IN WARD'S MOTEL ROOM at the Buffalo Head, Ruby doesn't know what to do with herself. September it is and should be cooling, but it's late afternoon and 106 degrees outside. The sky is hazy white with no clouds but a relentless sun. It feels good to sit in the cool room with the curtains drawn. The air conditioner rattles and whirs, blowing the lips of the curtains. Ward keyboards their bird counts into the data files on his laptop, leaning forward, his eyes squinting.

She can tell he thinks of this as his office. To her, it's still a motel room. And she's still an unmarried girl only seventeen years of age, alone in a motel room with a man. Underage and already a mother: What could be worse? She sits in an upholstered chair near the window and pretends to be engrossed in the bird identification book in her lap.

I think I saw a Pine Grosbeak the other day on a fence post, she says. But I'm not sure. Mom was driving me to town and I just got a quick glimpse of it.

Where was it? Maybe we could go back and find it in the area.

Maybe, she says. It was on the edge of town, the other side of that little park near the Arkansas. Where it's all dusty and raggedy-looking.

I know where you mean, says Ward. That's the place I got lost in the dust storm my first day in town.

I bet I passed not far from you, says Ruby.

Ward smiles. If I'd found you in the storm, I could have given you a lift.

Ruby looks up at the bad painting of a white wolf and an Indian in a snowy forest that hangs above the bed. She squints at it like an art critic. She smiles and asks, Is that the worst painting ever?

Oh, come on, says Ward. I kind of like it.

You like it? Ruby makes a face. Why is it that men have no taste?

I have taste. It makes me think of snow. Which is a good thing to think in this heat wave.

That wolf looks more like a rabid dog. Look at its face! Like it's wearing an evil grin.

It's symbolic, says Ward.

Of what?

Like in "Little Red Riding Hood," only with a Native American twist? The wicked white man ready to pounce on the good Native people?

It's corny, says Ruby.

The phone rings and Ward frowns, giving it a look. The sound is loud and jarring in the small motel room, the old-fashioned phone on the nightstand between the two double beds jangling. Ward doesn't move to answer it. He keeps his eyes on the laptop screen, keyboarding in bird counts from his notepad. On the second ring he says, Now, who in the world could that be?

On the fourth ring Ruby puts down her book. Shouldn't we answer that?

It's probably a wrong number. I don't know anyone here.

She picks up the phone and says, Hello, Ward Costello's room. She listens. Her face stiffens slightly. He's right here, she says. She holds out the phone to him. It's for you all right. A girl.

Ward gets up, takes the phone, and says, Hello. After a moment he says, Hi, Nisha. I'm fine. Thanks for asking. And how are you doing? He sits on the bed beside the nightstand. That's good to hear. So what's this problem?

Ruby feels herself blush and her heart beats too fast. She stares at the distorted face of the white wolf in the painting and tries not to listen to Ward's conversation, but she can't help it. Something about a house and paperwork. Her hands sweat and the dampness makes her feel clammy and slimy as she wipes them on her jeans. She gets up and purposely does not look at Ward as she opens the door and steps out onto the breezeway.

Ruby walks down the stairs to the vending machines and buys a Pepsi. The air smells of tortillas and diesel exhaust. There's a semi in the parking lot with its engine running. A pair of teenaged boys passing by call out to her, *Que pasa, chica? Dame un beso! Me gustan los pelirojos!*

Ruby ignores them and keeps walking. She has no destination in mind but away. Away from the Buffalo Head. Away from Ward talking to some girl on the phone and away from the crummy box of her life. She goes the opposite direction of the jerks walking down the sidewalk. Behind the motel is a small public park with kids playing on the merry-go-round and slides. A little girl maybe five years old stands at the top of a steep, twisting slide. A couple of other kids jostle behind her and she shakes her head and grips the metal rails fiercely.

Come on, Stacy! calls a boy at the bottom of the slide. Hurry up! You're blocking everybody else.

You shut up, says the girl.

Well, if you don't want to go down, stand aside and let them pass.

The little girl shakes her head again.

The scene touches Ruby and she can't take it, she keeps going. In a few years Lila will be that little girl on the top of the slide and she won't have any brother urging her on or coaching her or helping her against the other bullies on the playground. She'll be all alone. It makes Ruby sick to think of this. Her stomach turns queasy and she's sweating now from the heat.

She doesn't know where to go so she returns to the motel lobby. She sits on the sofa near the buffalo head and reads an outdated *People* magazine. The TV set is on a talk show with guests getting advice about how to make ends meet in economic downtimes. The dirty blond at the check-in counter calls out, You need any help, honey?

Ruby tells her no, she's just waiting for someone.

That's fine. You just sit there as long as you like, says the woman.

But Ruby doesn't like the tone of her voice. She waits a few minutes, then goes back to the room and knocks softly.

Where'd you go? asks Ward.

Can you take me home?

Well, of course I can. But I thought we were going to get something to eat as soon as I finish keyboarding.

I have to go now. Lila needs me.

Ruby stands at the door with her hands at her sides. Ward starts to say something but an ambulance passes down the street and the siren wail drowns his voice. When it's gone he says, What's the matter? Is it the phone call?

I have a daughter, remember? says Ruby. I told Mom I'd pick her up by five at the latest. I don't have time for this.

Ward sighs and asks her to come inside and give him a minute to get ready.

I'll stand out here, says Ruby.

After he gets his keys and wallet they walk down the stairway to the parking lot, Tejano music blaring from one of the motel rooms. The heat envelops them, makes them sweat. As they climb into the hot car Ruby puts her hand to her forehead and says, O, Jesus. I feel like I'm going to faint.

Ward rolls down the windows and turns the a/c on high, tells her he'll roll them up once they get the hot air out of the car.

That's okay, says Ruby. I'll be dead by then.

They head south on Elizabeth Street. Ruby stares out the window at the stucco houses with neat yards and flower gardens.

Pueblo is half pretty and half ugly. Nice houses with colorful flower gardens on one block, and a mile later the freight yards of the old rail lines, and beyond that the pawnshops, liquor stores, and massage parlors. Their route to her home takes them through this devolution. Ruby doesn't say a word once the car cools off. Ward frowns and pretends to concentrate on his driving. She can tell she's gotten under his skin.

After a few minutes Ruby says, Who was that on the phone?

My sister-in-law. She's living in my house back in Houston. She wants me to pay the electric bill but she must be running the a/c constantly because it's over six hundred dollars for August. I don't know what to do. I guess I have to pay it, but I wish she'd leave.

Ruby makes a face. And why is your sister-in-law living at your house?

She lost hers. The bank took it back. Plus she used to work for me. She was my assistant, I guess you'd say. At least that's what she called herself. But she didn't work much. So she didn't really assist me in anything.

Like I'm your assistant?

Well, no. I mean, I hired her when she was being laid off from her computer job. That was a year ago and it didn't work out. I still felt bad about it and she's still out of work. So when I left I told her she could stay in the house as long as she liked.

How male of you.

Ruby? Come on. The woman is out of work. All her family have passed away and she has nobody to help her out. I'm just doing what's right.

So how many other assistants do you have? One in every state?

Ruby.

It makes me feel real good, that it does. When you leave will you let me stay in your room here at the Buffalo Head? I'm sure Lila would love crawling around on the crappy carpet. I mean, free HBO. What more could we want?

Nisha doesn't mean anything to me. I wish she'd leave, but I don't mind helping her out. It's the right thing to do.

You're probably telling her the same thing about me.

Oh, Ruby. Come on. She's just an insecure, down-and-out person who needs some help.

Sounds like me. We should start a club.

She's nothing like you.

Right. Nisha. What kind of name is that, anyway?

I told you. Her family came from India.

Oh, right. But then they moved back.

Well, yes. Her parents did.

That's funny. People are leaving America for India now.

Ward shrugs. This won't last forever.

I hope not, says Ruby. She points at the parking lot of her mother's apartment complex. I hope Lila napped today. She won't sleep lately and it wears me out. She tosses and turns in the bed all night long.

Ward pulls into a parking space and leaves the engine running. Can I call you later?

No, says Ruby. She gets out of the car but before she shuts the door, she leans in and says, Well, if you want to. I'll be home.

A SHINY BLACK pickup appears in the driveway like a country-western hearse. A locomotive of dirt-road dust surrounds it in a redbrick glow. Ruby is washing dishes and when she turns to look out the window there it is. She and Lord God head to the porch. She puts on a face like a plaster mask. Be polite. Show no emotion. Get through this.

A man gets out wearing a white cowboy hat. He walks with a cocky strut like he owns a small-town casino with sixteen slot machines and a bouncer with a mean streak. Ruby thinks he looks like somebody's rich uncle. White-haired and well fed. His belly pooches taut above his belt buckle.

Good afternoon, Reverend Cole, says the visitor, his voice deep and smooth as chocolate pudding. He nods and spreads a smile Ruby's way, holds out his right hand and says, I don't believe we've met. I go by the name of Hiram Page.

Ruby shakes his hand and feels the strength of muscle and bone pulling her toward him almost imperceptibly. I've seen you at church, she says. Nice to meet you.

Lord God stands rigid and unsmiling. Take a seat, Mr. Page, he says, indicating the old sofa on the porch.

Hiram thanks him kindly and sits down with a burst of dying energy, revved up in the wrong gear and with the desert sunlight streaking in bands of God's light behind him, Ruby watches a light cloud of dust rise and float above his cowboy hat like a cartoon speech bubble. Lord God eases himself down onto the wooden bench beside the sofa.

Here, says Ruby, let me take your hat.

No, thank you, darlin'. He removes his hat and smooths back his white hair, slaps it against his leg. I'll keep ahold of it in case we take a walk and I need to keep the sun out of my eyes.

Can I get you something to drink? she asks.

Oh, I'm fine, says Hiram Page.

A glass of iced tea maybe?

Well, now, you're sweet-talking me. I think that would hit the spot.

Papa?

Nothing for me, says Lord God.

In the house, Ruby gets glasses from the cupboard, opens the refrigerator, and listens. Hiram Page asks Lord God how he's been feeling lately, if the leg has been bothering him. Lila is in her playpen in the kitchen, spinning a Winnie-the-Pooh mobile over her head. Ruby tousles her hair and reaches down to check her diaper. She hears her father say, I've been out of sorts lately, Mr. Page. If it's not this leg it's the drought, how dry everything is, all the dust in the air. It's like living in an hourglass is what it is.

It'll break soon, says Hiram Page. The Wet Mountains had a good rain just last week. Not enough but it's something.

She returns to the porch and hands Hiram Page the glass. I put some sugar in it, she adds. I hope you like it.

I do have a sweet tooth, he says. Hiram smiles and looks down at his boots. I assume your father told you why I'm coming here, didn't he?

My father mentioned you'd be coming for a visit. But he doesn't tell me much.

A wise man is closemouthed by nature. But here's what I'm thinking. What I'd like to do is take you to dinner. No strings attached. Someplace nice and cozy. You wouldn't be averse to that, would you? I imagine it would be a relief, not to have to cook dinner one night?

Ruby nods. I could do that. I'd have to get someone to watch Lila.

You know I will, says Lord God. I always do.

A pretty girl like you deserves to be spoiled, adds Hiram. Raising a child all alone must be hard work.

It is, she says. But Papa helps. And Mom does too. I'm not all alone.

I know that. You're in good hands. Why, your father's a hero. He fought in the war and protected our way of life.

That's one way to put it, says Lord God. Way of life? I guess. All I know is I lost a leg over there.

God bless, says Hiram. A good man defends his country when he's called.

I risked everything is what I did. And this is what it got me. Lord God pulls up his pants leg to display the working end of his prosthetic limb. I say I don't regret it but I do. Others don't give a fig.

Some do, says Hiram. The good ones do.

Maybe, says Lord God. But most of the others just want to get drunk or watch TV or cavort in a swimming pool somewhere in California. And be disappointed if they can't.

I hear you talking, says Hiram.

The country's gone to hell and enjoyed the fast ride, far as I see it.

I've given some thought and you know what's the heart of the problem? Fat-cat bankers in New York City. Somehow the whole country got turned the wrong way by that crowd in New York and now we've pledged the good blood of our young men to protect a handful of kooks and money-grubbers in Israel. It's the parable of the moneylenders all over again. It ain't right but there's not much fixing it.

Lord God rearranges his pants cuffs to cover his metal leg. That's one way of looking at it.

And now the illegals are taking over our neck of the woods. Or want to. But I've pledged my blood to stop them. The only way it will happen is over my dead body. And there's others just like me who have guns and will to boot.

In the kitchen Lila starts to cry. To Ruby the sound is plaintive, faint and beautiful. She hears in it relief and knows it as the only reason to wash the dishes, to wake in the morning. The only reason to listen to these two men without screaming.

She stands and pushes her hair out of her face. I better go, she says. I think my girl needs a bottle.

I'll come see, says Hiram. I love babies. Treasure from the Lord, you know?

In the dusty living room, with its Goodwill Industries furniture and scattered toys, Hiram Page pauses and looks around. He stands there with his ridiculous cowboy hat in hand. He says they have a fine home here and should be proud.

Hiram lifts Lila and holds her up to his face. Her crying hits a higher note. Her skin's so pretty, says Page. Her father of Spanish blood?

Ruby nods. His last name was Hermosilla.

Lord God rubs his good knee and frowns. He's a high school boy with no more brains than a piñata. He left you and he left his daughter and I don't want to hear any more about him.

You scared him off, she says.

Now, let's play nice, says Hiram. I wasn't trying to stir the pot.

It's our business, says Lord God, not yours.

Hiram strokes Lila's cheek and bounces her. She's just a little tanned, isn't she? Nothing wrong with that. I dated a mixed woman once. She was so pale-skinned you wouldn't know she was half blood. Looked as white as me. But I didn't hold it against her.

Hiram smiles as he says this and stares into Lila's dark brown eyes like she's his date to a picture show.

Ruby takes Lila from his arms and pulls her to her chest. You didn't hold it against her? Why would you?

You forgave her for who she was, says Lord God. Is that what you're saying? Did her a favor?

She didn't have a choice, says Page. She was born that way. Same as your daughter here.

How kind of you, says Ruby. I'm glad you can be so forgiving.

Now, Ruby, says Lord God. I don't believe Mr. Page meant anything by that.

No, I'm sure he didn't. Ruby tosses back her hair and picks up Lila. It's just the way of the world, isn't it? She nods at Hiram Page and takes a step away. I think baby girl here has a wet diaper and I've got some wash to do, so I better get to it. It's a pleasure meeting you, sir.

Oh, please call me Hiram. He reaches out to shake her hand

but she motions with her chin, indicating her hands are full. He smiles at her and adds, The pleasure's all mine.

Lord God stands. Mr. Page, I'll show you outside.

Are we done already? asks Hiram. His smile is forced. Oh, I suppose you two have work to do.

Ruby turns away without a word and carries Lila down the hall. Lila starts to cry, opening her mouth wide. Oh, baby, says Ruby. You're hungry, aren't you? There, there. What about I get you some milk and cookies?

She puts Lila on the floor in her room and strokes her curly black hair. She hurries to the kitchen and fills a sippy cup with milk. The wind whistles through a crack in the windowpane. She inhales deeply and stares out at the tan fields of prairie beyond the crooked fence that marks the end of their backyard. Buzzards trace a circle in the blue sky above. When she returns to the bedroom, Lila has a polka-dotted horse in her hands, saying, Horsey, horsey.

Okay, baby girl. Here you go, says Ruby.

Lila takes the sippy cup and says, Thank you, in a faint voice. She sits against a pillow on the bed and grabs a chocolate-chip cookie with her free hand.

On the front porch Hiram Page shakes Lord God's hand. We'll have to meet again, Mr. Cole.

Lord God walks to the edge of the porch and says, We could do that.

Hiram pauses. You think I have any chance here? he asks.

He squints in the bright sunlight, turning his hat in his hands, holding it by the brim. The hat is so clean it looks like a stage prop.

The moment stretches thin. Lord God's face does not react. It's not for me to say. I'll talk to Ruby and get back to you. The best I can do.

Okay, then. Hiram smiles and shakes his hand again. I can ask for no better than that.

Lord God wobbles slightly in the wind at the edge of the porch. She's a young thing with pride and honor and dignity, he adds. She needs a good man. I know that.

She needs someone who can care for her and that child too, says Hiram. I'd be glad to do that, Reverend Cole. Honest.

Like I said, I'll have a talk with her.

After Hiram Page drives off, Ruby hears Lord God approach. Lila has fallen asleep with her sippy cup in her hands, her lips loose, her belly full. Ruby lies beside her on the bed, one arm bent with Lila in the crook of her elbow. Lord God comes into the room slowly and smiles down at both of them. He jerks his head in the direction of the road and says, That man's a piece of work, isn't he?

Ruby rolls her eyes. I felt like hitting him.

Lord God sighs. I held my tongue. He's a rich man and I don't want us to be making enemies.

I know, Papa.

If I were half the man I used to be I'd kick him down the steps. But how could I tell the truth? How could I tell him no fool is going to marry my daughter? Lord God shakes his head. Or ever see her again, for that matter.

Oh, Papa. After a moment, she blinks tears from her eye-lashes. I'm glad you think that.

Ruby, Ruby. Lord God stands in the doorway, a band of late-afternoon light stretched across his pants legs, dust motes floating like atoms. I only want what's best for you two.

I know. Ruby smiles at him and he looks away, as if he can't take the moment. Outside the window behind him a flock of Grackles clatters about the roof of the faded woodshed. Ruby wonders what Ward is doing right now, if he's going to call her later. She wants him to. She'll have to tell him about Hiram's visit. Ward knows her father is trying to marry her off. Maybe if he hears what Lord God did, he might respect him more. She looks up from these thoughts and there he is, her father, still standing in the doorway.

I'm sorry, he says. I had a vision from the Lord that you should be married to a good man. I thought that might be him. I was mistaken.

Thank you, Daddy.

Lord God's face is penitent. He gazes at Lila. I envy the way she can nap. So peaceful and serene. She hasn't a care in the world, has she?

Not yet.

I'm going to town soon. You make a list of things you need at the supermarket and I'll take care of it.

We're about out of diapers.

She goes through those things, doesn't she?

Ruby nods. She's growing so fast, too. I think we need to get the next size up.

Lord God reaches out and touches Ruby's cheek. Well, you just tell me what to do, I'll do it.

RUBY SAYS SHE can't make it and ward says he understands.

Really. It's okay, he adds.

I want to go, but Lila has a fever and an ear infection, I think. St. Mary's has a free clinic that you can go in the afternoon and it's first come, first served. We're headed there in half an hour. I think she needs some antibiotics.

Do you need a ride? I'll be glad to give you one.

No, Papa offered to take me, and he'd be hurt if I said no. He's already jealous of you as it is. I don't need to cause more trouble there.

Ward can hear crying in the background. Okay, he says. Well, I guess I'd better let you go.

I miss you, whispers Ruby.

I miss you too. I'm not going to be able to get any work done without you.

You better.

The wind has picked up by the time Ward crosses the prairie west of Lake Pueblo, a flock of geese marking an uneven vee in the gray sky. He can see for miles around and not another soul is in sight. Jets scar the sky with white vapor trails. Now and then the wind blows the sound of trucks off the highway to the south.

He cuts through the rabbit bush and sage until he reaches a canyon that drops fifty feet, with a dry wash in the center. Cliff Swallows scatter as he nears the edge. He opens a collapsible deer blind, colored in brown-and-gray camouflage pattern. It's a simple thing, with shock-corded aluminum poles that snap together and fit into nylon sleeves of the blind's shell, popping it into a cone-shaped little hut. Tent stakes secure it to the rocky shelf of cliff face he's chosen as the blind location.

Once he has it set up, he sits inside and watches the Great Horned Owl nesting site across the canyon. He watches for two hours, his lower back aching from the awkward squatting position he must remain in to see out the window. The nylon covering of the blind pops and luffs in the wind, and Ward finds himself thinking of Ruby, wondering if he should call her later, wondering if he could get her to sneak away tomorrow night. But she's never been out at night with him and would probably think him crazy, with her baby girl's ear infection and her biblical father stomping across the floor with his peg leg and Book of Mormon nonsense.

He finds himself passively watching a flock of White-Crowned Sparrows, surprised to see them on the plateau. Cliff Swallows swoop in and out of cone-shaped mud nests in the canyon walls. A pair of Mountain Bluebirds perches in the branches of a cottonwood below.

He forgets to count any of them. He tries to recall the exact time span since his wife and daughter died, two years, ten months . . . eleven days? Or is it ten months, eight days?

He stares dully through his binoculars, wondering if Ruby

thinks he's too old for her. There's twelve years' difference, which isn't much if you think about it, really. It's not like he's old enough to be her father. But still, she's young enough to have the world before her, and sometimes he feels he's set in his station of life. He's a defined person. True, when she was eight, he was a sophomore in college. But that's comparing apples and oranges, isn't it? He's older and wiser, isn't he? Older, yes, but he's not so sure about wiser.

In late afternoon he watches as a trio of illegals passes by on the path of the canyon below, carrying *bolsas* and bottles of water. The cool taste of night is coming on by the time he stands and stretches. His leg has fallen asleep and tingles when he climbs off the ledge where he pinned the deer blind. He hobbles homeward across the prairie plateau, a solitary figure in an immense landscape, mountains to the west and the smokestacks of a coal-burning power plant to the east, the other side of Pueblo. Home to his empty motel room, to the shouts and clutter of the parking lot, the wailing of sirens that marks the city's heartbeat.

JACK BROWN ENTERS HP Pawns with a hangdog look. Page's witless nephew Ezra is slumped over the gun counter reading a magazine. When he sees Jack Brown he says, 'S'up, dog, and gives him a fist bump.

It's a sunny morning, 90 degrees outside, Jack Brown already sweating. Hiram tells Ezra to go make himself useful. I think our kinfolk here has some money for me, he adds.

Jack Brown tells Hiram it's been a bad time. He says he's

sorry. He missed last month and doesn't have this payment either, but he thinks he can get some cash in a week. I've got a deck job coming up, and it should be a big one.

A deck job?

Yessir. Some rich guy is getting me to build him a deck off his house in the foothills, out toward Penrose. It's a sweet place, and the deck he has in mind will cost a pretty penny.

Hiram nods. He's wearing a starched white shirt and turquoise bolo tie, his white hair combed back, an expensive watch on his wrist.

I have a business proposition for you. Page stares at Jack Brown with a shrewd look, as if he's about to name the price of an acre of land. You do me a favor and I'll forget these two lapses. Plus I'll knock five thousand dollars off your debt.

A favor?

A favor.

A five-thousand-dollar favor? Brown grins. Whatever it is, it must be either a lot of work or somewhat the other side of legal.

Hiram Page raises his eyebrows and purses his lips. It might be both. But that doesn't change the proposition. You can of course turn it down.

You're damn right I can.

All you have to do is come up with the twelve thousand four hundred eighteen dollars left on your note by next Monday. Plus the ring, of course. That's all.

I got two years left.

Read the contract, cousin. You miss one payment, the terms change. As of today, you're missing a second payment, correct?

Jack Brown rubs his neck and hisses through his teeth. What are you, the devil?

Hiram Page makes a finger pistol and points it at Brown, who can see Ezra in the caged-in office grinning at him. There you are mistaken, says Hiram. Read Joseph Conrad. He once said, The belief in a supernatural source of evil is not necessary. Men are quite capable of every wickedness.

You're telling me, says Brown.

Yes, I am telling you what you already sense. Conrad was a Pole but a smart one. Me, I'm not wicked. I'm just a businessman. Perhaps one with more acumen than most. I hope.

What's this favor?

Ah, there's the rub. Hiram Page walks over to the glass pane of his door facing North Avenue. He's quiet for a moment, then says, Notice how many Mexicans are coming up from the south and worming their way into Pueblo?

Sure. Now and then I do. Most times I ignore 'em. Shit, this town's half Mexican to begin with. What's a few more or less?

I generally don't appreciate this sociological development. In these dire economic times, they're driving down real estate values, which isn't good if you own anything. Hiram makes an expansive wave with one hand, indicating the shop, still looking out the door. And I do.

So what is it? You want me to rat out some illegals?

Hiram Page cocks his head to one side and slides a finger down the frame of the large glass pane inset into his front door. He looks at the dust on his finger and shakes his head. He turns to Jack Brown and says, No, nothing of the sort. What I want you to do is relocate a child. He nods as if to show Brown that he has heard correctly. Painlessly, he adds. She can't be harmed. But that's what I want you to do.

Relocate?

That's one way to put it. Her family must not know of it.

I'm no choir boy, but shit. I've never kidnapped no children and I'm not about to start now.

You took that ex-sweetheart of yours against her will, did you not?

That was different. Others did that. Me? Mainly I tried to see none of them harmed her.

You are guilty nonetheless. It's only different in that she's of greater age.

Well, that's different.

You have principles, is that what you're telling me?

Yes, goddamnit. That's what I'm telling you.

I see. Perhaps those principles are malleable. As they say, every harlot was a virgin once.

I'm no harlot and no virgin either.

True. I'm guessing you're somewhere between. But for five thousand dollars, perhaps just this once? Hiram Page smiles. Adaptation is one of the finer human talents.

Jack Brown shakes his head. You must be crazy.

He gives a curt wave with one hand and walks toward the door. Before it shuts Hiram Page calls out, Suit yourself. You just drop that truck off by five o'clock, you hear? That's a good vehicle. I'll be glad to have it back.

· · ·

Jack Brown tries to reach Hiram on the phone for a talk, but he won't take the call. He returns two days later and is made to wait almost an hour before his cousin appears. He kills time in the caged-in back office, by the video monitors, Ezra complaining to him about how boring the job is, how there's nothing to do. When Hiram arrives they both hop up and look busy. Brown leans against the pawnshop counter until finally Hiram comes to him and asks, Are you here to see me?

Let me get this straight, whispers Brown. You're saying she won't be hurt? No way I can hurt a baby, no matter how much money you pay me.

You think I'd hurt a child? She'll be better off in the long run. You'll be in her presence for no more than a half hour, then drop her off in the care of a good woman. For a day she'll be treated like a princess, then returned to her mother.

What's the story here?

Not your concern, says Hiram. Suffice it to say that it's in my personal interest to relocate this child and see her reunited with her mother in a timely fashion.

You wouldn't be setting me up for something, would you?

Jack? Would I do that to family?

Jesus H. Christ. Kidnapping is a felony. I know that.

You're my relation. This is no setup.

I've heard that people never get away with kidnappings.

That's because they ask for ransom. We won't. All you'll do is

217

take the child and drop her off where I tell you to. For you? End of story.

And nobody will ever hear tell of this?

Trust me. It will be our little secret. I'll have more to lose than you.

Jack Brown shakes his head and walks out the door, his hat in hand, jingling the bell. In a minute he returns and puts his cowboy hat in place. What if, he starts, then pauses, breathing hard. What if we make it the whole shebang? All I owe you? I do this and we're square?

What if? repeats Hiram. I don't know. You tell me.

If I do this for you, we're even. I get the title for the truck, free and clear.

Hiram nods. That could be arranged.

They shake hands awkwardly, Brown making a face, as if he's sold his soul and now thinks he should have gotten a better price. After Brown departs, Ezra asks if he can leave early. He has some errands to run. That Cousin Jack is a goofy sumbitch, isn't he?

Hiram nods and tells his nephew yes, he can leave early. Just don't make it a habit, he adds.

After Ezra leaves, Page fixes himself a bourbon and Coke, savoring the syrupy burn. He takes out a bottle of Windex and sprays the glass counter above the sidearm display, where Jack was slouching. He's not one to countenance smudges or slouches. As he wipes the glass clean he muses that he puts the odds of success for this little caper at a hundred to one. But the odds it works in his favor? Four out of five, maybe.

The worst that could happen? Brown is caught and fingers him as the kingpin. Unlikely result. Brown knows he has friends of friends, in prison and out. Plus, he's family. In case Brown does squeal, he denies it all, of course, makes his cousin out to be a disgruntled relative trying to blackmail one of his more successful kin. He resells the truck, makes more money, the ball keeps rolling.

One way or the other Ruby Cole gets a taste of just what the word *vulnerable* means. Could be she falls into his lap like ripe fruit.

PART THREE

Whatever God requires is right, no matter what it is, although we may not see the reason thereof till long after the events transpire. If we seek first the kingdom of God, all good things will be added. So with Solomon: first he asked wisdom, and God gave it to him, and with it every desire of his heart; even things which might be considered abominable to all who understand the order of Heaven only in part.

—*Joseph Smith*

The Kidnapping of a Child

DOWNTOWN IN THE SHADOWS OF INTER-state 25, prickly pear cactus grows in dusty vacant lots and the fat symbols of loopy-script graffiti decorate concrete highway pillars. As the traffic whines like a chain saw running in his brain, Officer Israel James finds himself ticketing parking violations, which is pretty close to the lowest of the low. What next? Scraping the gum off benches in Gnome Park? Elray scribbles a love note of bad news on a car parked too close to a fire hydrant, wondering exactly where and when he took a wrong step in life. What has led to this—this what? Dwindling? Step down? Christ, two floors down, it sometimes feels.

He doesn't want to admit it but secretly he knows his undoing occurred the night he failed to get the name of Rebecca Cisneros's ex-boyfriend, the yahoo intent on reclaiming the engagement ring she mock-swallowed, when her pretty face and come-hither invitation made his head spin so fast he forgot to ask the man's name, returned to hear of her abduction, and then the whole matter was taken out of his hands. Later to be covered up like the sins of a favorite uncle.

So it goes. He stands on the corner of Abriendo and Polk Street, tucking a pink parking ticket under the windshield wiper of a bent-fendered Nissan, when a pickup pulls up beside him and there he is, the legendary George Armstrong Crowfoot, black ponytail and all, wearing mirrored sunglasses and a plaid western shirt, giving Elray a smile, saying, Long time no see, Deputy Dawg.

Elray slow-walks over to the passenger-side cab window and gives the door a soft bong with his fist. Well, if it isn't the badass himself. Last I heard you were giving free haircuts to wayward Saints and galloping off into the sunset with a filly on your saddle.

I deny the charges, Officer, says Crowfoot. But I do owe you an apology. I remember way back when this all started you claimed that said young filly had invited you to dinner and that you felt cheated. So I guess I owe you one.

You mean for stealing her?

Well, it doesn't sound so noble, put that way. I didn't steal a soul. But we have become somewhat inseparable.

I'll take that as a thank-you, then.

You didn't tell me she was a looker.

Sounds like you found out for yourself.

I did. Crowfoot grins. She thinks I'm her savior, and seeing as I've never saved anyone before, I'm not about to argue.

Don't blame you.

So I heard through the grapevine you been looking for me.

I have, I have. Elray takes off his hat and climbs inside Crowfoot's pickup, moving a crate of bottled water on the floorboard to make room for his boots. I understand you and your lady friend are cozy as bedbugs now, but I still want to give her ex-boyfriend a little payback. Who is this clown?

Jack Brown. A nobody related to that pawnshop owner Page. He's a fool. Becca told me the whole story, and it sounds like he got into something over his head. She gave him back that ring and we don't want any hand in any payback now. Let sleeping dogs lie, Wyatt Earp.

George? You going soft on me? I figured you'd be putting the hurt on him big time.

Maybe I mellowed with a woman whispering in my ear. I don't know. But I'm the one who told her to give the ring back. Since then, what's done is done. Haven't heard a peep out of the Saints and hope I never will again.

You hear about that tanker hijacked and a trucker killed?

Nope.

Elray frowns. You don't watch the news much, I take it.

Hardly ever. Up on the mesa, we watch the sunset.

That's nice and gooey and all, but us law-enforcement types, we stay up on things. This hijacking gone wrong wasn't that long ago, and seemed to me like a plot the Saints would hatch. An entire tanker full of gas. A lot of money to be made if you can sell it. Who else but Saints is what I'm thinking. And just the other day the tanker shows up empty at a rest stop in Nevada. I'm thinking these outlaws sold the gas somewhere in the polyg back alleys of southern Utah, then crossed state lines and dropped the truck off to wash their hands of it.

Those freaks got too much time on their hands, says Crow-foot. Never mess with a people crazier than yourself.

Yeah, well, I'm writing parking tickets now. I got some time on my hands too.

But you're not crazy.

That's debatable. I'm a horse cop in the shadow of a freeway. Can't be that sharp or I'd be making the big money.

Do what you want. Me and Becca, we're over it. I know they say revenge is a dish best served cold, but ugliness begets ugliness. The best way to end a feud is to walk away, forget about it.

I wish it was that easy. But maybe. I'll sit on this for now. If Jack Brown runs afoul of the law, I'll be there to greet him. Elray nods and gives George an *adios,* returns to Apache, tied to a chain-link fence. He climbs on the horse and watches Crowfoot drive away, sees the pickup disappear in traffic, thinking that as much as he hates to admit it, the man is right. Let it go. Sometimes that's what you have to do. Sometimes that's all a man can do. Let it go.

Except when you can't.

ATOP WILD HORSE MESA, Crowfoot packs a row of eighteen-by-twelve-inch wooden frames with mud, clay, and straw, leaves them in the sun to bake dry. The wooden frames are made from scrap two-by-fours. He's building a round adobe house, Santa Fe style. Becca Cisneros brings him sausage-and-egg soft tacos wrapped in aluminum foil and a thermos of coffee. How's it going? she asks.

Good, good. He wipes mud and clay from his hands and takes the foil packet she's offering. At this rate I'll have enough bricks done to start laying and mortaring the walls before the worst of the cold sets in. I'm thinking of putting a big window in here. He points. What do you think of that?

It's a great view. She rests one hand on her belly, her face sublime, untroubled in the sunlight. She's carrying a baby girl and is happy in this knowledge, at this moment, on top of this mesa, the blue sky above dotted with clouds white as clean pillowcases. She smiles and gives Crowfoot's belt loop a tug. Is that the bedroom?

He nods. The sun will wake us up every morning.

We can lie in bed and watch it.

Or do something else, he says.

Or that.

And I can watch you. With the morning light on your skin.

Now, you better quit thinking that way.

What?

I see that look on your face. You keep giving me that look and you'll never get this finished.

He laughs. I saw Elray James yesterday.

You did?

I did.

What was he doing?

Putting parking tickets on cars of the unfortunate, downtown.

You say anything about us?

Well, I said thanks for being the one to introduce us, after a fashion, I guess.

You did.

I said I felt guilty for stealing you away.

You didn't steal me from him! I only met the man once.

I know that.

It's like another lifetime ago. I don't even want to think about it.

Then don't.

I want to think about what kind of tile we're going to put on the floor. We're going to use stone tiles, aren't we?

We are.

It will be beautiful.

Crowfoot nods. And a lot of work. But by the end, beautiful.

That's what matters, isn't it?

Yes, it is. Everything worth doing takes work.

Crowfoot stares southwest, the landscape stretching beyond like a painting of the legendary Anasazi cliff houses. A high, treeless plateau of tan and russet fields rising to forested mountains jagged against the horizon. Burned patches of scorched trees still standing on one of the closest hillsides. The sharp drop-off of the cliff edge a hundred yards beyond where the south-facing house plot lies. He pictures the adobe home, a fire in the corner fireplace hearth, snow on the mesa lovely out the windows. He pictures how the golden sun rays will fall onto the flagstone tiles of the room. How Becca will look as she wakes in bed, the light so clear and true he'll be able to see the fine hairs that cover her lower back. A plan for a life worth living. Something whole and different.

.   .   .

Later that day Crowfoot bounces his pickup down the steep road on a supply trip to town. When he stops just outside the cattle guard to open the gate at the foot of Wild Horse Mesa, he finds a cardboard box. He regards it for a moment, the odd vision of a box in the desert, sitting next to a clump of cactus. He gives it a tentative shove with the toe of his boot. There's a note scrawled on the top flaps in black marker: *Adios, amigo. Here's a present for you and yours. Keep it to scare the Saints.* Crowfoot hefts the box in the air and gives it a shake. Knows what it is without looking.

WARD WALKS UP the street from the buffalo head to the parking lot of a Sonic Drive-In. It resembles an open-air *mercado* in Tijuana. The kitchen still sells hamburgers and fries, but the customers order at the walk-up window. The rest of the space functions as an after-the-fall flea market.

Vendors sit on folding chairs behind card tables covered with ragtag wares for sale: dusty bootleg DVDs, plastic dinosaurs, scuffed tennis balls, sunglasses, old shoes, footballs, recycled car batteries, five-gallon jerry cans of deep-fryer grease, beeswax candles, and cans of calcium carbide for mining lamps. Piles of used clothes, jars of honey, and *nopalitas*. A stretch of five stalls selling locally grown fruit and vegetables: spotty oranges, avocados, corn, and tomatoes. Another vendor specializes in Mexican candies:

Chiclets, sugar candies shaped like Day of the Dead skeletons, and sweet devils.

Wearing wire-rimmed glasses, baseball cap, plaid shirt, and jeans, Ward mingles among the crowded stalls, jostling with everyone else for space below brightly colored sun umbrellas or the old awnings for the drive-in carports. The air smells of pork tamales, caramel popcorn, beer, and diesel fumes.

The day is hot and dry, the sky bright blue and relentless as a heat lamp. A radio blasts Tejano music full of accordions and trumpets while children run through the crowd squealing and laughing and begging for sweets, for coins, for papier-mâché piñatas—*burros, caballos, y tigres*—hanging from the metal awnings of the old carports.

Ward wanders through the crowd for half an hour until finally buying a fruit drink, a pair of turquoise bird earrings, and a handful of *empanadas* wrapped in newspaper. He's shooing away the flies from his paper cup of fruit punch when he hears a familiar voice behind him say, You're here.

He turns around and it's Ruby, her curly hair bound in a ponytail and a floppy straw hat on her head. He smiles and says, You want a taste?

She looks at the meat pie and squints. Where'd you get those?

Over there. Ward points through the crowd. She has a stack of them in a metal bucket. I don't know how hygienic it is, but the price is a bargain.

Ruby takes a bite and smiles. That's pretty good.

They make their way through the crowd, having to lean in close to hear each other.

On the walk over I was half thinking that you weren't going to show, says Ruby.

No, you weren't.

I was too! Really. I didn't want to get my hopes up too much.

Well, of course I was going to show. I mean, I wouldn't miss it for the world.

Ruby stands on her tiptoes and kisses his cheek, a funny look on her face. Guess what today is.

Saturday?

My birthday.

Close your eyes and hold out your hands, says Ward.

When she does, he places the turquoise bird earrings, in a tiny ziplock baggie, in her hands. Now open them.

A present? Ruby smiles and thanks him. How'd you know?

My secret. Plus I have other presents for you at the car.

She turns and heads into the crowd, calling out, That's even better.

They wend their way back to the Buffalo Head parking lot and walk up to Ward's Subaru.

What's a canoe doing on your roof? she asks.

Waiting to be used, he says. Waiting for you. I mean, it's yours.

Atop the Subaru's roof rack is strapped a green canoe with the legend MAD RIVER in white letters on its side. Ruby reaches up to touch it. I can't accept that, she says. It's too much.

I bought it used, he says. Besides, nothing is ever too much for a birthday. I have something else.

Ward opens the car and comes out with a shoebox. In it are four tail feathers from a Red-Tailed Hawk—graceful, cinnamon-colored. Ruby says, Now, this I can accept. She holds one up to the sky. They're perfect.

Plus we're having a picnic, he adds. I went all out. I got special olives and special cheese. The whole shebang.

Special olives?

Ward nods. And special cheese.

Ruby grins and climbs in on the passenger side. She turns on the radio and starts searching for a station. She can't look at him. I guess I should thank you, she says.

You don't need to. I see that smile on your face.

It's too much. She fiddles with the radio, not looking at Ward. But thank you. I always wanted a canoe.

You're welcome.

They drive west out of Pueblo through the canyons and prairies that mark the end of the Great Plains, where the flatland meets the foothills of the Rocky Mountains, the smaller peaks of the Sierra Mojada and the Green Horns. After the ghost town of Wetmore— all boarded-up buildings, tumbleweeds clumped against a shuttered general store, dust drifts upon sidewalks and against the foggy glass walls of dead service stations—they turn onto a country road that cuts a winding route through the forested hills and canyons. They cross two rocky creeks and a number of ranch gates, white-faced cattle in the fields, prairie dogs on the roadsides. Backwoods homes with satellite dishes and solar panels on their roofs. Aspens cover the hillsides, their leaves bright yellow and gold, shimmering in the wind. Ruby says she has never been to this lake before.

Ward shakes his head. That's a shame. Then again, neither have I.

But I have hiked west of here. In a couple months, when it gets really cold, I want to take you into the mountains to see the ghost trees. In storms the snowflakes coat the trees solid white, and as the snow falls it becomes like a curtain. Or a fog. Where you can only see a short way. So the trees become a solid wall of white. Like a forest of ghosts.

Okay, then. You'll have to take me there.

Look, a Red-Tail. Ruby points out her window toward a hawk beating its wings, a rodent clutched in its talons. It caught something.

Ward pulls onto the shoulder and leaves the motor running, then leans over Ruby's side to get a line of sight low enough to see out the windshield. He smells her apricot shampoo and sees the veins pulsing in her neck.

The buteo lands atop a telephone pole. Ward catches a brief look before it spreads wide its wings again and glides away, flying low before them and across the road, over an open field, and into the forest of ponderosa pine and white fir.

A female, he says. That's a good-sized bird, and with Red-Tails, the females are bigger than the males.

I like that, says Ruby. If women were bigger than men, that might solve some of our problems, right?

Ward stops twice more on their way to point out birds. They see Black-Billed Magpies on fence posts, with foot-long tail feathers and white wings, and lustrous Mountain Bluebirds perched on barbed-wire fences.

Evergreens surround White Baby Lake except where the aspen leaves have withered yellow and gold. A historical marker near the parking lot explains that the lake was named after Isabel, the first white child born in the area, in 1854. A band of bright color follows the creek that feeds the lake. Besides Ruby and Ward, the only other visitors are an older couple sitting in lawn chairs and fishing. Ward buys soft drinks from a small convenience store at a motel next to the lake. A plump woman rings up his purchase and tells him to watch the weather. The fire danger is high. He asks her if they've seen any ducks on the lake yet.

Stragglers, she says. Not many but a few. She says the weather has been funny. The migrating birds arrive earlier every year. If you're lucky you might see some Pelicans. She points to the western edge. Over in the shallows.

Enjoy yourselves, she adds. And make sure to wear the life jackets. The Fish and Game man comes by pretty often. He'll give you a ticket for no jacket faster than your head can spin.

Ward and Ruby unstrap the canoe from his roof rack and carry it to the landing dock. Ruby stands uncertainly as Ward puts his binoculars and a knapsack with lunch beneath the thwarts. He tells her to get in and move toward the bow, then take a seat.

Ruby situates herself in the bow of the canoe, on the forward thwart, and tells him she's ready, now what. Ward steps into the canoe and drags the stern off the sandy shoreline until the entire keel is in the water.

Just sit still and hold on to the gunwales, don't stand up or anything silly like that. With a quick movement he steps into the canoe and takes a seat, causing the canoe to wobble for a moment. He grasps the wooden paddle and pushes off the bottom of the shallows.

Do you want me to paddle?

Not yet. You just sit still and don't rock the boat.

Ward guides the canoe in smooth strokes across the lake, heading for a cove near the west shore, where the ducks and waterfowl cluster. The wind blows Ruby's hair in her face as he shows her how to paddle, explaining that she should keep her paddle to the port side of the canoe and he will take starboard.

What do you mean, port?

The left side.

Why don't you say that?

Because that's not seaworthy slang. On the water you say port and starboard, bow and stern.

She frowns. This is a lake.

Well. It's appropriate.

Bruised clouds darken the sky until the pines and firs look like stencil cutouts. At first both are quiet, although Ward points out birds on the shoreline, Sandpipers and Egrets. Ruby concentrates on paddling. Finally she says, I'm getting wet. Every time I paddle, I splash water on myself.

Ward laughs. Don't paddle, then. Just sit there and enjoy yourself.

After a moment she answers, I don't know how to do that.

Oh, come on. Enjoy yourself. It's not that hard.

She shakes her head. My father tried to marry me off to a pawnshop owner. Now that isn't working out, he told me the other night he's going to find someone else. Someone worse, I imagine.

Ward paddles, watching the dark clouds above. You deserve

a man who loves you, he says softly. I think your father will see that in the long run.

In the long run I'll be gone. She turns to look back at him, holding her paddle. I'm eighteen. She smiles. I. Am. Eighteen.

By the time they reach the west end of the lake the surface is rough with waves pushing them forward. Lightning flashes and a roll of thunder follows. Ward says they had better take shelter. He shoots the canoe onto the shore with a heavy crunching sound against the gravel.

He hops into the water as Ruby says, We better not get hit by lightning. Lila can do without any shiftless father but she needs me bad.

Hurry, then, says Ward. We're probably safest away from the water.

Ruby climbs out and both of them drag the canoe onto the shore.

They pull on jackets and walk the shoreline, collecting goose feathers in the flotsam and jetsam. It thunders but no rain falls.

When he thinks perhaps they should return to the parking lot, Ward turns to find Ruby standing behind him, her face framed by the hood of her rain jacket, smiling, her curly hair bunched around her cheeks and forehead. A clap of thunder splits the air and a lightning flash illuminates the darkened trees as Ruby huddles closer. Ward puts his arms around her and holds her. He wants to kiss her but doesn't dare. Ruby puts her head on his shoulder and laughs for no reason.

I think we should head back, he says. Let's at least get to the other side of the lake in case the storm gets worse. That way we'll be close to the car.

They paddle across the lake, staying close to the shoreline to watch the birds. Tall pines sway and shudder in the gusting wind. The bluster of rain but no drops fall.

The smell of smoke.

Faint at first, like the ghost scent of a backyard barbecue. Ward notices but doesn't mention it. They're in a canoe. The water like a blanket, a wall. Canada Geese waddle on the shoreline, white-cheeked and black-backed, honking and shuffling, dozens swooping over the banks, wings cupping the wind, black webbed feet splayed at the last second. Ruby counts thirty-seven, thirty-eight. A pair of Audubon's Warblers flits in the whippy branches of willows. Steller's Jays in the fir trees that line the creek cascading down to feed the lake.

Are those Mallards? asks Ruby. Over there? They must be Mallards.

Ward says she's probably right. You see a duck, guess Mallard.

Do you smell something? she asks.

Ward nods. I think it's the forest. Burning.

South of the lake, across the road, a plume of dark smoke rises into the sky. It drifts west to east, like belch from a volcano.

We better go, says Ward. He turns the canoe toward the landing dock. Paddles harder. Feels the burn in his shoulders.

I don't want to leave, says Ruby. What about our picnic? We've got sandwiches. She turns, swiveling on the thwart, smiling back at him. We've got special olives. And what about the special cheese?

Gouda, he says. The best.

Maybe it's nothing.

We better go. Ward is watching the smoke thicken, closer to the road. A starburst of cinders floats in the sky break above the road, the shoulders now smoldering. Pine needles glow like July 4th sparklers. The wind shifts and smoke roils toward the lake. They can no longer see the opposite shore clearly. Stronger and sharper now, the smoke stings their eyes and throats.

It's slow going, paddling against the waves, watching the fire touch the crowns of the ponderosa pines on the opposite side of the road, embers drifting in the wind, and soon both sides of the road are cloaked in smoke. They beach the canoe, dump the water out, collect their things—lunch and water, the camera, the notebooks. They lift the canoe onto their shoulders and portage it up the hill to the parking lot, coughing.

By the time they have it lashed onto the roof rack, the wind is blowing cinders and floating embers onto the car and the asphalt of the parking lot. One lands on Ruby's neck. She swats it like a mosquito, and it leaves a red scorch mark. From the south, from the direction of the road out, the smoke pulses toward them like black, scratchy fog.

Ward's hand trembles as he puts the keys in the ignition, turns to Ruby. So much for a peaceful picnic at the lake.

We better scram, she says.

At the intersection to the main road, the way home to Pueblo descends downhill into a cindery cloudbank. The sound of a helicopter chops overhead, its body invisible in the murk. Ward turns left and says, We'll take the long way.

They slow to a stop in a queue of pickups fleeing the fire. A black dog stands upon a hay bale before them, barking at butterflies of ash that drift into the truck bed. The road switchbacks down the mountain, and the dog doesn't stop barking. Ruby holds a gauze mask over her face. The line of cars moves on and slows, moves and slows, until finally they are beyond the smoke drift.

In the rearview, once they have passed out of the fire zone, a long black cloud stretches eastward, glimpsed through gaps in the serrated teeth of the mountains. On the road shoulder stands a herd of bighorn sheep, ewes and lambs, feeding in the grass, unsettled by the fire.

Later they pull over at a scenic viewpoint to eat lunch. Ruby leans over and strokes Ward's face. Relax now, bird man. The only time you seem happy is when you're around Lila. That's maybe the only time I've seen you smile. Or maybe sometimes when you look at me.

I can't help it, he says.

I don't mind. It makes me feel good.

Ward is quiet for a while, sitting atop a picnic table, staring down at his boots on the picnic bench. I guess there are things I regret, he says. I don't think I've done much with my life. I wish I had.

What in the world are you saying? Look at you. You're a scientist. That's important, isn't it?

It all seems so tedious, actually. If I had to do it over again, I'd try to be better.

What would you do? You're not dead yet, you know.

I'd like to sail around the world, he says.

Oh. Well. I don't know anything about that. Are you a good sailor?

No. Not really. I've been on a sailboat a few times.

Maybe that's not the best idea.

I could learn. Lots of people sail. It can't be that complicated.

True.

I used to want to be a great ornithologist. A savior of birds.

What are you saying? It's, like, you know every bird in the state. Isn't that something?

Not really. I'm average, is what I am. Sure, I know more than most people. But in my obituary no one's going to write that I was great or anything. When you're just average, they don't say much about you. You have to be extraordinary for anyone to remember you.

I don't know about that. I remember people who weren't really extraordinary. Isn't pretty good enough?

Ward shrugs. I guess.

Then I think you're setting your goals too high. What would make you extraordinary? What would that even mean for a bird expert?

The Lord God Bird. That's what I'd like to find. It's been

sighted, and people believe it still exists, but they don't know for sure.

Ruby doesn't know what he's talking about. He explains about the Ivory-Billed Woodpecker, the largest woodpecker in North America, not sighted in the wild since the 1930s, believed to be extinct. Some claimed to have seen it in 2005, but it was never conclusively photographed.

It's magnificent, says Ward. It has a huge beak the color of ivory, white bars on its wings, and is so big it was nicknamed the Lord God Bird because when people saw it in the southern woods, they'd say, Lord God.

Makes me think of my father, says Ruby. My father as a bird. Now, there's a scary thought.

JACK BROWN HAS NEVER kidnapped a child before and the more he thinks about it, the more his stomach churns. Hiram insists that no harm will come to the little girl. She'll be returned to her mother the very next day. I give you my word, Cousin Jack. Trust me. What you are doing is only self-preservation. As George Bernard Shaw put it, Lack of money is the root of all evil.

Still Jack can't imagine actually doing the deed. He's not a pervert. He's not a bad person. And somehow he will have to touch this little girl, pick her up, put her in the car, drive away? While her mother and grandfather sleep? Just thinking about it gives him a headache. He tries to block it out of his mind. He eats half a pizza. He watches another episode of *The Deadliest Catch*. He falls asleep and when he wakes, it's dark out. His hands sweat as soon as he remembers the little girl.

At midnight he drives across town, queasy as if he's just stepped off a Tilt-O-Whirl carnival ride. His mouth waters with too much saliva. His heart pounds so hard he feels weak. At stoplights his legs tremble as he pushes in the clutch.

A bright sliver of moon hangs in the eastern sky like a bleached bone shard. It's Halloween night and the streets teem with drunken people in costume, many of them dressed for *El Día de los Muertos*. Low-rider muscle cars hop up and down at intersections. Teenaged boys catcall at girls in skimpy costumes taking pictures of each other. A crowd of kids smokes weed in a convenience-store parking lot, throwing water balloons at other teens in pickups.

It feels like Guadalajara on festival night. Jack shakes his head as he passes a series of billboards in Spanish, advertising Coke as *La chispa de la vida* or *Se compra casas feas*.

At an intersection he stares as a college girl in a devil costume miniskirt runs to make the light, splashing beer from the plastic cup she's carrying, looking back at her friends and laughing, a mouth painted vampire red. Jack Brown tells himself he's doing the wrong thing and he's in the wrong place. The wind gusts and lifts the girl's skirt, showing off her bright pink panties. The light turns green and cars behind him honk.

Jack Brown passes the freight yards and crosses the Arkansas River, heading west through the moribund business district on Thatcher. After he crosses Pueblo Avenue it's like he's fallen off the edge of the known world. No streetlights shine and the prairie yawns into a wide darkness so black it's as if his headlights no longer work. He has handwritten directions from Hiram Page to the Coles' house. At one point he pulls off the road near Lake Pueblo and reads them over again by the cab light.

After the highway turnoff the road resembles a pale riverbed dividing a horde of stick-figure cactus people, the black shapes of junipers. He rumbles along in second gear until he reaches the Cole mailbox and driveway. A hundred yards off the road looms the dim outline of this woebegone Little House on the Prairie. He does a cramped U-turn, parks the truck with two wheels in the ditch. He leaves the key in the ignition, douses the interior light as soon as he opens the door. When he steps out his boots sound too loud in the rocky dirt and gravel.

He hears a high-pitched barking and freezes. Did Hiram tell him whether or not this grandpa has a dog? He listens closely, sitting on the pickup's bumper to keep a low profile. The house is dark but for one bathroom window aglow with amber light.

The buffet and keening of the wind fill his head until he hears the barking again, a high-pitched yip. Coyote. Now it's coming from farther away, faint and muffled by the wind. He lifts the pair of night-vision binoculars and scans the prairie distance. Nothing moves but a white apparition, floating like a ghost, jerking to a halt on a cactus. After a moment Jack realizes it's a plastic grocery bag blown by the wind. He turns back to the house, a green box in the night-vision glow.

The second window on the right-hand side of the house is the nursery. His instructions are to jimmy open that window and crawl inside. Take the baby girl from her crib, wrap her in blankets, and hightail it out of there. What if she cries? Duct tape, said Hiram. Jack has a roll in his pocket, but he hopes it doesn't come to that. Maybe she won't even wake up? Maybe it will be easy as pie? Then why does it feel as if he's watching a horror flick through the eyes of the killer, everything illuminated in this spooky green light?

An old adage from Gata de la Luna pushes him on: *No glory without pain.* He moves quickly through the yard to the side of the house below the girl's window, stops to catch his breath. His tongue is dry now and his heart lurching. He stands pinned against the side of the house with his mouth open, struggling to breathe, his lips chapped.

Lord God awakens in the guts of the windy night. The bed reminds him of nothing less than a freshly dug grave. He blinks and stares into the purpled darkness, listening for Ruby and Lila. The refrigerator hums, the bedside clock ticks. He calls out for Ruby and as his voice dissipates in the empty rooms he feels the roller-coaster sensation of remorse.

He has driven away his only daughter, the person he loves most fiercely in the world. The last time they spoke he told her that pawnshop fool had not changed a thing. He had received a vision from the Lord and would find another man for her to marry. She sassed him and grabbed Lila, stormed out of the house, and slammed the door. He limped to the front door, only to see her walking down the dirt road, talking on a cell phone. Later she called from Juliet's to say that she and Lila were staying there now, for good.

He refuses to believe this. She'll come back around. Still he can't shake the feeling that his world is coming apart. Forests burn night and day and strangers come to the door asking for food or money. His daughter now wanders alone in this desert. Her only hope for comfort and protection is a man who counts birds on their way to extinction.

He sits up in bed and fumbles for his prosthesis, the funk of his body polluting the chill air. He will not prostrate himself before the devil and beg his benediction. He will fight to the end and if it comes to it lie down in the road to save his daughter's life.

Another stormy night and the air too warm for this time of year. Aspens and junipers rattle and sway, scratching the wood-shed walls with a rasp and a hiss. Lord God grimaces as he at-taches his leg, willing himself not to curse the God and nation for which he has given too much. With his leg attached, he thumps to the kitchen window. He stares outside as if the wind-strewn leaves will tell his fortune. As if the clouds will open wide and a voice offer guidance when he needs it most.

A shriek from the direction of the woodshed. Tossed by the wind, the high-pitched sound is little more than a brief bleat. Lord God doubts his ears, doubts he actually heard it. He waits, his breath caught in his throat. A bar of light streaks his cheek, tangle-bearded and furrowed. A gust of wind sends a clatter of leaves against the back door. He hears the sound again: a quick, sharp shriek.

Loading a handful of shells into his twelve-gauge pump shotgun, his hands shake. Outside, the wind is hot and blustery, tinged with the smell of smoke. Fires burn in the Sierra Mojada to the west, twenty thousand acres, it's said.

Lord God places his prosthetic shoe carefully on the dark path, the moon a faint glow above. He remembers how he had hoped Ruby would become a good man's celestial wife. To be welcomed into a large family, surrounded and protected, embraced. Now he has come to doubt all of it. The Saints glory in their own inherent goodness and in this glory became swollen with pride. Lord God fears that pride and self-righteousness blind them to the wickedness of their blood.

Clouds rip across the sky and for a moment the path brightens. He sees a neighbor's cat crouching in the shadows. Again he hears the shriek. This time it's louder, closer. Behind the woodshed and toward the back corner of their lot, where the land opens onto the prairie, near the gulch that cuts the plateau.

He shines the flashlight beam on an aspen, sees a Barn Owl staring back, its curious, heart-shaped face appearing to glow. The white owl bobs its head but does not fly away. Lord God wonders how many years it's been since he's seen one. What shift in fate does this apparition portend? What omen this eerie night bird? He doesn't know. Trouble. A sea change ahead. He would like to think hope but in his doubtful mood he doesn't trust any instinct toward optimism.

Jack Brown watches as the back porch light comes on, a screen door creaks open. A sound of scuffling and a rhythmic hiss. The beam of a flashlight crosses the backyard and points into the aspens. It points away from him. Jack ducks and scuttles across the sideyard to hide behind the propane tank.

He crouches, his face jammed against the cold metal of the tank, something jabbing him in the back and sides. A mass of tumbleweeds huddles beside the tank, windblown and prickly. Brittle branches sharp as cactus spines. He peeks above the edge of the propane tank. A man limps across the backyard, carrying a flashlight.

Jack Brown watches as the beam spotlights the aspens, shining on something in the bare branches. After a moment he realizes it's a white owl. It swoops and glides into the prairie blackness. The man limps away from the house, following it. Must be some kind of nut, following an owl in the middle of the night.

How does a geezer like that take care of a child? I might be doing her a favor, setting her free, like Hiram said. He's a polygamist nutcase preacher and for all I know he'll marry off the girl when she's ten years old to some doddering lecher.

The flashlight beam flickers and flashes over the prairie. Jack stands up and moves around to the corner of the house, his knees burning, one leg asleep. Before long the light disappears completely, as if it and the man have vanished off the face of the earth.

At the back door Jack pauses, listening. He steps inside and closes the door. The wind whistles through the doorjamb. An old coffee pot steams atop the woodstove. An aluminum cane rests against the kitchen table. A half-eaten sandwich on a plate. On the wall a rough wooden plaque with the legend AS FOR ME AND MY HOUSE, WE SHALL SERVE THE LORD. JOSHUA 24:15.

Jack tiptoes down the hall to the nursery. The room is dark and musty. He hesitates. He doesn't want to wake the baby girl if he can help it. Hiram said to wrap her in blankets and whisk her away, drive to the drop-off house, and that's that. Jack creeps to the crib and reaches down to lift her out, but he can feel nothing. After a few moments of searching, he crosses the room and turns on the light. The crib is empty.

Lord God watches the white streak of the owl swoop through the flashlight beam and disappear. The faintest sound of human voices reaches him, elusive in the wind, voices mystical and un-clear, incomprehensible. He follows the path out his back gate and across the high desert prairie, through the field of yucca and Spanish dagger, until he reaches the blackness of the gulch. A murmur of people in the floor of the gulch, traveling. The clink of provisions and scuffle of passage.

Down into the gulch he goes, stumbling forward like a blind man in the darkness, his rough hands on rocks rougher still, un-til he's close enough to hear their voices. Their tongue is Spanish, and he can tell there's some problem. He shines his flashlight on a trio of women crouched over a young boy and asks what's the matter.

Está enfermo, says one of the women. *Tenemos miedo que muera el niño.*

Lord God hears the ragged breath of the boy, his lungs full of liquid. It sounds like a drowning. I've got a house up here, he calls out. What can I do to help?

The Mexican women huddle over the boy and whisper among themselves. Lord God holds the flashlight and waits. The boulders and cactus catch and shimmer in the flashlight beam, a glow of yellow spines. Lord God feels as if a caul of spiderwebs is woven upon his face.

The young boy coughs, loosing a rattle of phlegm in his throat. His mother thanks Lord God. They're bedraggled and need shelter. His flashlight beam freezes the line of refugees in place—a queue of misery extending as far as Lord God can see.

Lord God leads the way up and out of the gulch. He slips and stumbles halfway to the top. His face and arm dirtied, he lies on his back and works his prosthesis into position to stand. The crowd behind him sees the metal peg leg revealed, the thin aluminum tube like the limb of an android.

I'm fine, says Lord God. I just need to get my good leg under me.

As he struggles, a man steps forward. He takes Lord God's hand, gives him a yank, hefts him up and over his shoulder.

Lord God smells wood smoke and sweat on the man's clothes, his face pressed into the man's back. His feet dangle in the air like a child's, with the prosthetic shoe resembling that of an oversized Pinocchio.

I can walk, says Lord God, his voice muffled against the man's back. I can walk. I just need—

The Mexican man doesn't respond. He climbs goatlike up the steep trail. Lord God's head hangs awkwardly to the side, his eyes focused on brief glimpses of the trail illuminated by the wavering flashlight beam now jostled in his left hand, cutting wildly across the gulch—here casting a circle of yellow light upon a shimmer of wet prairie, there shining into the darkness above.

They reach the plateau and the Mexican lowers Lord God to his feet. Lord God thanks the man, dusts himself off, then leads the procession that carries the ailing child toward his house, feeling like a gimp-legged Moses leading illegals out of the desert.

After a frantic search of all the rooms, Jack Brown leans against a wall and sucks on his inhaler. He returns to the nursery and wipes the doorknob and window frame with his sleeve. About to leave the room and this wacko hellhole forever, he notices his black footprints, gets down on his knees, and wipes up the mud with a baby blanket. He's just finishing when he hears voices and the back door opening. He peeks out of the nursery and glimpses a Mexican standing in the hallway, holding a child in his arms.

Jack backpedals to the closet and closes the door. He squirms into a mass of coats and boxes, sweating and breathless. Has Cousin Page double-crossed him? Sent some Mexican to do the deed and set him up for a fall? It doesn't make sense. Why would all these people be involved, making all this hubbub?

Jack burrows into the nest of coats, wheezing, dizzy. He has to suck his inhaler to keep from passing out.

Lord God brews a pot of tea. One of the women tells him the boy has been sick only for a day or two, that he became weak and feverish the day before. She says they were living in the boxcars of the old train yard but were driven out by vigilantes with baseball bats. Now they need to find a place to stay. Their only choice is a tent city west of town. That's where they're headed, using the gulch as a hidden back way to avoid *los vigilantes*.

A crowd gathers in Lord God's kitchen, close to the wood-stove. The women lay the boy on a sofa in the living room. The knee of Lord God's good leg is now swollen and stiff. He limps to and fro between the living room and kitchen, afraid he's about to collapse in pain. He must have twisted the knee when he fell. He realizes he might not be able to walk in the morning.

From the closet Jack hears a confused burble of voices, most talking in Spanish. One hoarse voice asks questions in English. At one point he hears someone enter the room, a heavy footstep, limping, rhythmic thump and hiss, searching for something. Jack tenses and is ready to bolt, run like a madman through the house and out the door. The door creaks shut and the thumping fades down the hallway.

Jack closes his eyes and prays to Jesus that he not be found. He promises he will change his dumb-ass ways and sin no more. He drifts into a half-sleep state and dreams of devil girls with Taser guns torturing him. . . .

On the sofa, the Mexican boy's young mother sits beside her feverish son. She wears an old sweater wet from the rain and dirty from the gulch. She looks about the same age as Ruby. She wipes tears from her eyes and pleads for God almighty to help her son, not to let him die in pain, in this house of strangers.

Her face resembles that of women Lord God saw in the Arab desert, huddled over their bloodied children after the explosion of a car bomb in a market, asking Allah for forgiveness and protection. He wonders if any in the room would blow themselves apart for an antigringo jihad. He wonders if they're to be trusted. A teenager among them turns on the television set and watches a sunblock commercial—blond, bikini-clad girls playing volleyball, high-fiving in the sand.

Lord God limps into the kitchen and places a saucepan on the stove. He opens a can of tomato soup, stirs in a splash of milk.

His knee throbs as he leans against the wooden kitchen counter. Dirty dishes fill the sink, a stack of plates clutters the counter, and the faucet drips. Flies buzz and light on spilled bacon grease on the stove. Without Ruby and Lila in the house, Lord God is lost and vacant. A Mexican woman steps through the doorway and asks, *Le ayudo?*

Lord God says no, he's doing fine. He just needs to get this soup heated and find where he put the saltines. I know they're here someplace. *Galletas*, he adds.

The woman says something he doesn't understand, begins pulling pots and pans from the sink. Lord God tells her she really doesn't need to do that.

She drains the mucky water, rinses the sink clean, and fills it with hot, soapy water. She goes to work on the pots and pans, stacking them in the dish drainer as he stirs the tomato soup.

Lord God feels ripples of weariness wash through his body. He struggles to make his way with the bowl of soup and crackers to the living room, where the boy is now propped up on pillows on the old, faded, flower-print sofa. Lord God's hands tremble, the spoon tinkling against the bowl and saucer on the tray. One of the migrants takes the tray and thanks him while another makes a place for Lord God to sit on the sofa. The boy's lips are cracked and discolored, his nose leaks a thin dribble of blood.

I don't know that I can do anything, says Lord God. I wish I could but I don't know. He shakes his head and watches the boy as a woman spoon-feeds him the soup. The boy's eyes are pink and he moans after he swallows, his coughs high-pitched and painful-sounding. He puts his head back on the sofa cushion and pants. He closes his eyes and calls for his mother.

Later Lord God awakens in the rocking chair, disoriented. The crowd in the room stands hushed and weeping. He feels a weakness in his bones and heart, a burning sensation on the skin of his throat and neck, the small of his back. It's all he can do to stay awake as the crowd filters out, carrying the boy's body, thanking him for trying to help, not daring to look in his face. Lord God urges them to stay the night, but he takes to coughing with a roughness that frightens the migrants. He tells them to take his water, a collection of fifty gallons in plastic jugs beneath the kitchen table.

They thank him and form a line from the kitchen out the front door, passing down the one-gallon jugs as if manning a fire-brigade line. Lord God urges them on, telling them, Don't be shy. Take it all. I can get more.

Lord God falls into a coughing fit again, leans forward to clear his throat, the mucus thick and gluey. When he looks up the last of the people are walking away, only the flickering beams of their flashlights visible as they head back toward the gulch and the path toward their shantytown. The dead boy's body fades into the darkness, draped with the white bedspread, held high by the illegals.

After three hours in the closet, Jack Brown tries to stand but his leg is asleep. He leans against the closet door and rubs until it begins to tingle. Outside, all is quiet. He hasn't heard a peep for a long time. The house seems empty. He creeps down the hallway and reaches the kitchen. A saucepan on the stove, a glass of water on the table. He gulps it down quickly, the first thing he's had to drink in hours. He tiptoes through the passageway, glancing into the living room. There sits an old man with a hooked nose and a gray beard in a recliner, his head leaning back, eyes half open.

In a feverish sleep, Lord God dreams himself inside the vortex of a whirlwind. Images of Ruby and Juliet swirl and float above him until he opens his eyes and sees the apparition of a stranger in the hallway of his house. He tries to focus and speak, to call out to this interloper.

For a moment their eyes meet. Jack tenses, a tremor passing through his body as if he's looking into the eyes of an angry God. Next he's running out the back door, through the windy yard, and fumbling for the keys in the truck cab. He shoves the truck into gear and lets out the clutch, his legs trembling.

He rushes down the dirt road, bouncing over cattle guards and ruts, almost flipping the truck on a high-sided curve, slamming back down to earth, holding on to the steering wheel like the crossbar of a roller coaster, tires squealing as he gets back on the highway. He wheezes and gasps, struggling to get his inhaler out of his pocket while speeding to put as many miles as he can between that crazy old man and his miserable hide. Still he can't suppress a shit-eating grin that he got away without a load of buckshot in his ass or worse.

He plans to get up early and tell Cousin Page just what went wrong. But the next day he has a wicked fever and his body aches so bad he can't get out of bed. By afternoon he lies in bed sweating, staring at the television with scorching eyeballs. He wishes he could just die and get it over with. In his fevered delirium he remembers Gata's advice for remorse: *Close your eyes and don't look back.*

L O R D   G O D   A W A K E N S   to the sound of Lila playing with her blocks in the living room. Simple wooden blocks embossed with letters of the alphabet, numerals, and images of fish, birds, bears, cats, and horses. He sits in his easy chair and tries to peel an orange in one continuous piece, a trick that always brought a smile to Lila's face. He wears pajamas with moose on them and Lila points to the moose pattern and says, Cow.

No, says Lord God. That's a moose. He holds his fingers out from his head to pantomime antlers. They're much bigger than cows, with big antlers. And they're wild.

Cow, says Lila again. She blinks slowly, with both eyes, and then clacks two wooden blocks together as if they are cymbals. They make a hollow, wooden sound. She keeps doing this for several minutes.

Lord God hears Ruby call his name. Papa? she calls out. Papa? Are you there?

He turns and looks for her in the kitchen doorway, but there is only blackness in that direction. He looks down at his legs as he wills himself to stand. Both of his legs are whole and firm, and he stands as if weightless. Only now Lila holds a wooden block in her hand, and on it is a hideous wrinkled face with the horned forehead of a devil. She frowns at him and says, You are a stupid, selfish man. I hate you and hope you die. You will roast in hell for your sins.

He tries to speak, to tell her he loves her and ask why she would say such a thing. He can't move his mouth. He holds out his hands to pick up Lila but she scurries away quickly, like a rat, crawling beneath the sofa and hissing at him.

He feels Ruby's hand on his forehead. Papa? Are you awake? Wake up, Papa. You need to eat something.

He opens his eyes and stares at Ruby's face. She has her hair pulled back and her head looks too small for her body. His breath is hot on his lips. He wheezes and feels a wave of fevered weariness move through his veins and arteries. The room smells unwholesome, as if something is rotten.

Where's Lila? he asks.

She's in town, says Ruby. Mom's taking care of her.

She told me I was selfish. She said she hoped I rotted in hell.
Why did she say those things?

She didn't, says Ruby.

Yes, I heard her. She was in the living room playing with
blocks—

Hush, says Ruby. She puts a cool washcloth on his forehead.
Everything will be fine. It must have been a dream. A nightmare.

Lord God's lip trembles. There was a stranger here. The devil,
it was. Or one of his minions. I saw him.

Hush, Papa. Here. Ruby maneuvers a TV tray onto his lap
and fluffs his pillows, tries to get him to sit up. His fever is so
high she can feel it radiating off him as if from a space heater.
She holds a glass of orange juice to his lips. Drink.

He has no strength to swallow. He coughs and chokes, his
face turning red, a vein down the middle of his forehead swollen
and pulsing. Ruby makes him lean forward and pounds his back.

Breathe, Papa. You have to breathe!

After a moment he catches his breath, the air making a wheezing, high-pitched whistle when he exhales. He coughs again and
Ruby sees blood droplets on his pillow. Orange juice spills on the
tray and leaks onto the patchwork quilt. Papa, she whispers,
what's the matter? Your knee is swollen. What happened?

Why does Lila hate me so? he answers. I love that child. You
should never have taken her from me.

She doesn't hate you, Papa. She loves you. Only I had to take
her for her own good.

You left her. You left her to me and she's mine now. And now you try to take her back I won't let you I won't—

I had to. Lie back. You're getting yourself worked up for—

Lord God closes his eyes and leans over, coughing again, struggling for breath. Sprays of blood droplets speckle his pillow. Ruby bunches a corner of the sheet and holds it to his mouth, patting his back. The room is cold and through the window she sees the gold autumn sunlight fading to dusk on the prairie. The phone rings in the living room. She holds his head to keep him from falling forward, the heat from his face like something un-natural, otherworldly. When he can speak again he tells her that yesterday he tried to help a sick boy in a crowd of migrants.

What happened to them? Where did they go? asks Ruby.

He didn't make it, says Lord God. He died in the living room. They carried him away.

Oh, Papa. You shouldn't have done that. I think you caught his sickness.

A man has to help his brother, says Lord God. A man has to do the right thing.

I know, says Ruby. You're right. Only you should have been more careful.

It doesn't matter, says Lord God, his eyes closed. The lids are bluish and have deep circles of shadow beneath. My knee is kill-ing me. Nothing matters.

Ruby finds an old humidifier in the closet, fills it with water, plugs it in, and turns it on. The steady whirring sound makes her feel better, as if something is being done. It convinces her there's hope. She sits on the wooden chair beside his bed until he falls asleep, until her tailbone aches and the small of her back burns.

She goes to the kitchen and fills the teakettle with water, the flow from the kitchen sink barely a trickle. She notices there are no gallon jugs beneath the table. Staring out the window at the faint glow above the Sierra Mojada, she watches a single Grief Bird perched on the woodshed roof, near the witch-on-broomstick weather vane. She corrects herself and renames the grief bird Raven, or *Corvus corax.*

The weight of a threatened world presses down upon her with its ugly might. She calls her mother and talks to her. Juliet wants to come but they agree she should stay in town and care for Lila, that both of them should stay away. After hanging up Ruby sits stunned, bereft in this prairie quarantine. She has no answers to all these problems. Her mind feels blank. She puts the teakettle on the stove and falls asleep in the kitchen, her head on the table. She wakes to see steam shooting out the spout, a screaming whistle.

Lord God fades and moans, his eyelids a deep purple color, his eyes sunken as if he has aged years in the few days since Ruby saw him last, a withering too fast for sense. She tries to fluff his pillows but he whispers that she should leave them be. Ruby has never seen him look so spent and drained. She comes to stand over him and feel his forehead. The sour smell of urine is strong in the air. I think you had an accident, she says.

I've got no strength, he says. I can't even make it to the bathroom now. He's crying. I'm just an old goon now, peeing on myself and waiting to die. I'm not good for anything. Listen. I want you to shoot me.

Oh, hush, says Ruby. Nobody's shooting anybody.

You have to do it, says Lord God. He coughs blood again and struggles to breathe.

Ruby asks him what happened to the water jugs.

I gave them to the migrants. They were thirsty.

But you don't have any water yourself. There's barely a trickle left from the well.

Lord God makes a noncommittal motion with his bloodshot eyes. He starts to raise his hand and lets it drop. What does it matter anyway? Soon I don't think I'm going to need anything to drink.

Don't say that. You're going to get better. You're just under the weather.

We're all under the weather, says Lord God. Some more than others.

STANDING AT THE STREAKED and dusty windows of his pawnshop, watching the traffic rumble and roll down Northern Avenue, Hiram Page is in a blue funk, experiencing a crisis of belief. The iron bars that protect the shop windows from vandals and thieves cast shadows across Hiram's white hair and dignified face, as if he's staring out the windows of his own Folsom Prison.

He's always believed in his inherent superiority. Always thought he was top dog. Not the kind of seer or genius whose quotes he memorizes to trump whatever scant knowledge his customers might presume to attain, but savvy enough.

His intellectual competition includes the strays who wander through a pawnshop on any given day. That's not a high bar to clear. Consider the sad sacks, burnouts, disgruntleds, lowlifes, snaggletooths, and food-stamp misfits among whom he mingles. Bottom feeders. Most of them are lucky to button their shirts in order. If they can pay their power bill it's an accomplishment of note.

But of late a pack rat of worry has crept into his brain and made a nest.

For one thing he has come to suspect it may be time for the Wagon. He rejects the idea that alcoholism is a disease. Dylan Thomas had it right: An alcoholic is someone you don't like who drinks as much as you do. Of course Thomas was a famous drunk who died in a tavern, falling off his bar stool dead. A happy man you might say.

Hiram is not an indiscriminate, wayward sort of tippler. He likes his bourbon. It makes him feel good. It loosens up the bolts that keep him in place. When it wears off, the bolts are still there, still as tight as ever. He thinks the fools who attend AA meetings and make a public spectacle of themselves are losers and deadbeats. Any man with a strong sense of discipline knows when to stop, when he's had enough.

Lately Hiram does have his suspicions. Could be his time to call a dry spell is nigh. He worries that some of his decisions may perhaps have been made with a clouded mind. This kidnapping caper with Cousin Jack is not an action of which he should be proud. He takes another drink from his silver flask of Maker's Mark and savors the warm mist in his mouth. Still. If all had gone well the plan would have been a stroke of genius.

He rinses the smell with mouthwash and spits into the sink, telling himself that it's time to turn over a new leaf. Tomorrow will be different. The cobwebs are thick. At times his mind is cloudy. He forgets things.

What he does remember is that he instructed Cousin Jack Brown to waylay the child of that preacher's daughter. Which may or may not have been a wise move. But after repeated and unreturned calls to that hillbilly's cell phone he has come to the conclusion that said cousin is slightly more unreliable and incompetent than he imagined. He hasn't made his monthly payment and he refused to do what Hiram asked? A simple favor that any nitwit could accomplish? Who does he think he is? A nobody who can defy Hiram without retribution?

At the end of the business day Hiram asks Gracie Benavidez, his store manager, for a ride to the east side of town.

I have an unfortunate errand, he says. A client is several months behind on his payments. I believe I have to take custody of a vehicle under loan.

Gracie is too soft for this job. A motherly Hispanic woman in her forties, she gets a look of tender sadness on her face as she stares at her boss.

You're going to repo it?

I'm afraid so, Gracie. I'm afraid so.

I don't have to do anything, do I?

Hiram closes his eyes and shakes his head. He's a little unsteady on his feet, and perhaps he shouldn't be bothering with this errand at the moment, but he has a busy day planned tomorrow. His second wife, Honey, has a doctor's appointment. It appears the nubile young woman is with child again. And Hiram insists on doing the right thing and attending the doctor's visits, sitting beside her in the waiting room, holding her hand if need be.

In his deep Gregory Peck voice he says, If you can see fit to drop me off at the home of said vehicle, I'll be on my way and you on yours.

Well, okay, says Gracie. She gets her purse and heads for the front door. But I feel sorry for him, you know? No one wants his car to be taken away. What do you do without a car? You're like a nobody. Like less than nobody.

A man has to pay his bills, says Hiram. That's one of those unfortunate facts of life. If not, they come and take away what you have.

Still, says Gracie, I don't like it.

It's not the end of the world. He comes up with the payments, he gets the truck back.

Gracie says nothing on the drive to Jack Brown's house. Sitting in the passenger seat, Hiram feels emasculated and out of sorts. He's not used to the right side of a vehicle, to not being in control. The odd position, plus the bourbon fuzz on his brain and tongue, takes him back in time.

He remembers riding the bus to school, so many years ago, sitting next to a red-haired girl named Gail. He floats off on the currents of that memory, how they had a caterpillar exhibit in their sixth grade classroom, a gallon jar full of leaves and green caterpillars, how he liked to stand next to the comely teacher as she explained the life cycle of a moth—the pupae, the larvae, the cocoon, the big unfolding.

What was Gail's last name? McCarthy? Gail McCarthy? Yes, that's it. Red hair like soft copper. Hair the same color and luster as that of the preacher's daughter. Who doesn't want a thing to do with him. Whom he wanted to marry and keep in his bed and home. Who thinks he's disgusting no doubt and makes fun of him to her friends. Can you believe that old fart? That's what she says. What a lech he is. I wouldn't touch him with a ten-foot pole. That's what Ruby Cole says to her friend. Ruby Cole, who reminds him of Gail McCarthy. Who deserves to be taken down a notch. Who is unworthy.

Where do I turn? asks Gracie.

Hiram blinks out of his reverie as the car idles at a traffic light before the concrete pillars of I-25. Out his window a shantytown with cardboard-box people scuttling among the pigeon flutter and whine of tires on asphalt. Grimy hard-luck lost souls stare and hold makeshift signs asking for food or work.

Mr. Page? I know it's not my business but I can't help saying something. You shouldn't be doing this. It's not right.

Hiram turns away from the overpass denizens and their re-enactment of Christ's birth night in Bethlehem. He looks in the visor mirror and smooths his white hair beside his ears.

It's not a matter of right and wrong, he says. The boy has failed to make his monthly payments. He's three months in arrears now. Three months.

Yes, well. I understand that, says Gracie. But this is America. A man needs his car. Needs wheels to get around.

He could have paid me on time. I don't like doing this either.

In this country, without wheels you're not even a man. And you're about to take them away.

Hiram says nothing to that, watching the world go by from this odd spot on the passenger side. East of I-25 Pueblo takes on a dilapidated and dusty look. Tumbleweeds cluster against weathered storefronts. Spanish signs advertise Coca-Cola and bread. Beneath the billboard proclaiming *Se compra casas feas*, Hiram directs Gracie to pull over.

The white pickup sits in front of Jack Brown's shotgun shack just asking to be reclaimed. A German shepherd gets to its feet and heads toward them, barking, chain rattling as it scrapes on the wooden porch steps.

Don't do it, Mr. Page. Gracie shakes her head. It's going to come back to haunt you. I'm warning you. It's bad mojo.

Don't you worry, Gracie. Hiram steps out of the car and takes the keys from his pocket. Things like this happen every day.

She frowns and says good-bye, her expression pained and flinching. A shrug as she rolls up her window. Hiram stands on the road shoulder, waiting for her car to move so he can cross the street. He watches his distorted reflection in her window glass, a stretched-out image of a white-haired man alone in a bad neighborhood.

Maybe she's right. Maybe he should just let this one go. But if he did that, no one would respect him, right? He needs to make an example with Cousin Jack. You don't miss payments and leave your vehicle parked in the drive without a guard. A dog on a short chain isn't good enough.

The cold November air cuts through Hiram's linen shirt. A white coral reef of clouds casts a pall of chill. At a break in the traffic flow Hiram hurries across the street, reaching into his pocket for the keys. Jack Brown's cur barks and scrabbles at the end of his chain, cutting side to side like a snagged sailfish. The curtains are drawn. Hiram unlocks the truck door, slides into the driver's seat, and has the engine running in a heartbeat, expecting Cousin Jack to come running out in his underwear, waving a gun most likely, shouting all their business to the low-life neighbors in hope of a sympathetic mob.

It isn't until Hiram has pulled onto the road that he allows himself to glance back. The front door is closed, the dog still barks. At the stop sign a block later, he checks the rearview and sees no movement behind him.

Still his heart pounds and he guns the truck through a series of yellow lights, feeling short of breath and light-headed, feeling as if he's stealing the coffin for his own funeral.

ISRAEL JAMES SITS NAKED in the back of the buffalo head's office. He watches out the windows through a gap in the Venetian blinds, pensive and guilt-ridden. Down inside where it matters, he knows his soul is corrupt. He even suspects that one day, perhaps in the not-too-distant future, he will burn in the everlasting fires and torments of hell. But seeing how he's not exactly a saint to begin with, the underworld might be full of *compadres*.

The motel manager, Denise, aka Fufu, sits beside him on the

worn dog-brown sofa, her dirty-blond hair mashed flat on one side and a mess of split ends catching the late-day light like an alcoholic halo. She wears a loved-up look on her pie-pan face, half a lazy smile on her lips, sweetly swollen now and asking for more. Elray tells himself that he has to quit this woman but he just can't. She won't win a mother-of-the-year award but then, nobody's perfect. Her virtue is prickly as cactus but her nipples are like velvet sombreros.

He knows himself to be a career criminal, lovewise. When he sauntered into the lobby an hour before, he was all business. He rang the bell on the counter and when she appeared, he said, Afternoon, ma'am. Sheriff said there were municipal violations taking place in the Buffalo Head and told me I better ride over to do some undercover work.

He did, did he?

He did.

But Fufu was the one who pulled his belt loops and led him toward the inner office, walking backward, unbuttoning her blouse, saying, Perhaps I was going over the speed limit, Officer? She licked her lips and slid her hand down her shirt, popping the snap buttons one by one. Is there anything we can do so that little old me doesn't have to pay some nasty old fine?

O, sweet Lord, he said. You do make it hard to uphold the law.

From the lobby came the babble of Diego, Fufu's eighteen-month-old, penned in a plastic crib with mesh walls. He tugged at an electronic mobile of airplanes. The batteries were dead and, after a few minutes of batting the arms of the mobile in a circle, he yanked it loose. Soon he busied himself with methodically taking apart the wings. Meanwhile, in the back office, on the ratty brown sofa, his mother bit Elray's ears and squirmed in his lap like she was getting a tooth pulled without anesthesia.

That afternoon Elray is called to investigate the firebombing of an adult bookstore. He walks out to untie Apache, drowsy with the late-afternoon heat and the lingering of Fufu in his blood. The wind has picked up since morning. A high-pitched whine follows his every move as he puts his boot in the stirrup and swings onto Apache, patting her neck and telling her he's sorry to be moving in weather like this but he has a job to do and he can't sit on his ass in the back office of a motel fornicating all day.

The air is colored a dim brown, a khaki haze making the sun up high no stronger than a streetlight at dusk. The wind buffets a wall of grit and paper trash into which Elray rides, down the alley behind the Buffalo Head Inn, beside the train tracks. Apache nickers and bucks her head, cantering sideways as he urges her into the stinging murk. Migrant squatters living in the boxcars go about their business, some of the children waving, the women pretending not to see him. A couple of kids not more than nine years old each push a shopping cart full of recyclable cans and bottles, an old desktop computer monitor atop the mess, its cables and wires hanging like robot tentacles.

He skirts a newly formed shantytown of illegals and refugees, labeled by a bright red, white, and green banner stretched between two telephone poles that sports the legend AQUÍ EMPIEZA LA PATRIA. The squatters are mainly Latinos from the East and

South, construction workers and laborers who have left the suburbs of Georgia and Florida. Left or been chased out. The South is driving out its Mexicans, by hook or by crook. All the extra work has dried up, the locals saying it's now returning to a place that looks halfway like home. Or a halfway home for a fallen world. A small crowd of smiling boys trots beside Apache, chanting, *Monedas, por favor! Monedas, para comida! Por favor, señor! Tenemos hambre!*

They want coins for food.

Lo siento, says Elray. Apache clops on the pockmarked pavement. Sorry, kids. I got a job to do here.

They don't respond. A half-dozen boys reach up their hands, pleading, *Por favor! Monedas! Monedas!* One of the boys shouts, *A dónde va?* He stands in Apache's way. The boy is maybe thirteen years old, his hair cut short and jagged, one eye swollen as if from a punch. He wears a bandanna over his mouth, a Texas Tech hoodie. *Dame la pasta!* he shouts, scampering backward, holding a tree-branch spear, its tip whittled to a sharp point. He makes as if to stab Apache, shouting, *Le falta permisión pasar!* The horse doesn't stop but slows, raises her head, and nickers. Elray gives a slight tug on the reins. He pats her neck as she sidesteps, avoiding the boy.

Escuchame, muchacho, says Elray. *Soy la policía.*

No me importa, says the boy. You listen to me, he adds in English. I am king of this street. *Soy el rey.* Give me five dollars and you pass.

More boys gather as he speaks, massing behind him. All wear ragged clothes and hold baseball bats, pool cues, or tire irons.

They wear bandannas as face masks, like a ragtag group of child outlaws with no trains or banks left to rob.

Apache flares her nostrils and pins her ears. Elray strokes her neck and pauses, staring down the little gang. He tells them he can't be paying five dollars to pass every street. It's his job to patrol this road. They're in his way.

You little gang o' pissants had better move, he says. Now. While I'm still smiling.

It's early evening, a bite of coolness already in the air. Behind the boys a woman burns scrap two-by-fours in a campfire, the orange flames casting the boys' shadows across Apache. The tang of wood smoke smarts in Elray's eyes.

No puede tocarnos, says the boy. Five dollars or you do not pass.

Elray asks his name. *Dime tu nombre, rey.*

Me llamo Balthazar Cardenas. *Eres estupido si no lo sabes.*

Some of the other boys laugh. Most don't. Apache shakes her head and does not want to go forward. The crowd is over twenty strong. Some have machetes.

Pues, Balthazar. *Quieres conocer la carcél?*

He shrugs. *No tengo miedo. Tengo amigos allá!* The campfire flares as the cooking woman stokes it. The sharp air smells of diesel exhaust and wood smoke. One of the boys takes off running and several are talking so softly Elray can't make out what they're saying. Balthazar's face is lost in shadow. *Somos reconquistadores*, says Balthazar. *Tenemos hambre*, he repeats. You got some food, horse cop? he adds in English.

Claro, says Elray. *Hay tortas en los cojones de mi caballo.*

Balthazar jabs his spear and strikes Apache's nose.

The horse flinches and snorts. A boy grabs at the reins as another leaps into the air and reaches for Elray's pistol in its holster. Apache veers to the right, knocking one of them to the ground, and the boys scamper backward. They hurl rocks at horse and rider. Apache rolls her head back and twists to turn around. Elray struggles to control her, and before he has time to pull his sidearm, he hears a sharp sound and suddenly feels dizzy.

The boys are shouting, throwing chunks of loose asphalt from the potholed road. Elray's forehead is wet and warm, and his right eye feels funny, buzzing and gone dark. Apache wheels around and bolts away from the group, into the shaggy lawn of an abandoned apartment complex, before Elray manages to regain control. Sitting astride Apache with only one eye working, he pats her neck to calm her, passing a Dumpster littered with old mattresses and stinking plastic bags of trash. His heart pumps wild and fast. Right eye swollen shut and face streaked with blood from a scalp wound. Like a cyclops he is, and will be, and will have to explain how he's been bested by a gang of junior high *reconquistadores*, bless their black hearts.

He rides on, taking the back route to the Buffalo Head Inn, wiping blood from his face, holding his gauze face mask over the wound and pressing hard to staunch the flow. He passes beneath the buffalo and cowgirl lariat of the neon sign. He dismounts and ties Apache to the breezeway pillars outside the office. His ears yet ring and his head buzzes.

Inside the office Fufu says, O, good Lord. What happened to you?

I had a run-in with some troubled youths.

She shakes her head. You look like hell. She goes to the back office of the motel and returns with a bottle of hydrogen peroxide, rubbing alcohol, Band-Aids, and gauze.

Sit over there on the sofa. I think that lamp gives me the best light to clean you up by. She stares at him a moment, then adds, You're downright gory, you know that?

My hands are still shaking, says Elray. He holds one out. That's a hell of a thing, a cop's hand shaking.

Fufu pats his back. I know the idea of a horse cop sounds romantic and all, but I think you might be more of a target than anything else.

I was attacked by a gang of kids, he says. He closes his eyes and lays his head against the sofa arm in the lobby. They must've been twelve, thirteen years old, tops.

I heard the council wants to get rid of that crowd. They're planning to burn down that shantytown asap, says Fufu. She puts a rag at the top of the alcohol bottle and turns it upside down. Out the window a family of illegals passes by, riding a hobo wagon made of an old pickup bed pulled by a burro.

Hold on, now, she says. This will hurt for just a sec. She dabs the wound on his forehead with the alcohol rag, cleaning the blood from it. She uses a butterfly bandage to close the wound and says she thinks that will do it, no need for stitches. Elray flinches at the sting. Hush, she says. I'm almost done. Once his face is clean, she makes a square eye patch from the roll of gauze and tapes it into place.

There, she says. You can tell them it's just laser eye surgery gone wrong.

Elray winces. You know what? I'm thinking maybe it's time for a new career path.

THE DAY HE FEELS HEALTHY enough to stand on his worthless two feet for more than a few minutes Jack Brown leaves his shotgun shack and heads across town to Gata de la Luna's. He's on a mission to buy a curse. He doesn't care how much it costs. It will be worth whatever the cost, even if he has to sell his soul. If Gata will buy it.

The worst part about walking is the utter humiliation. Walking across town you might as well wear a sandwich sign shouting, LOSER. You know you're no longer scraping bottom but living in it. You stare up at the light above, a world beyond your touch, the light of the Normal World. You're in a dark and stinking hole. Nobody cares.

People with jobs pass you and cringe. They stare as if you're some kind of hitchhiking weirdo they want to identify later on the Crime Watch segment of the nightly news. Or they ignore you like a plague victim who might infect the rest of the healthy population. Which is not far off the mark.

Walking down the cracked sidewalk, heading west, Jack Brown doesn't know what to do with his hands. He feels like a goon swinging them as he walks. When he puts them in his pockets, it's like he's got something to hide. His feet hurt. Cowboy boots aren't meant to hike crosstown. The friction chafes a blister on his heel by the end of mile one.

Beneath the interstate he winds his way through a village of cardboard-box shanties and overpass dwellers. They seem like extras from an apocalypse survival film. Through the bands of weak shadows and jaundiced sun he passes, stepping over sleeping rag folk who clutch galvanized pipe in blackened nails for protection. Already his body stinks from a cold, unhealthy sweat. Jack realizes now these are his people: He even smells like them. A bearded misfit in a smeared and filthy hoodie stares out at him with yellow eyes.

Yo, pretty boy, he calls out, you got some spare change for a vet?

Jack Brown hurries on, ignoring the catcalls of the box people. He imagines a curse that makes Hiram Page impotent. Better yet, a curse that makes his penis shrivel until it's a small, limp thing no bigger than a Vienna sausage that breaks off, to his howling dismay. A curse that makes his tongue swell until he can't close his mouth. A curse that paralyzes him from the neck down. Or only his eyeballs can move, darting back and forth.

You take my truck and think you'll get off scot-free, do you? You try to use me and stab me in the back? You're going to get what you deserve, is what you're going to get.

Traffic rumbles and honks and hisses. Jack finds himself admiring and sizing up the vehicles, the grace of this one's chassis, the girth of that one's exhaust pipe. What he would give for fine upholstery to sit on, a steering wheel to grab. Kias, Toyotas, Ford pickups pass by like a parade of what Jack would like to drive. A vintage Thunderbird pulls into the Loaf 'n Jug at the corner of 4th and Evans. A bald dweeb gets out and starts to pump gas. Jack tells himself it should be he driving that car, not some fat, bald fart.

On the back side of a Walgreens parking lot, a scraggly mutt sidles up to Jack and sniffs his leg. Jack gives him a pat and rubs his ears. The dog wags his tail and tries to jump up and lick Jack's face, but Jack pushes him off. Go home, he says.

Jack turns his back and cuts across the parking lot to Evans, heads south. He refuses to look around, but soon a little white terrier trots ahead of him and the mutt chases it, both of them stopping to roll and nip at each other on a nearby lawn. Jack Brown keeps moving, feeling absurd. The dogs wag tails as he shouts and cusses at them to go home. It's as if he's taking these two strange dogs for a walk. He worries that they'll follow him too far and not remember their way home. If they even have one. He picks up a rock and throws it halfheartedly at the black mutt, who skips to the side, wagging his tail.

By the time he reaches Gata de la Luna's palm-reading shop the dogs lurk a block away. Jack hurries inside the door, the bell tinkling above him. The dogs creep him out, like a cloud of guilt. Like sins he has tried to forget.

Inside, it's dark and pungent. Jack takes a seat on a wooden bench and tries to get a good look at the photo of Gata on the wall opposite her Tarot-card table, but the beaded curtain is in his way. Through the curtain he can see a middle-aged Mexican woman seated in a ladder-back chair, leaning forward to look at the cards. The sweet smell of incense makes him feel dizzy. He hasn't eaten or showered, and after walking across town, he stinks something fierce. He worries that Gata will find him too repulsive to endure. A glass fish bowl filled with peppermints tempts him, but he fights off the urge to stuff a handful in his mouth, tries to retain a shred of dignity.

He can't shake the feeling that he's entered the lair of a *bruja*. He sits on a squeaky wicker chair and wipes his sweaty hands on his jeans. On the end table beside him sits a small box that appears to be made from alligator hide. A small, yellowed claw as a hook for the lid. He lifts the hook and peers into the box. Inside lies the bone-white shape of a raven's skull, resting upon a pair of gnarled black talons. Brown lifts the skull and stares into its hollow eye sockets. The grisly bone gives him confidence: It looks like something that could cast a spell itself. On a shelf across from Brown's chair is a large gray slab. After looking it over for a few minutes he realizes it's a dinosaur bone encased in rock.

The beads tinkle as the middle-aged Latina woman leaves, not even glancing in Jack's direction, as if they are both here to score drugs and don't want to recognize the other in a lineup.

The air inside the dark shop is cool. Jack has goose bumps when Gata steps through the beaded curtain. *Dios mio*, she says. You look like death warmed over, cowboy.

Jack rubs his arms and tells her he's been sick. But I'm feeling better some.

I hope so. You want a cure, is that it?

No, ma'am. I want to put a curse on someone.

A curse?

Somebody done me wrong. I aim to make him pay.

Oh, *qué lástima*. Gata shakes her head and leads Jack inside. She wears a low-cut white blouse decorated with embroidered flowers, long black hair on her shoulders like a black river. She sits him down and pours a cup of black tea.

A curse is a terrible thing, she says. You can't do this lightly. A curse is only to be used to right great wrongs.

This is a great wrong. I can't say what it is. But it's bad. Serious bad.

Gata scrutinizes Jack's face as if reading his fortune in his shaggy eyebrows, spiky hair, and dimpled chin. He meets her gaze at first, as he's always been told to look a man in the eye and even if Gata isn't a man, she sure acts as strong as one, far as he's concerned. But her gaze and beauty make him squirm.

It was horrible, what he wanted me to do.

I tailor a curse for the wrong that it intends to right. I don't have some generic, one-size-fits-all wickedness to call down on him. What was it?

I can't say.

She keeps staring, as if trying to hypnotize him. Jack can't stand it. He turns away and meets the yellow-and-black eyes of a stuffed owl up in a corner of the room. The next thing he feels is the touch of Gata de la Luna's hands on the back of his neck.

Relax. You've had a great pain and it shows.

He goes squishy all at once, his lips trembling when he says, I got no job and no money and now this. I been down before but lately I hit some kind of new low.

You stink too. Gata looses a soft, throaty laugh, patting his cheek with a warm hand.

I know. He sniffles. I'm just in a hole. I just got to dig myself out of it.

Come on. She tugs his collar. Come with me.

He gets to his feet and stands there like a child at day care, waiting for directions. She takes his hand and leads him through a door and down a hallway, up a flight of stairs, and into a small bathroom with a checkered tile floor and a window looking out on a pine tree in the backyard. There's a shower cabinet and a toilet, incense holder and candles on the windowsill. She leans into the shower cabinet and turns on the hot water, shows him where the towels, shampoo, and soap are. Get yourself cleaned up, she says. And hurry. I've got people coming later.

O, Jesus, he says. I'm so dirty you have to clean me up.

Es verdad! She laughs. Get in there, she adds. You'll feel a hundred percent.

A half hour later he's clean, wrapped in a robe, sipping from a mug of hot tea. They sit in her kitchen and she's got a fire in her woodstove. She makes him a bowl of posole and fries up tortillas for chalupas.

He tells her the whole story as they eat dinner. She makes him stop and backtrack several times, asking who did what and why, shaking her head in disbelief.

He wanted me to kidnap a baby, insists Jack.

Who?

Hiram Page. You know him? He's got a pawnshop a few blocks west of here. HP Pawns.

I know this man. He's good for nothing. Gata stares at Jack. Eat some more, she says. You look like a scarecrow.

Good for nothing is right. He sold me a truck and took me to the cleaners is what he did. First he made me give up my grandmother's diamond ring. Then I missed a couple payments and he repo'd me, but before that he said he'd let me keep the truck if I kidnapped this baby girl.

Gata hisses. You don't look like the kind of man who kidnaps babies.

I couldn't do it, says Jack. I just couldn't. So he took my truck and now I got no job and no truck and no ring neither. I'm up shit creek without a paddle. All because of him.

This is *muy loco*. Who did he want you to kidnap?

A little girl who lives on a ranch out west of town, off Red Creek Road. I think he's mad at her parents or something. He said she wouldn't be hurt. That they weren't even going to ask for ransom, just give her back in a day or two. But I don't know what he had planned. He's a liar, that man is.

Gata sighs, sips a spoonful of her posole. She has three grown children, two girls who already have children of their own.

Tell me more, she says. Why would he do such a thing?

He wouldn't tell me much, but she lives with her grandfather. I saw him. Scary old graybeard is who he is.

This is *la verdad*? You swear?

On a stack of Bibles. The man told me to do it and when I didn't, he took my truck. That's why I had to walk here. And that's not even the worst. His nephew, he killed a man. And got away with it.

Gata shakes her head and hisses through her teeth as Jack tells the story. I saw him do it, he adds. I swear to God. He shot that trucker dead.

Who knows about this?

Hiram Page knows. He even hired that dipshit to be his body-

279

guard. It's his brother's kid and some kind of cousin to me, I guess. But he acts like his shit don't stink.

Pues, bien. What kind of curse you want? Blindness? Impotence? Financial ruin?

What about all three? asks Jack.

Gata shakes her head. Don't get greedy. A curse is a dangerous thing to wish upon anyone, even a *cabron.* You will pay a price for a curse. More than you think.

Well, I don't have much money, says Jack. I might have to owe you.

That's not the price I mean. There's a price that goes beyond money. Gata reaches over and taps Jack's chest. The price of your soul, maybe.

You want me to sell my soul to buy this curse?

You cannot sell your soul for such a thing, but you must pay for it somehow. Nothing in this world is free.

You're telling me. Money is how I got into this mess.

Gata closes her eyes as if dissolving into a trance. Her face resembles that of a stone idol, cryptic and remote. Jack starts to speak and she holds up one hand to stop him, eyes still closed, as if she's attempting to commune with the dead and the phone is ringing. The darkness of the room blurs her features, the lines of her neck erased, the wrinkles at the corners of her eyes lost in the shadows.

Jack stares at her breasts and wonders what it would be like to nurse them. A fly buzzes against a window. It's late afternoon by now, and in the shadows of the kitchen, Jack notices the gaping nose hole of a human skull on a shelf above the window-unit air conditioner. Did the owner of that skull sell his soul too? And that's all that's left of him now, a trinket? The moment he glances back at Gata she has her eyes open wide. Go now, she says. It is done.

Jack's mouth hangs open for a moment. Gata rises from the table and pushes her coal-black hair over her shoulders.

What kind of curse is it? asks Jack.

It's the right kind, says Gata. Now go. We must not speak of it anymore.

After Jack Brown leaves her shop, Gata stands beside the window and watches him walk away, followed by a pair of dogs. She taps her long red fingernails against the sill. She fixes herself a cup of strong tea and massages her temples.

Is that fool lying? She doesn't think so. She remembers hearing about that hijacking on the news. That's bad trouble, prison trouble. And why would the pawnbroker want to kidnap a little girl? The world is inscrutable and infested with evil. What if it were her baby, or her daughter's? She sips her tea and watches traffic on Northern Avenue, most of it headed west, the direction of HP Pawns. George Crowfoot would like to hear about this. Plus his friend Elray.

Before long she's on the phone and telling the world.

LORD GOD SQUIRMS in his bed, his eyeballs bloodshot and burning, lips cracked and face scorched. He tells Ruby to load the shotgun and keep cartridges at hand. The bears will be coming soon, he says. They have nothing to eat in the high country. It's their nature, he adds. They are neither good nor evil. But hungry.

Don't worry, Papa, says Ruby. She presses a cool, wet washcloth to his forehead. Don't worry about any bears.

Have you burned the garbage? If they eat the garbage they'll expect food from you.

We can't burn it, she says. It's locked in the shed. Like always.

They'll rip the shed doors off. You have to burn it. It's the smell. They'll come for the smell.

The wind is too high for a fire. We can't go outside, Papa. The dust is too thick.

It's the end of the world, says Lord God.

Ruby squeezes out another wet washcloth and replaces the one on his forehead. I hope not, she says.

Hope doesn't make a difference.

I thought you always told me to have faith? Aren't hope and faith the same thing?

Lord God closes his burning eyes and grimaces. Faint light from a gap in the curtained windows softens the wrinkles and furrows of his face. The tendons and windpipe in his throat resemble loose roots beneath his pale, slack skin, covered with gray stubble. The dome of his skull seems a talisman, his eye sockets stark rings of bone. From beyond his bedroom door comes the sound of his granddaughter crying.

What's Lila doing here? I don't want her to get sick.

Mama had to work. We talked to the hospital and they think

Lila's immune after being around me and not getting the fever. They think she's safe enough.

Who's taking care of her?

Ruby hesitates. She wants to lie but can't think of anything convincing. Her father is always able to smell a lie.

My friend is here, she says. He's good with Lila and he's watching her while I take care of you.

Your friend?

Ward. The bird scientist.

Lord God breathes roughly, his hollowed eyes staring into space, into Ruby's future without his presence.

What kind of man is he?

He's a good man.

How can you trust Lila with a stranger?

He's not a stranger. He's the man I've been working for, remember?

Since when?

I've been counting birds for him.

That doesn't make sense. Counting birds.

Yes, it does. How else would you know how many there are?

That's like counting motes of dust. It's impossible.

No, it isn't. They're bigger than that.

This man in there with Lila. What does he do for money?

I told you. He counts birds.

Lord God twists his head and makes a face. That's ridiculous. He's a fool if that's what he does for a living.

Hush, Papa. He's a scientist. He's studying bird populations.

What kind of job is that?

He's an ornithologist. The birds, they're a sign of other things. They're dying out.

Lord God chuffs. I could've told you that. Without no counting.

Well, that's what he's doing. Being exact about it.

The birds are a sign, yes, sir. A sign of things to come. But science won't help us. Nothing will.

Hush, Papa. I have to go now. I'll be back in a while with some tea, okay?

Don't worry about me, says Lord God. I'll be gone soon.

Don't keep saying that.

It's the truth. You keep an eye on your child. She's young and she doesn't deserve any strange men around her.

He's not a stranger. He's a savior.

A savior? Ha, says Lord God. That's even worse.

In the kitchen, Ward is trying to feed Lila pasta shells. She has stopped crying but is having none of it, twisting her head when he tries to put the pasta in her mouth.

How's the little monster? asks Ruby.

Fussy. Ward leans back and shrugs. She's not thrilled with pasta, I guess.

Lila smiles and scrunches up her face, sticks out her tongue and sputters. She looks at Ward and then at Ruby, holds a spoon in her small hand and dangles it over the edge of her high-chair platform, then lets it drop.

The wind gusts and whistles at the kitchen window, the yard outside blustered and unkempt, a Raven perched on the wood-shed weather vane, its shaggy neck feathers ruffled.

How's he feeling?

Awful. Ruby picks up the spoon Lila dropped and sits beside her in the creaky wooden chair. She gives Lila the spoon and puts a pasta shell in her mouth. Lila takes the shell and waves the spoon in the air, chewing with her mouth open.

You think he's getting better or worse?

He's talking about the bears again.

The bears?

They come down from the mountains during droughts. When there's no food up where they live.

And?

They come down to feed.

On what?

On little girls who don't eat their pasta.

By afternoon the wind eases to gusts and sudden squalls. The vista beyond the woodshed and their property opens to the juniper plateau. A layer of dust coats the yuccas and cholla, as if the land itself is an old thing left to gather dust in an abandoned home. Ward watches a murder of Crows flap and squawk past the yard, diving and swooping at the wide wings of a Red-Tailed Hawk. The hawk glides and beats its wings, fades into the tan sky.

Ward takes these sightings as a good sign, as a sign of hope. Ruby has told him about her conversation with Lord God. Now the blades of hope and faith turn in Ward's head like a windmill. Too often *faith* is the word preachers use to ask for money. When he questioned the idea of a benevolent God who would let so many suffer and let his daughter die in pain, he was told the

Lord works in mysterious ways. That he had to have faith. That he had to let go of his earthly hopes and dreams and put his soul in the hands of the Lord, who would reward him with ever-lasting life.

Ward can never lose the suspicion that the reward of blind faith is blindness.

Hope is a smaller, more reliable thing. You don't have to bank on the idea of a supreme being to hope for a better day, for Lila not to come down with the fever, for Ruby to keep a shelter over her head, for rain to come in the summer, as it has in the past. Faith is a shield, an excuse, an alibi.

Hope is something you can carry in your pocket. Something you can give to others. Something you can act on.

JACK BROWN HEARS his German shepherd barking in the unkempt yard of the bungalow for which he has not paid rent for three months now. After a moment he looks out to see a policeman dismounting from a chestnut horse. Monster lunges at the end of his chain, spooking the mare, who backsteps a few feet until the cop ties the reins to the chain-link fence.

Brown stares, standing frozen in his underwear, then takes to cussing and pulling on his pants. Before he can decide what to do first—bolt out the back door or step outside to quiet Monster—the cop is on the porch and knocking, sharp and loud, like an FBI agent. Brown shouts, Just a minute, rushes to his bedroom for a T-shirt, dons it, and opens the door, hair spiky and unwashed, eyes crusty.

Are you William Henry Brown?

Well, yes. I suppose so.

Israel James smiles and says, Remember me?

AT EVENING LORD GOD'S throat closes up. His breath rattles in raspy pops and gurgles. Ruby ministers to him with soup, wet washcloths, and apple juice. He shoos her away.

Bring me that man you have in our home. I want a word with him.

Ruby stares at her father. Don't say anything ugly to him. He's a good man and he doesn't deserve any hatefulness.

Bring me that man. He's under my roof and by God I'll say what I want, to him or anybody else.

His name's Ward.

Lord God leans forward and looses a wet cough into a ball of tissue. When he can breathe again he says, Okay, then. I want to meet this Ward. He falls back on his pillows and composes his craggy face. Let's have a look-see.

Ruby finds Ward in the living room, showing Lila a stack of flash cards. He bought her the deck the last time he was in Denver. Images of birds.

This is a Hooded Oriole, pretty yellow-and-black feathers. And this is a Painted Bunting, he says, holding up the card. It's a beautiful, showy bird, but a shy thing. You have to get close to it to see all these colors. Or look through binoculars. That's what most people do. Isn't that a pretty bird?

Lila points at the card and says, Kitty.

287

Ruby watches them and waits. That's her favorite word. Everything is *kitty.*

Ward nods. I like the sound of that. It could be a motto. *Everything is kitty.*

Lila grins and bites the edge of the bird card. Ward tries to pull it away from her gently, saying, Don't eat the card, Pinky. It's not good for you.

Papa wants a word with you, says Ruby. I'll take her.

Ward looks up. How's he doing?

I don't know. He's having trouble breathing.

Okay. Anything I should be careful not to say?

Ruby lifts Lila and nuzzles her cheek. Avoid the Jesus jokes?

Ward nods. No problem.

Otherwise, be honest. He'll see right through anything that sounds false or fake.

I'm not good at lying anyway.

Don't be scared, says Ruby. He won't bite.

Ward carries a candle in a ceramic Mexican candleholder for light. The flame casts an amber light down the hallway. The power is out again. Here in the boonies, power outages are becoming frequent. As he enters Lord God's room, with its smell of mentholatum and sickness, it seems as if he's going back in time—bowing before a biblical father, holding a candle, heading into darkness. He can hear Lord God breathing before he sees him. When he nears, the old man's face is craggy and harsh. Ward doesn't shake his hand but introduces himself and says he wishes they could have met in better circumstances. Times will be better, he adds. You'll pull through this.

Lord God gives a slight, almost invisible shrug. He breathes through his mouth, but his eyes are bright and liquid in the candlelight. We'll all be gone at some point. I'm just closer than most, I guess.

It seems you're under the weather.

Is that what you call it?

Well.

I'm on my deathbed and you call that under the weather?

Ward asks if he can get him anything. Are you thirsty?

Lord God closes his eyes. Ruby takes good care of me. That's what she's here for. What about you? What are you here for?

Well, I guess I'm here to take care of Ruby. Do what I can. I help with Lila.

You guess.

Well, yes. It's an expression.

Lord God shakes his head. If you're spending time with my daughter you better be more than guessing.

Yes, sir. I see your point.

And what about Lila? You help with her? You're old enough to have a wife and daughter of your own. Why don't you?

I did. I had a wife and child.

You did.

They passed away two years ago. From the fever.

Lord God waits. Ward puts his hands in his back pockets and leans against the wall. So I don't have anyone anymore. Ruby started working for me, and she needs somebody.

That she does, says Lord God. Are you that somebody? Are you a good man?

I try to be.

You don't try. You either are or you're not.

It doesn't seem that easy to me. But I'll care for Ruby and Lila. I'll do my best to keep them safe from harm.

You believe that Jesus Christ is the son of God?

No, sir. I don't.

Well, then. What do you believe?

I don't know.

You mean you believe in nothing? Is that it?

I don't think it's an either/or. Not a choice of one or the other.

It's the choice of Christ or Satan.

I don't think so. I don't believe in Christ or Satan. I think those are legends or ideas, ways we try to understand the mystery of the world.

Ideas, ha. Lord God makes a motion with his chin, gray-stubbled, a wattle of throat skin beneath. You think ideas are going to take care of those girls?

No, sir. I think actions are. My actions, best I can.

You can be damned to the fires of hell for your actions.

I think hell is an idea. A human idea to serve as a warning for bad behavior.

Is that what you think? For a moment Lord God wears an ugly smile. The sinners roasting in hell are full of ideas, I betcha. He begins to laugh and soon he's leaning over the side of the bed, coughing jaggedly, spitting blood.

Ward reaches to hold his body upright and Lord God pushes

him away. He wheezes and gasps and leans back on the pillows. I don't need your help. I got a daughter, a good daughter, takes care of me. Now you say you want to take care of her. And you believe in no God, no nothin'. Makes me think she be taking care of you before long.

I have a career, says Ward. I make a living. I'll make sure Ruby and Lila won't want for the important things in life.

A career? Lord God grimaces. Counting birds. You call that a career.

I'm an expert at it. I make sense of things. They pay me for it.

Who does?

I work for an institute.

Lord God pushes back his blankets and squirms, shivering in pain. I guess that's good for now. We'll see, though. Things going to get worse.

Maybe so, says Ward. I hope not.

What you hope won't make a hill of beans. A few years from now there won't be institutes enough to pay all the fools in the world.

I'm not a fool, Mr. Cole.

That's what you say. Lord God closes his eyes, a thin trickle of blood below one nostril, in the tangle of his beard.

Ward says he'd better go get Ruby.

That's right. What do I know? You best be leaving this dying fool. Lord God's voice is hoarse and clotted with mucus, barely a wet whisper. But before you go, let me warn you about something. Ruby tell you about that Page fella who's got an eye for her? She might have said I tried to get her to marry him.

Yes, sir. She did.

Well, I wised up. Watch out for him. I think he got his sights set on Ruby, fixed on the notion and hungry for her. I was a fool listening to other fools to have anything to do with that man. But I did and once I saw the light I broke it off. He took it personal. He finds out I'm gone he might come calling.

I'll keep an eye out, sir. My word. And I'll take care of both Ruby and Lila.

You better. Lord God sinks back into his pillows, the skein of blood trailing down his upper lip. Now, go on. Watch out for my girl. You don't, I'll come back from the dead. Make you believe hell's a lot more than an idea. That's for damn sure.

Lord God takes to coughing again, hunched over, body tensed and wracked with pain. Ruby is in the hallway when Ward goes for her. You go watch Lila, she whispers. I'll stay with him now. She squeezes Ward's hand and steps into her father's room, shuts the door.

Ward forgot to grab his candleholder. The hallway is pitch black. He moves forward, feeling the walls, until he turns the corner and sees the lantern light in the kitchen, hears the light voice of Lila saying, Kitty kitty kitty.

THE FIRST THING Hiram Page notices when arriving at work is a patrol car in the parking lot, his dimwit nephew with his legs spread wide and hands on the hood, being cuffed by a Pueblo County sheriff's deputy. A chestnut horse stands off to the side, with a cop in the saddle. It clomps its hooves nervously when Hiram pulls in and kills the engine. He gets out and holds the door open for his dachshund, Weenie, helping the short-legged dog down from the pickup cab. He stares at the arrest in progress, asks what this is all about.

Officer Israel James grins. I believe this young buck has run afoul of the law. Me, I'm just here for moral support. To make sure all is on the up-and-up.

Uncle Hiram, you'll get this straightened out, won't you?

Hiram removes his sunglasses and doesn't say a word. It's early and he won't open for another hour. It's a pleasant morning, too peaceful for hubbub and mayhem: The sky is a sinless blue and the air has the cold taste of winter on its way.

I take it my employee here is being charged with a crime?

The patrolman is a short, thick-necked deputy whose uniform is too tight around his belly, wearing a regulation cowboy hat and black belt complete with sidearm and can of mace. You take it right, he says, leading Ezra by an elbow to the rear passenger-side door. You might say this boy's in some deep shit, but I suppose that's jumping the gun.

Has he been read his rights?

He has, says Elray. You want us to read them again, Mr. Page?

Ezra shakes his head. No use in that. I ain't saying a word.

What are the charges? asks Hiram.

Oh, just a little case of murder. Apache dips her muscular neck down to scratch her cheek against her leg. Elray tugs at the reins and pulls her head up. I think your nephew here has been hanging out with the wrong crowd, he adds.

You'll post bail for me, won't you, Uncle?

Hiram turns away and says, I'll see what I can do. He walks toward the pawnshop entrance, clicking his tongue for Weenie to follow.

Another vehicle pulls into the lot before he can even get the keys in the door. A blue-and-white van with a small dish antenna mounted on its roof and its sides emblazoned with the call letters and legend of the station, KXDO NEWS—LIVE, LOCAL, LATE-BREAKING. A junkie-thin techie gets out, wearing a ball cap backward, carrying a video camera. He's followed by a short, dark-haired Asian woman. The woman straightens her outfit and tucks her hair into place as the techie shoulders the camera and focuses on her, the two discussing how to set up the shot.

Hiram watches them for a moment, says, Good God. It must be my lucky day.

Both stop talking and turn to him. Pardon me? asks the woman.

Hiram nods and says in his best godlike baritone, Looks like I won the Lotto this morning.

The young reporter touches her hair and steps forward, holding a microphone out as if offering Hiram said prize. She asks if he's the owner.

Hiram smiles and answers, Guilty as charged.

Do you have any comment on the graffiti?

The bony cameraman shoulders his video equipment and trains the lens on Hiram, who does his best to wear a poker face, as if looking at a pair of deuces. Ezra's arrest distracted him from the words scrawled across the bars and windows of his pawnshop. He regards his ex-convenience-store-cum-pawnshop now with momentary shock, seeing a mess of freshly spray-painted accusations: Child Molester, Kidnapper, *Pervertidor.*

The red paint drips and dribbles bloody punctuation at the ends of letters, like horror-movie credits. It starts at the lower left-hand corner of the building, on the brick base, then splays across the iron window gates and makes dashes on the glass behind.

Hiram's face struggles to suppress any disgust or dismay, anger or outrage. He smooths his white hair at his temples and jingles the keys in his pockets. At his feet is a pulpy mess of French fries spilled from a white Wendy's bag. Weenie sniffs at it. Hiram steps aside and scrapes the mess from his cowboy boots. Looks like someone's been using my parking lot as a dump site, haven't they?

Hiram walks to the door and unlocks it, feeling the presence of the reporter and her sidekick behind him, Weenie at his heels. Does he have any idea why his shop would be targeted? Is it the work of street gangs? Who might be the "pervert" or "child molester" in his shop?

Hiram pauses before he steps inside. I have no idea what this is all about. He smiles into the camera. I'm just a tax-paying citizen whose shop has been vandalized.

The young Asian reporter starts to speak and he cuts her off. I'm sorry, you'll excuse me if I don't have more time to chat. He furrows his brow and frowns. It appears I'll have to research the whereabouts of a paint-removal specialist.

Inside the dark shop, Hiram's brain throbs from a sudden, sharp headache. Weenie's claws tap on the tile floor as she waddles to her doggy bed behind the counter. Hiram feels faint and short of breath, limps to the back office and, with trembling hands, removes a liter of Coca-Cola from the small refrigerator. He has to crouch to retrieve the bottle from the bottom shelf of the fridge, which is tucked between a pair of file cabinets below the counter.

He rises quickly, feeling a rush of blood to his brain. All goes black and dizzy. Hiram grips the counter and steadies himself until his vision comes back. The veins in his temple thud as he fixes himself a stiff drink of bourbon and Coke. The cool, syrupy taste warms his throat, coats it with an alcoholic afterburn. He watches through the window bars as outside the reporter speaks into her microphone, the cameraman recording, a crowd of onlookers gawking behind her, kids jumping and waving.

After Hiram manages to steady his breath, he comes to stand behind the gun counter. He tries to calculate just how deep this trouble is and to imagine how he's going to wreak his vengeance on Cousin Dipshit.

But who did this? Jack would never be that bold. He got someone else to do it for him? Perhaps. How would he entice others to do his dirty work? Does Preacher John Cole know anything about this little caper gone wrong?

When Gracie arrives a quarter hour before opening, Hiram Page is already on his fourth drink. She gives him a wary look as he stands there sipping from his plastic cup, as he calls out to her in an unnaturally loud and cheery voice, Well, don't you look ravishing this morning!

She frowns and asks about the reporters, the graffiti. Someone's trying to get back at you, Mr. Page.

The many disgruntleds, he says. Any idea who it is?

She goes about her business without a reply, putting her purse in the back office, where she keeps it during work hours, checking her makeup, arranging things by the checkout counter. Hiram weaves and burps, standing behind her. He tries to focus. The world is getting a bit fuzzy around the edges.

Pervert? he says. Well, I suppose I'm no angel, but that's going a bit far. Like Mae West said, I generally avoid temptation unless I can't resist it.

Gracie asks would it be possible for her to leave early? Will Ezra be here today? She promised her daughter she would take her to the hospital. She's having an ultrasound to find out what her baby is. Hiram starts to make a joke about what the baby is today might be something different than what it will be tomorrow, but he holds his tongue.

It appears that my nephew has run afoul of the law, he says. In fact they had him in handcuffs when I pulled in this morning.

Gracie clicks her tongue. I don't know about that boy. I don't like the way he looks at Elena.

Yes, well, he's family. We have to look out for our own, don't we?

Hiram goes on to tell Gracie yes, she can leave early, even offering her an hour earlier than she asked, saying that way she won't have to be rushing around to get there on time. He's being extra nice. Gracie will remember this later, push comes to shove.

Any idea who might have done this artwork? he asks again.

Gracie shakes her head. Looks like somebody put *el mal de ojo* on you.

Late in the afternoon Hiram Page finds himself alone in the shop, feeding Weenie a doggy treat, when the biggest Indian he has ever seen enters carrying a bowling-ball bag. He's unsmiling and mean-ass-looking, wearing his long black hair in a ponytail, a death's-head belt buckle, and black cowboy boots with metal toe ornaments the shape of longhorns. Hiram's hands start sweating as soon as he sees him.

Afternoon, friend. What can I do you for?

George Armstrong Crowfoot hefts the bag in the air, then sets it on the counter. I've got something you might be interested in.

Hiram gives Weenie a final rub and shoos her to the red-plaid pillow of her doggy bed.

Sorry, but I can't help you there. I've got a dozen already and it appears the bowling craze may have—

As he's talking Crowfoot unzips the bag and pulls out the withered human head.

Friend of mine told me this was the head of Black Jack Ketchum, famous outlaw hanged in New Mexico years ago. I don't buy it, but I figured pawnshops like oddities.

Hiram regards the head for a moment, even leans in close to get a better look without touching it.

I've seen that head before. A Mr. Rodriguez offered it to me.

When was that?

I don't recall.

You seen him lately?

Nope. Hiram gives Crowfoot an all-business smile. As I said before, I think I'll pass.

Crowfoot raises it in the air. You sure? You could place it on a pike. Wow the onlookers.

Sorry, pal. I said I'll pass.

Crowfoot shrugs and places the head back on the counter. Tell you what. I'll give you a minute to reconsider. I even have a price in mind. One thousand dollars.

Hiram scoffs. A thousand for that? Do I look stupid?

Crowfoot allows that perhaps they could barter. He says he'd like to look at the handguns.

Hiram squints at him and says, Easier said than done.

How so? You wouldn't be refusing my business, now, would you?

If you plan on purchasing a firearm, we'll have to do a background check first. Fill out some paperwork.

Humor me, says Crowfoot. He points at a Beretta beneath the glass counter. I like the look of that one.

The afternoon sunlight gushes through the jaundiced shop windows and fills the room with a golden glow. Hiram moves slowly to the gun counter and places the Beretta atop the display case.

Looks like you had a visit from the spray-can patrol last night, says Crowfoot.

Pardon me?

We got a joke name for you, says Crowfoot. He Who Sells Crap to Suckers. But now that's changed. Now you're the man who tells others to steal children for him. You're the man who owes me money.

I'm at a loss here. What's your name again?

You're a smart guy. Always quoting this and that. You know what this is about.

This what?

This visit. I came up with that figure of one thousand dollars because it's what you owe me.

For what?

For services rendered. My part in a cattle delivery I was never paid.

I tell you what, Hiram says, I won't call the authorities if you walk out the door while I'm still in a good mood.

Call them. Be my guest.

It's my shop. I have the right to refuse—

We can talk about how you tried to con some halfwit name of Jack Brown into kidnapping a little girl, daughter of a woman who spurned you. Out Red Creek Road. That's the story I hear. They might be interested to know a few of those details. 'Less you bought off so many of them the whole corral is in your pocket.

Well, that all sounds rather dastardly. It's the first I've heard of it.

Crowfoot twirls the Beretta and says, A lying man always denies the truth.

You think you know everything, don't you?

I know enough.

You must know who did this little mural on my storefront, then, don't you?

Crowfoot stares without blinking. You want to pin some vandalism on me? That's funny.

You're the one making threats here.

No threats. Crowfoot scratches his neck with the barrel of the gun. His high cheekbones and full lips give his face a fearless expression. He seems prepared to wait. I'm here on what you might call a last-chance mission, he adds. Thought you might appreciate knowing what you're dealing with.

You thought wrong.

I was the one stomped by a steer and left to my own devices. Now I'm back.

I've had enough of this. Hand me the gun and take a hike.

Be my guest. Crowfoot places the Beretta on the counter, then reaches behind his back and pulls out a similar pistol. I got my own anyways. He fishes in his pocket and brings out a small clip, slides it into the pistol. And I just happen to have a loaded clip right here.

Hiram stands still. I asked you to leave, he repeats.

I asked for the thousand you owe me.

In what could be his last moments among the realm of the living, Hiram Page experiences a twinge of guilt and remorse, a sense that things have taken a wrong turn, he's miscalculated the variables. He puts his hands on the counter, an attitude of submission.

Looks like you've got me. But we've all got something. I've got two wives and three children, another one on the way. You want to spend years in prison, writing "I'm sorry" letters to those orphans?

His rich Gregory Peck voice quavers as he speaks. The world is turning too fast. There's no time to think. He stares at Crowfoot, who holds the loaded gun with the barrel pointed toward the ceiling, until finally he drops his gaze.

I'm locking up, he says. You do what you're going to do. Me, I got kids to feed.

Here, says Crowfoot. He offers the pistol in his wide hand, fingers splayed, palm up. If you think that's the difference between us, you can have it. You could shoot me right here. Say I was robbing you.

I could, says Hiram. He can feel his hands shaking, his palms slick with sweat.

But you won't. You're chicken.

Don't tempt me.

I want that grand, adds Crowfoot. It's what I'm owed.

Hiram goes to his cash register, turns a key, the drawer pops open. He counts out ten twenties and places them on the counter in front of Crowfoot. That's two hundred, he says. All I have on hand at the moment. And then we're even.

Crowfoot picks up the money and flings it in Page's face. What do you think I am, stupid? You owe me a grand. I know where you live. Little Pueblo, right? You got little pissant guards protecting those pretty wives? I bet they're lonesome in the daytime.

Hiram turns and heads to the back office, opens the wire-mesh gate door. Behind him he hears the sound of Crowfoot's boots on the tile floor, the jingle of the front door opening. Hiram enters the office cage and closes it, the clang ringing unnaturally loud in the empty pawnshop. He resists the impulse to duck and hide.

He has some dignity left. It may be tiny. It may be meaning-less. But he's not diving beneath the desk like a frightened child. Not after the man just gave him the chance to take the pistol outright.

In his cage in the now silent shop, the bottle of bourbon is golden and lovely, like a flask that holds an elixir that offers eternal life. He fills a shot glass and gulps as if it's his last drop. When he can't stand the suspense any longer, he peers behind a pillar and through the wire mesh. Crowfoot is gone.

Hiram Page notices his hands are still shaking. On the counter sits the head of an infamous outlaw or more likely Morris Dinwoody, a world-class nobody, the lipless mouth gaping wide to show its awful teeth.

By the third jigger of whiskey Page's nerves have calmed. A hot mist fills his mouth as he collects the twenties off the floor and returns them to the cash register. He puts Weenie in the crook of his arm and scratches her floppy dog ears, douses the lights, and steps outside into a chilly November dusk in this di-lapidated edge of Mexican town. He heads toward his pickup, fishing the keys from his pocket. As he backs out of the parking lot, he can't help but stare at the spray-painted legend of accusa-tions, a wave of shame washing through him, realizing too many people know his blackest heart, too many to strike back at or wish away.

No matter: All will pass with time. He has another gulp of whiskey from his silver flask as he fiddles with his radio. He's go-ing home to his wives, one of whom is going to have another baby.

God will forgive. It's his job.

Hiram drives past a used-car lot where an enormous inflatable yellow gorilla sits, tethered by guy wires. The wind sings in his windows. He floats and drifts and forgets he's at the wheel. This too shall pass. There's always time. Time to make up for mistakes, to turn over that proverbial new leaf. Everything happens to everybody sooner or later if there is enough time. Time is but the stream I go a-fishing in.

By the intersection of Pueblo Boulevard and Thatcher Avenue, he's talking to himself, quoting this and that, forgetful of what he's doing, lost in his labyrinthine mind full of blind back-alley deals and Indians with tomahawks, preachers' daughters and deadbeat cousins.

The next thing he knows the airbag explodes in his face, the world turns over and over and over. He comes to upside down, the inflated airbag jamming his neck against the head rest. Outside his window all he can see is grass and dirt. The truck's alarm blares. The warm, wet feel of blood on his face. He struggles to move. From above him somewhere a voice calls out, Hey, mister! You all right? Are you all right in there?

He tries to speak but no sound comes out. I'm okay, he tries to say. I'm okay.

He hears a soft whimpering, feels the warm, wet touch of Weenie's tongue licking his neck.

Any minute now, he'll get out of this jam.

RUBY ASKS WARD to dig Lord God's grave in the back-yard. He wanted to rest close to home, she says. He showed me a place near the corner of the fence, behind the woodshed. The ground's kind of hard there, but that's where he wanted. There's a shovel in the woodshed.

Softly Ward tells her that's not legal. There are laws about the removal of the dead. He'll need a death certificate, a county-approved method of interment. Usually it's a cemetery or cremation.

He didn't want any of that. He wanted me to bury him there in the yard and I plan to do it, do what he wants.

Ward shrugs. With the fever across the country, maybe what one family does won't matter.

The morning sky is pink and hazy. Ward must leap onto the shovel blade with both heels to loosen the baked-dry topsoil. At first he wears a gauze mask to keep the dust out of his mouth, but he can't catch his breath and pulls it off. By the time he gets half-way, three feet down, his back burns and his hands are blistered. He stumbles once and brushes against a cactus, impaling his leg with a cluster of spines. It hurts to stand upright when he has to pitch the dirt out of the grave and onto the mound. The wind keeps blowing it back into the hole. He has to keep at it, can't rest or come back to finish it later.

Ruby brings him a sandwich for lunch and says she's sorry. I appreciate you doing this, she adds. I don't know what I'd do without you.

Ward leans close and kisses her ear. We have anything for dinner?

There's some soup and cornbread.

That sounds good. I'll be hungry, I know that.

By the time he has the grave six feet deep, long and wide enough for a man the size of Lord God, it's late. The sky is layered in strata of pink and blue, a deep purple over the Sierra Mojada in the west. Ruby tucks and pins Lord God's body in a sheet. She helps Ward carry it outside. He stands in the grave and does his best to lower it over the edge gently.

Juliet has arrived and stands bundled in a black dress and wool coat, eyes bloodshot, face grief-stricken. Cool wind sends the prairie dust into Ward's face and Ruby's hair into her eyes. Once he gets the body in the ground and laid out in repose, Ward struggles to climb out. Ruby leans over to give him a hand. He almost pulls her into the grave.

They stand for a moment. The only sound is the wind in their ears. Ward winces from back pain, and his hands sting and throb. Ruby recites the twenty-third psalm. Juliet struggles to say a few words, how he was a good man who gave too much away, too soon. She stops in mid-sentence, Ruby's arms around her, holding her up. They start for the house and Ruby turns to Ward.

I have to get back, she says. I put Lila in the crib and she was crying. She's been fussy all day. She knows something's up.

Go to her, says Ward. I'll finish up here.

Ruby leads her mother back to the house and asks if Juliet can give Lila a bath and get her ready for bed.

At the grave, Ward picks up the shovel with his bandaged, aching hands and goes to work. Every bladeful burns. When he's done he has trouble walking to the back door. His back so stiff he can barely stand. The wind in his ears and face makes him stupid. He struggles with the screen door in the wind and stumbles inside, blistered and spent. Ruby warms up a bowl of tortilla soup on the woodstove, with three wedges of buttered cornbread wrapped in foil.

This will take a few minutes to get nice and hot, says Ruby.

Lila squeals from the bathtub, and Ruby hustles down the hallway, saying she'll be right back. Juliet is perched on the edge of the tub, one hand in a sock-puppet duck, quacking at Lila, who sits in a shallow pool of soapy water, a pink rubber duck in one hand and a seahorse in the other.

She wants more Rubbadubbers, says Juliet. I told her we'll have to ask Mommy.

Oh, I know where they are. Ruby retrieves a walrus and penguin from her toy basket, comes back and tickles Lila's tummy with the penguin before kissing the top of her head. Thanks for watching her, Mom. I'm trying to fix Ward something to eat.

Go on, she says. She pinches Lila's nose with the sock puppet. We're having fun, aren't we?

Ruby returns to find Ward asleep with his head down on the kitchen table, breathing deeply. She pats his back until he wakes and sits up.

Come on, Tiger, she says. You need something in your belly. We have work to do tomorrow, right?

He smiles and nods. I'm okay, he says. This is just what I need.

Ward chews his cornbread and says, My hands are blistered. I should have worn gloves.

I'll put some Neosporin on them, says Ruby. You'll be good as new in no time.

She washes the dishes and stares out the window. The junipers on the distant hillside look black. Nearby the ghostly white trunks of the aspens shimmer by the woodshed, their knots like Cleopatra eyes. Sunlight glows above the mountain ridgeline. Over the yard it casts a blue sheen. A breeze waves the brown stalks of grass by the water pump.

From the kitchen window Ruby can just see the mound of loose earth on Lord God's fresh grave. She thinks the words, *It's over.* The phrase sounds odd. The word *over.* Life without Lord God. How to grasp such a thing?

She remembers him years ago, full of energy and hope. He was always building something: a birdhouse for swallows, a rock wall. He planted aspens by the woodshed, nursed them with water and a wire fence to keep the deer from eating all the leaves. He was a force of nature, relentless and indomitable. He chainsawed dead trees and split wood for winter. Every night and morning he'd rise early and make a pot of coffee, have the fire going and the wood box full before anyone else was up. He fixed the leaks in the roof and varnished the hardwood floors.

Lila runs into the kitchen, wrapped in a yellow towel. She tugs on Ward's left hand, wants him to come with her to the living room to play. He tells her he will, soon as he finishes dinner. He lets her tug his hand absentmindedly, as if it's the most natural thing in the world. To get his attention Lila puts an orange plastic bucket shaped like a pumpkin atop her head, for trick-or-treats. She keeps repeating, I get lollipop? I get lollipop?

He smiles and says, Only if your mom says it's okay.

Ruby feels tears swell and she wants them to stop, her heart so full it's cracking. She wipes her eyes with the back of a wrist, her fingers sudsy and pink. Lord God loved Lila and was always there for her. He said the world was hers to inherit. He was right. Whatever happens to her from here on out, Ruby knows she must be strong and fierce for her baby girl, to give her a good life.

But what does that mean? A good life? It's like some rare bird that we know exists but have never yet glimpsed. Like the Yellow-Breasted Chat—a lovely, musical bird that hides low in thickets, that you can hear and know it's there but rarely see.

And in this moment, a blue-winged Kestrel kites above the backyard, hunting mice. *Falco sparverius.* It opens its wings wide and glides in a low, looped arc before alighting softly on the wire clothesline, its black face stripes barely visible in the fading light.

Acknowledgments

I'd like to thank Anne Edelstein, Greg Michalson, Fred Ramey, Kent Haruf, Mike Merschel, Caitlin Hamilton Summie, Libby Jordan, Rich Rennicks, and Glenn Blake for their enormous support and help. And most importantly, I give my greatest thanks and love to Elizabeth May, for holding my life together, and for helping me find the time to write.